BLIND JUSTICE

When a fireman or a police officer visits his school, most of his classmates' heads fill with childish aspirations of growing up and catching bad guys or saving someone from a blazing inferno. When these moments came for Ethan Cross, however, his dreams weren't to someday be a cop or put out fires: he just wanted to write about it.

Now his dream of telling stories on a grand scale has come to fruition with the release of his thrillers, *The Shepherd*, *The Prophet* and *Blind Justice*.

Ethan Cross lives in Illinois with his wife and two daughters.

Praise for Ethan Cross

'Fast paced and all too real'   Andrew Gross

'Fast and furious and will leave you breathless to read more'
Lisa Gardner

'Gory, gruesome stuff that you will read in one sitting'   *Sun*

Also by Ethan Cross

The Shepherd
The Cage (a thriller novella)
The Prophet

ETHAN
CROSS

BLIND JUSTICE

arrow books

Published by Arrow Books 2013

2 4 6 8 10 9 7 5 3 1

Arrow Books
Random House, 20 Vauxhall Bridge Road,
London SW1V 2SA

www.randomhouse.co.uk

Addresses for companies within The Random House Group Limited can
be found at: www.randomhouse.co.uk/offices.htm

The Random House Group Limited Reg. No. 954009

A CIP catalogue record for this book
is available from the British Library

ISBN 9780099588375

The Random House Group Limited supports the Forest Stewardship
Council® (FSC®), the leading international forest-certification organisation.
Our books carrying the FSC label are printed on FSC®-certified paper.
FSC is the only forest-certification scheme supported by the leading
environmental organisations, including Greenpeace. Our paper
procurement policy can be found at:
www.randomhouse.co.uk/environment

Typeset in Palatino by Palimpsest Book Production Limited,
Falkirk, Stirlingshire

Printed and bound by CPI Group (UK) Ltd,
Croydon, CR0 4YY

To my daughter, Calissa, for introducing me
to the world of *special needs* . . .

Acknowledgments

First of all, I want to thank my beautiful wife, Gina, and my daughters, Madison and Calissa, for their love and support (especially Gina who has to endure a lot of craziness in the name of research and put up with me in general).

Next, I wish to thank my parents, Leroy and Emily, for taking me to countless movies as a child and instilling in me a deep love of stories. Also, thank you to my mother, Emily, for always being my first beta reader and my mother-in-law, Karen, for being my best saleswoman.

And, as always, none of this would be possible without the help of my UK editor, Tim Vanderpump, my wonderful agents, Danny Baror and Heather Baror-Shapiro, and my mentor and friend, Lou Aronica. In addition, I wouldn't be here without the guidance and friendship of all my fellow authors at the International Thriller Writers organization.

A huge amount of research went into this book, which would not have been possible without the help of the following people and groups. My friend and fellow author, Anthony Franze, for being my partner-in-crime during my DC trips and helping to arrange some of the behind-the-scenes access needed for the book. Michael Sozan for his wonderfully informative tour of the US Capitol Building and the Senate office buildings. Carl Woog for arranging a private tour of the Pentagon and PFC Yates for being my guide. Major Bruce H. Norton for helping me to understand the mindset and tactics of a Recon Marine. And all of those at the Mary Bryant Home for the Blind, especially Allan J. Rupel, Dave Jackson, and Howard and Janice Thomas, for providing insight into the world of the visually-impaired.

To all of these and my extraordinary readers, thank you so much. I couldn't be living my dream without your support.

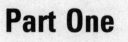

Part One

1

General George Easton woke up covered in blood.

He tasted the coppery liquid on his tongue before he noticed it on his hands and arms. Glancing around, he tried to clear his thoughts and determine where he was. An exact copy of the Resolute desk rested in front of him, its top stained with dark red handprints. He had commissioned the creation of the intricately carved replica shortly after the Senate had affirmed his nomination for Commandant of the Marine Corps. The original desk, built from the timbers of the British Arctic Exploration ship *Resolute*, sat in the Oval Office as a gift from Queen Victoria to President Rutherford B. Hayes. Easton had felt the replica fitting since his large white colonial home, located in the Marine Barracks at 8th and I in Washington, DC, was truly the White House of his chosen profession, and this was a marine's equivalent to the Oval Office.

As Easton tried to stand, pain shot through his limbs. He had seen combat many times. He had watched men die, had killed men himself. Training had conditioned him to keep his head in situations such as this, and his mind ticked off the possibilities as if reading from a checklist. He sniffed the air. There was no trace of smoke or gunfire, just the smell of old leather – and fresh blood.

As he pushed himself up from his black leather chair, his feet slipped on the hardwood floor. His shoes left bloody smears on the dark wood as he stumbled forward and steadied himself against the side of his desk. And that was when he saw the woman's crumpled body in the corner of his office.

Easton rushed forward, knocking over a lamp and chair, falling on his knees in front of the mangled body of his wife. Crawling forward, he took her lifeless form into his arms and cradled her like a child. He didn't bother to check for a pulse. There was too much blood. Her face had been beaten into an unrecognizable pulp. With shaking arms he pulled her close to his chest as he sobbed, the tears flowing down his cheeks and mixing with the blood.

The realization of what had happened came slowly at first, then thundered through his mind, flooding him with anger and guilt. In that moment, he knew exactly who had killed his wife and why.

"I'm sorry for your loss, general."

The gravelly voice startled Easton, and he spun in the direction of the sound. A copper-skinned man with coal-black hair stepped from the shadows. Nondescript military fatigues covered the man's large frame, and his right fist gripped a silver decorative Colt 1911 pistol. The general recognized it as his own gun that normally rested inside a display case on the mantelpiece of his office.

Easton began to stand, but the other man aimed the weapon at him and said in a South American accent, "Please don't move. I would hate to kill you before we've had a chance to speak, but I will. I'm sorry that it's come to this, general. You were just trying to fulfill your duty, to do the right thing. But so am I."

Easton clenched his teeth so hard that pain shot through his jaw. His eyes scanned the room for anything to use as a weapon.

"Don't get any ideas. Remember, you have four children and seven grandchildren to think of as well."

"You stay the hell away from—"

The man stopped him with a raised hand and said calmly, "Please, general, let's not make this any more painful than it needs to be. If I could get to you here, in a secure military facility within the heart of DC, do you think that I would have any problem snuffing out the lives of a few young couples in the suburbs? We'll start with your oldest son, the lawyer, and his family. It's his birthright, after all. Please understand that I don't wish you or your loved ones any harm, but don't question my resolve. Where is Wyatt Randall?"

"I don't know what you're talking about."

Another man, with the wiry frame and intense eyes of a special-forces commando, stepped in from the hallway. He held a dark Glock pistol.

The copper-skinned man said, "We know that's not true. If you do the right thing now, this ends with you. No one else has to get hurt." As he spoke, he circled Easton like a shark but stuck to the periphery of the room, away from the bloody crime scene. "A true military tactician realizes when it's time to order the retreat and save the lives of his remaining forces rather than needlessly sending them all to their deaths. Think for a moment. Look at this situation objectively. There is no nobler death than that of a father sacrificing his own life for his children. But let's say for a moment that you somehow overpower myself and my partner. What then? We're not working alone. Our associates will still visit the homes of your children and grandchildren. You have no choice. There is no way out for you."

Easton closed his eyes and hugged his wife's corpse tight against his body. Her warm blood soaked through his shirt and ran down his skin. Her hair still carried the scent of cinnamon from her favorite shampoo. "I don't know where Randall is, but he's supposed to meet me tomorrow morning at 8:30. In front of the Lincoln Memorial. He's going to turn over all the evidence then."

"And he hasn't given you anything yet?"

"He's showed me the files, but he kept them with him. As insurance."

The copper-skinned man scratched at the black stubble covering his cheeks and narrowed his eyes. Then he retrieved a cell phone from his pocket, punched the keypad, and placed it to his ear. "Yes . . . kill the son."

"No! I'm telling you the truth. Search my computer and my files. There's nothing here."

The man hesitated a second, searching Easton's eyes. "Hold that order. If you don't hear from me in five minutes, then kill him." The phone snapped closed. "We've already searched your files. I don't know that I believe you, but unfortunately, we're out of time. I'm sure you've guessed that we're not going to leave you alive, but I am going to give you a choice about how you die. You can either do it yourself, or we can force you and simply make it look like suicide. I'm not sure of your religious beliefs on the matter, so I wanted to give you the option."

Easton glared at the man, his hatred overshadowing his fear. "How considerate of you." His words dripped with venom. He raised his hand, palm out. "Give me the damn gun."

The man slid the decorative .45-caliber 1911 across the floor. It spun to a halt against Easton's foot inside the pool of red. Hesitating only a second, the highest-ranking marine in the United States picked up the weapon. The gun had been a gift from an Italian general that Easton had worked with while in Naples and during the NATO bombing of Yugoslavia. He had never fired it. "What's your name?"

The man cocked his head to the side. "Why do you ask?"

"I want to let the devil know to be on the lookout for you."

"My name is Antonio de Almeida. But I've seen a glimpse of hell during my life, general, and I truly pray that you're destined for a better place. You may have a moment to prepare your soul, if you need it."

The general ignored Almeida. The man's words about a father dying for his family being noble came back to his mind, but he didn't feel noble. He felt fear and helplessness and failure. Only two years left of his four-year term as Commandant, and then he and his wife had been going to retire to a farm in Tennessee. Forty-four years of marriage. More good years than bad. He stroked his dead wife's hair and hoped that he would get to see her again on the other side.

Then he raised the gun to his temple and squeezed the trigger.

2

Deacon Munroe couldn't see the flashing lights of the crime scene. He couldn't see anything at all, but he could hear it and feel it. The creaking of the flashers rotating in light-bars atop police cruisers. The murmurs of a crowd of onlookers. Patrol officers controlling the scene and pushing back the crowd. Feet striking the pavement, moving with purpose. Detectives. Crime scene techs. Reporters shouting questions. All of it overlaying the dull roar of the city. His city – Washington, DC.

The world was an intricate tapestry of sounds, smells, and vibrations that most people never noticed. But, in the years since losing his sight, Munroe had learned to weave the data from his remaining senses together. He intertwined each strand in his mind's eye and could usually stitch together a picture of his surroundings. Still, there were so many details that were lost to him. If he couldn't hear it or smell it or feel it, then it didn't exist in his world.

He had always prided himself on his attention to detail, and it was this affinity for minutiae and problem-solving that had led him to become a detective in the first place. Then, one day, half the details had just disappeared and the world had become a frightening place of darkness.

"What do we see, Gerald?" Munroe asked in his soothing

Southern drawl. He adjusted the dark designer sunglasses that rested on the bridge of his nose. He was seldom in public without them. Although his eyes appeared normal, people found his vacant stare to be unsettling.

"Crime scene," Gerald Dixon said. His voice was deep and smooth. "Lots of cops going into the commandant's house. I see some jackholes in windbreakers with white letters. Probably NCIS."

"Jackholes?"

"Yeah, you know. More than a jackass, slightly less than an asshole."

"I see," Munroe said. People often found it odd when he used verbs that referred to sighted actions, and conversations always grew awkward when someone accidentally used such a word around him. But, in reality, he used terms like that constantly in common speech, even though they were technically inaccurate. There was nothing offensive about it. In fact, he found it more offensive when people noticed the faux pas and apologized, as if he were some sensitive child that needed to be coddled.

"Check the crowd. Anyone suspicious? Anyone seem out of place or watching just a bit too closely?"

A moment passed, and Gerald said, "Nothing."

"Okay, let's make an entrance."

Gerald guided Munroe's hand to his forearm and led him up to the door. Agents and police stopped them a couple of times along the way, but a flashing of their credentials from the DCIS – the Defense Criminal Investigative Service – allowed them to pass.

Once inside, Munroe heard the voices of detectives and CSI crews echoing off the hardwood floors, but a loud nasal voice cut through the rest. "What are you doing here, Munroe? This is an NCIS investigation. We don't need help from a *special* investigator on this one."

"Hello, Agent Ashter. I'd try to insult you now, but I'm afraid

9

that I may lack the proper vocabulary for it to be effective or even understood."

"Screw you, Munroe. You're a liability, and I don't want you stumbling around my crime scene."

Munroe laughed. "*Your* crime scene? We both know Markham's never going to let you take the training wheels off. Speaking of Markham, don't you need to be picking up his dry cleaning, getting coffee, mowing his lawn?"

He felt Ashter push in close. The man smelled of breath mints and Old Spice. "You shouldn't even be an active agent. You're a cripple. I don't know what you hold over the heads of the big boys at the Pentagon, but if you ask me, your retirement's about ten years overdue."

Munroe was descended from Southern aristocracy, and like a true Southern gentleman, he reacted to the other man's comments with a calm, indifferent smirk. But on the inside, the remarks reverberated through his mind. He wanted to scream. He wanted to bash Ashter's face in. He had become accustomed to people discounting him because of his disability, but few were as blatant and rude as Ashter. Still, Munroe's father had always said that to show anger to those beneath you was to put your weaknesses on display.

"I do so enjoy our little talks, but I have work to do. Where's your boss?"

He could hear Ashter chewing on his bottom lip and suspected that the agent's head was shaking as well. Munroe continued, "Come on. You know that all I have to do is make a quick phone call, and this ignorant posturing will be for nothing."

Ashter hesitated but then said, "Stay here. I'll send him down to you."

A few moments later, Munroe heard NCIS Special Agent Dean Markham approaching. Markham had taken a round in the hip several years before, and it gave his gait a rhythm that Munroe found distinctive. Munroe stuck out his hand and said, "You need to keep your dog on a shorter leash."

Markham shook the proffered hand and replied in his Boston accent, "He's a good agent."

"If brains were dynamite, that boy wouldn't be able to blow his nose."

"Why are you here?" Markham said, all business.

"I was here to see General Easton. At his request. He called me and said that he had an urgent matter that he needed to discuss. I came as soon as I could."

Munroe heard Markham flip open a notebook and click a pen before the agent asked, "What did he need to talk about?"

"He wouldn't say over the phone. I really have no idea."

"What's your relationship to the commandant?"

"We're old friends. We get together now and then, drink some Scotch, smoke cigars."

"Did he often discuss personal issues with you? Marital problems, anything like that?"

"No. He wasn't looking forward to his retirement, but his wife definitely was. You want to tell me what's happened? Why are you asking about marital issues?"

Markham released a deep breath. "Because it looks like he brutally murdered his wife and then killed himself."

Munroe was silent for a moment. "That's not right. The man I know would never do something like that."

"It's too early to draw any definite conclusions, but that's the way it looks."

"Things aren't always the way they seem."

Markham flipped the notebook closed. "They almost never are, but this is our investigation. I'll let you in out of respect for your service to this country and your . . . sacrifice. But stay out of our way. If you see . . . I mean . . . *pick up on* anything, you come to me first."

11

Munroe once again fought to maintain his calm demeanor. It seemed that these guys always fell into two camps: one that thought he should be collecting disability and one that gave him undue respect for simply being in the wrong place at the wrong time. None of them respected his skills as an investigator or treated him as an asset. He was just thankful that the DOD and the Joint Chiefs didn't share the viewpoint of the NCIS and FBI.

Gerald led him up the stairs and down a familiar route, the rhythm of Markham's footfalls sounding on the hardwood in front of them. He knew that they were heading for General Easton's office. Munroe and George Easton had shared many glasses of fine Scotch in that room. As he counted their steps to judge the distance they'd traveled for his mental tapestry, he knew that the eyes of the previous commandants were looking down on him from the portraits that lined the hall. He could feel the weight from the gazes of the great men, urging him to find justice for their fallen brother. History was thick in this place. The home of the commandants was said to be the oldest continuously occupied public building in DC and one of the few not to have been burned by the British when they sacked the capital in 1814. Legend held that the British had spared the home of the commandant from the torch out of a gesture of soldierly respect. It occupied fifteen thousand square feet, including thirty rooms not counting closets or baths. Unfortunately, Munroe had never actually *seen* the interior of the great structure. Just one more detail and experience stolen from him.

The noise from the crime scene grew closer, and he heard and felt the sound alter as they entered Easton's office. It was like a change in pressure as the voices and footfalls no longer echoed from the walls of the corridor. "What do we see, Gerald? I know the layout. Just give me the details of the crime."

Gerald Dixon had been his best friend since they were children.

The large black man's family had worked for Munroe's forebears on the plantation for generations. Young Deacon Munroe hadn't known that Gerald was below his station in life. And older Deacon Munroe simply didn't care about such things. One of the crops grown on the farm was tobacco, and he still vividly remembered the first time that he and Gerald had decided to try to smoke some directly from the field. The two boys had been sick for what felt like a week.

Gerald took a deep breath. "The bodies are along the north side of the office. Easton's on his back with his wife cradled in his lap. It looks like she was beaten to death. Her face is . . ." Gerald's voice trailed off, painting Munroe an especially grim picture. "The entry wound on the general's head is to the left temple with the exit wound on the right. I think I see powder burns consistent with direct contact of the barrel."

"Did you say the entry wound is to the left temple? Gun in the left hand?"

"That's correct."

"Go on."

"The general appears to have scratch marks all over him, consistent with a struggle. The room's the same way. Lamp's overturned. A chair. Some papers and books are scattered across the floor. Bloody footprints leading to the desk. Bloody handprints on top of the desk. Blood on the chair."

"What about the murder weapon?"

"For the wife, it looks like she was beaten to death. I see a lot of blood and abrasions on the general's fists. It doesn't look good, Deac."

"Continue."

"The gun is a decorative Colt 1911. It looks like the one from his display case."

"Check the case. Is it bloody?"

"No, it looks clean."

"Good. Could you summon Agent Markham for me, please, Gerald?"

A moment later, Markham's clip-clop footfalls approached, accompanied by another set that Munroe guessed to be those of Ashter. Munroe said, "What do you think about the scene, Markham?"

Ashter's nasal voice said, "Are you kidding? It's clear that—"

"Adults are speaking," Munroe interrupted.

"What is your problem, Munroe?" Ashter said, playing the victim in front of his superior.

Munroe turned sharply toward the sound of the man's voice. "I don't like your face." Turning back to where he assumed Markham to be standing, he continued, "Your thoughts, Special Agent Markham?"

When Markham spoke, his words were slow and measured as if he were considering every syllable with care. "It's too soon to draw any definite conclusions. We haven't gathered all the evidence yet. But from what I've seen to this point, it appears that General Easton and his wife had a physical altercation, and Easton, a highly trained soldier, killed her during the fight. He then sat down at his desk, considered what had happened. Realized what he'd done and decided to end his own life. He retrieved the gun, cradled his wife's body, and shot himself in the head."

Munroe nodded. "At first glance, that is what appears to have happened. However, there are a few inconsistencies. First of all, the commandant is right-handed. Why would a right-handed person use his left hand to hold a gun and commit suicide?"

Ashter cut in. "Maybe he hurt it in the fight. That doesn't—"

"Second, if things played out as you described, why isn't the display case covered in blood? Have you checked the weapon? Any traces of blood on the magazine or the rounds that Easton would have loaded?"

Markham told them to hold on and went to check with his

people. When he returned, he said, "The real test will be done at the lab, but they checked with UV light and found no traces of blood on the magazine, bullets, or display case. But before we go off half-cocked with wild conspiracy theories, none of that necessarily proves anything more is going on. There are scratch marks on Easton and skin under the wife's nails and a whole lot of other evidence saying that the wife fought him for her life. It's too soon to come to any conclusions."

"Please, we both know that you came to a conclusion within thirty seconds of seeing this scene. I'm just saying not to let any preconceptions allow evidence to be missed or possibilities to be overlooked. Are your people checking for witnesses who may have seen anyone suspicious?"

"We know how to do our jobs, Munroe." Markham walked off with Ashter following on his heels like a new puppy.

Munroe said, "Let's take a walk down the hall, Gerald."

The big man led him out of the room and away from the others with his guide arm, the one Munroe was holding, sliding behind his back. The small gesture told Munroe to transition into a single-file line in order to maneuver through a tight space. "I don't like your face, says the blind man?" Gerald commented.

"I thought you might like that. I bet our boy's still chewing on that one."

"You think that somebody faked the scene? Is that why he's holding the gun with his left hand?"

"No, I think that it was a message. George was leaving us a clue. If a professional had faked the scene by forcing the gun to his head, they would have assumed that he was right-handed. And that's if they hadn't checked beforehand to be sure. But if they had threatened him in some way, forced him to do it, then he may have used his left hand in order to throw up a red flag. Do you remember the Sherlock Holmes short story, 'Silver Blaze'? We read it in Ms. Petrie's class when we were kids."

"Yeah, it was the one where Holmes solves the case because the dog *didn't* bark."

Munroe nodded. "Good memory. There's a dog *not* barking here too."

"What are you saying?"

"George had an ornate clock in his office that ticked with every second. A present from his grandmother or some such, one of those new clocks that are designed to look like antiques. It always annoyed the piss out of me, but George found it relaxing. He kept saying that he was going to send me one for my office at home, that I needed to relax a bit more. But where's that clock now? There wasn't any ticking in his office."

"Okay, wait here. I'll take a look. Maybe it was broken in the struggle."

Munroe listened to Gerald's footsteps as his colleague walked away. Waited. Thought. Listened to the same footsteps return a few minutes later. "I found it," Gerald said.

Munroe shook his head. "Damn, I thought I had something there."

"It wasn't in his office. It was in the study a couple doors down."

"Really? I don't hear it."

"It's not working. Batteries must be dead."

Munroe considered this. Why would the commandant have moved his clock and let the batteries run down? He loved that damn clock. Especially when he knew that Munroe was coming. Unless it was another message. One directed specifically at him.

"Check the battery compartment. Don't let anyone see you do it."

"That shouldn't be a problem. They're all focused on the office."

A moment later, he heard Gerald return. His partner's breathing pattern had changed noticeably. "You were right. I found something where the batteries should have been."

3

Jonas Black always pushed himself harder on the last leg of his run. Exhaustion pressed down on him and his legs burned, but he pressed forward, gaining momentum, arms pumping, teeth grinding down. He was in the best shape of his life, even better than when he had been a Recon Marine.

The training to become an elite special-forces operator had been difficult for him. Most spec-ops soldiers were small and wiry and quick. Jonas was none of those things. At six-foot-six and two hundred and seventy pounds, he was a freight train, not some kind of ninja. Most people thought that being big gave him an advantage as a soldier, but they were wrong. His size made everything about the job more difficult. It was hard enough to carry a fifty-pound pack through dense forest and up cliffs during SERE (survival, evasion, resistance, escape) training when you weighed a hundred and sixty pounds. He had nearly twice as much bulk to contend with and could never move as fast as his smaller counterparts.

Sometimes, though, his size did give him an advantage. Like when he had become an inmate at Holman Correctional Facility in Atmore, Alabama. In prison, size mattered, and Jonas Black was an intimidating opponent for even the craziest of his fellow prisoners. The others gave him his space, and he liked it that way. He just wanted to do his time and get back on the outside. The problem was that a big percentage of the inmates at Holman were serving life without parole. They had nothing to lose, while Jonas only had six months left on his sentence. Still, he knew better than to show any kind of weakness to the wolves.

That type of thinking wasn't anything new for him. He had learned that the strong survive and the weak get swallowed up and spat out. Fortunately, he had never been weak.

He finished his run around the prison yard and placed his hands on top of his head as he caught his breath. A little white guy known as Shorty peeled away reluctantly from a group of other inmates and approached him. Shorty stank of body odor and cigarette smoke. The little man's voice trembled when he said, "Yo, Black, think you can hook me up with some Julep?"

Jonas wiped the sweat from his forehead and ran his hand through his closely cropped hair. "How much you want?" he said in his gravelly baritone.

"Bottle'll do it."

"You have payment?"

"Got two Mrs. Freshleys."

"A bottle will cost you four Mrs. Freshleys and a pack of Bugler."

"Damn, Black! I thought you were in here for murder, not robbery."

"That's the price, Shorty. Don't waste my time. No credit, no loans."

Shorty shuffled back to his group, still mumbling curses. Black had made a decent business for himself while on the inside. The prisoners, of course, weren't supposed to have drugs or alcohol, but Jonas had never let a little thing like rules stop him before. He didn't deal drugs or use them, but he had acquired a special recipe for Julep, which was a kind of home-made whiskey in high demand at Holman. It was difficult to make and could often result in an alcohol content as low as two percent, but the batches that Black made were much stronger and much more expensive. The current going rate was a pack of Bugler, the brand of tobacco sold out of the prison store, and four Mrs. Freshley's Grand Honey Buns. Strangely, the treats had become a better prison currency than cigarettes. Black wondered if there was some correlation between this and the rise of obesity in America. He had never liked sweets himself, never had them while he'd been growing up, but here in Holman they were good for barter and for sweetening his Julep.

He made his way back through the prison yard, across the dusty ground dotted with occasional patches of grass. He didn't make eye contact with anyone, radiating an aura of intensity that told the others to stay out of his way. The air was thick with humidity, and the July sun beat down on the back of his neck, but a slight breeze carried a trace of something flowery and sweet, the hint of a better world beyond the fences. He passed the basketball courts and workout equipment and was heading for the blue gate leading to the general-population dorm – the place he called home – when Mel Franklin ran up to him.

Franklin was a skinny black kid with a tattoo fetish. He was bare-chested, displaying the artwork that covered his whole upper body like a shirt. Black had a few tattoos himself – one on a bicep from the service that showed a skull and crossbones and the number one over a blue triangle and the words *1st Recon Bn* and the motto *Swift, Silent, Deadly*, and then a pair of simple tattoos on his knuckles with the words *Pain* and *Life* – but he couldn't understand why anyone would want to ink themselves from head to toe.

"You gotta help me, Black." Franklin's body trembled, and fear gleamed in his eyes.

"I don't have to do anything, kid." He walked on, but Franklin followed.

"Please – Grier's coming for me. If you don't help, he'll kill me."

Jonas shook his head. He tried to keep to himself as much as possible, but he felt sorry for the kid. Franklin and his brother had broken into someone's house to get drug money, and his brother had shot the guy. Even though he hadn't pulled the trigger, Franklin had still been there, an accessory, and had taken the same rap as his brother. Then the kid had managed to piss off the resident white supremacist group, the Southern Brotherhood, on his first day. The Aryans weren't as numerous at Holman as they were in some other jails since the prison population here was made up predominantly of African Americans, but they were still a force to be reckoned with. And Grier was the worst of the bunch, a lifer with nothing to lose.

"I'm not your babysitter. Handle your own problems."

"Please, Black. He showed me the shank. Said he was gonna—"

Black swung back toward Franklin and leaned down to stare in his face. "That's not my problem. I've got six months left. I'm not screwing that up for you or anyone. It's a hard-knock life, kid. Get used to it."

A flash of memory shot through Jonas's mind. His brother Michael had always used that phrase – *a hard-knock life*. Michael had thought of the two of them as orphans like the famous Annie, even though their parents were technically still alive. His brother would have liked for some rich guy to come pull them out of the gutter too, but Jonas had liked things the way they were, liked his independence.

Black left Franklin standing there, alone and afraid, and headed back toward the dorm. Along the way, three men passed him, heading in Franklin's direction. They moved as a unit, quickly and with purpose. The one in the center was Grier, his prison jumpsuit untucked and open to reveal a white tank top beneath. A giant red swastika climbed from Grier's chest to his throat. The killer's eyes stared straight ahead in a laser-beam gaze directed at Franklin.

Black had seen that look before. He also noticed Grier slide something from beneath his shirt and cup the object in his right hand. Black could guess what the other man was holding: a home-made box cutter made from a razor blade glued between two pieces of wood. It was the weapon of choice at Holman – perfect for slicing a man's throat.

He tried to ignore the group. It wasn't his problem.

But words and phrases spoken at his own sentencing floated back to him . . . *same as pulling the trigger . . . life cut short . . . take responsibility for his choices*. Then he thought of the concepts engrained into his mind during his Marine training. Concepts like honor and never leaving a man behind.

A part of his brain told him to keep going. It screamed at him that he'd never been a hero and now wasn't the time to start.

But another more dominant part turned him around and moved him quickly back toward Mel Franklin.

4

Antonio de Almeida knelt at his mother's bedside and said a prayer over her frail form. The doctors had sedated her and called him after her most recent violent outburst. Her mental state had been sliding downward for months now as the Alzheimer's ravaged what was left of the woman who had given him life. He had moved her from a nursing home in Mexico to a temporary one in Virginia when he had learned that he would need to be in DC for an extended period of time. He couldn't stand the thought of her struggling through her disease without him by her side, whether she could register his presence or not.

He finished his prayer and then took her small hand in his. It felt like all bones, and her skin was thin as tissue paper. She was withering away before his eyes.

Her gaunt face turned in his direction, the eyes flickering with a brief second of recognition. "Nio?"

He patted her hand and smiled. "I'm here, Mama."

As her head lolled over and her eyes fluttered shut, she said, "Dónde está tu hermano?"

Almeida closed his eyes and fought back the tears. His brother, whom his mother had just asked about, had died when they'd been boys.

His phone vibrated on the nightstand and pulled him away from the pain of both the past and the present. "Hello?"

The angry voice of Brendan Lennix answered. "Have you found Randall?"

"No. General Easton lied to us. It must have taken a great deal of self-control to do so. He was a man to be respected."

Almeida held the phone away from his ear as Lennix screamed at him from the other end of the line. "I'm so glad that you made a new friend! But do you think that maybe you could worry less about being respectful and worry more about doing your damn job!"

Almeida let silence set in on the line before he replied calmly, "We'll find your scientist soon. It's only a matter of time. Things would have gone differently with the general if we'd had more time, but we couldn't raise suspicions by kidnapping a man in Easton's position. Besides, the important thing was to remove him as a threat, which has been accomplished."

"We're supposed to be going into production in two weeks, and DARPA has been asking questions. There are billions of dollars at stake here. We can't afford any more screw-ups."

"I am well aware of what's at stake, Mr. Lennix. John Corrigan will be executed in a few days, and Wyatt Randall's research and documents will be recovered. Stick to what you know best, and I will do the same."

"You listen to me, you lazy . . . jungle savage. I want to know exactly how you are going to find—"

Almeida killed the connection and placed the phone back on the nightstand. He took a moment to calm his breathing, then said, "Don't worry, Mama. That was my associate Mr. Lennix on the phone. His company has a new project that may be able to help you. Unfortunately, I have to kill a few people to make that happen."

His mother didn't acknowledge his words. She just lay there, breathing shallowly, wasting away. Almeida rested his head on her chest and said another prayer for her and for himself.

5

Grier had Mel Franklin backed up against a wall on the east side of the yard, and Jonas Black knew how it would go down. Franklin would have nowhere to run, and Grier's two goons would grab the kid by the arms. Maybe Franklin would fight and prolong things for a few seconds. Either way, Grier would slip in and slice the kid's throat. Maybe he and his men had some plan to try to slip away and not get caught and maybe they would just lie down and wait for the guards. In any case, Grier would never see the outside world again. The most they could do to him would be to stick him in Ad Seg and tack a few more years onto his sentence, a gesture that really only mattered on paper.

"Time to give the devil his due, boy," Grier said as he and his accomplices hemmed Franklin in.

Jonas stepped up behind Grier. His first instinct was to attack without saying a word. Announcing your intentions and drawing things out was usually pointless, but he still held some hope that perhaps he could muscle his way in and scare Grier and his boys off without there actually being a fight. But he doubted that would be the case.

"Leave him alone, Grier."

Grier turned slowly toward Jonas. His dirty mop of

reddish-brown hair flapped in the wind. Dust from the poorly kept prison yard swirled around them in the breeze. Jonas felt it collecting in the rivulets of sweat running down his neck and arms.

"This is none of your concern," Grier said. "Me and this boy's gonna dance, Black. Has nothing to do with you."

Again, Jonas's first instinct was to go on the offensive, but he restrained himself and decided to try reason first. "It's all of our concerns. There's already been one stabbing this month, and our total number is up from last year. You stick this kid, and the warden is going to lock this place down. He'll close the prison store, take away our yard time. All to prove a point. If all these gorillas in here can't buy things from the store, then they can't pay me for my product. I'm just looking out for my business interests."

Grier laughed. "Your business interests? You know, I've often wondered whose side you're on."

"What are you talking about?"

"White or black. You look like a white man, but your skin's dark enough that you may have some of their filthy mongrel blood mixed in there too. I think you might be a mutt."

Jonas stepped forward. "Leave him alone and push off. Now."

"You know what I did to the last man that tried to tell me what to do?"

"I don't care."

Jonas saw the blow coming from a mile away. Grier had decided to strike, and his body betrayed his intentions. His eyes went wide. His muscles stiffened. His lip curled. His weight shifted to the ball of his right foot. All of it telegraphed exactly how and when Grier was going to attack. And Jonas Black was ready.

Grier's right arm shot up toward Jonas's throat. The box cutter jutted out from his fist, ready to rip through the jugular. Jonas might have been outnumbered, and Grier might have been the one holding a deadly weapon, but he wasn't concerned. There were a lot of guys in Holman that Jonas wouldn't have wanted to tangle with, but these three weren't on that list. They were untrained and undisciplined thugs. They might have been scary to a kid like Franklin, but Uncle Sam had invested a lot of money in training Jonas Black to hurt people. And the taxpayers had gotten their money's worth.

Jonas's huge left hand caught Grier's forearm as it shot forward. His fingers wrapped all the way around the man's arm as he gripped it like a vise and twisted it. Then he rammed his right forearm upward against Grier's elbow, using it as a fulcrum, and pulled Grier's arm down.

He felt the joint give way with a crunch as the elbow snapped.

Grier dropped the cutter and howled in pain. The white supremacist fell to the ground, writhing in agony as his goons and Franklin scattered away from the fight.

As he rolled in the dirt, Grier screamed, "You're dead! Never be safe! A dead man!"

Jonas Black sighed, and a part of him wished that he had just minded his own business and kept walking. It was too late for that now. Guards in dark blue uniforms ran toward him. He put his hands behind his head and chose a nice patch of grass to lie down in so that the guards could slap on the cuffs.

6

The Phillips family had put their impressive art collection on display starting in 1921 in Washington's Dupont Circle neighborhood. The museum contained paintings by artists such as Renoir, Bonnard, O'Keeffe, van Gogh, and Diebenkorn. But, before losing his sight, Deacon Munroe had always enjoyed the museum's Rothko room. The Russian-American painter's work was simplistic – mainly consisting of only colors without a defined form – and could easily be overlooked when comparing it with the more grandiose and intricate paintings hanging within the collection. Rothko had wanted his paintings to be very intimate and human, and Munroe found them to carry a certain spirit. He could remember the power emanating from the subtle shades during his previous viewings. Although he couldn't gaze upon them now, he could still feel a strange energy coming from them, as if the artist had placed a piece of his soul in each painting.

Munroe recognized the sound of Gerald's shoes before his friend announced himself. Gerald had placed padded inserts into his dress shoes, and it added a slight creaking to his steps.

"When we were boys, did you ever think that we'd end up like this?" Munroe said.

He felt Gerald's weight fall onto the bench beside him. "Well, let's see. You getting into trouble, and me bailing you out and watching your back. Hell, Deac, nothing's changed."

"Everything changes, yet everything stays the same. It doesn't matter what our age is or what time period we live in or what our individual circumstances are, when you break it down, we all just keep making the same mistakes over and over."

"What's eating you?"

"I don't know. Easton's death, I suppose. He lived through multiple wars and conflicts, and then he dies bloody in his own home. I don't understand the world anymore. I keep thinking about his kids, his grandkids. Ripples, you know. All the people we affect in our lives. I wonder who will be there crying at my funeral – other than my girls, of course. And you and Annabelle."

Annabelle was Gerald's younger sister. She too worked for Munroe, handling all the back-office labor including converting documents into formats that Munroe could consume as well as assisting with investigations. Gerald had followed Munroe into law enforcement when they were still teenagers, and so when Munroe had been given the go-ahead to form his own team, he had wanted to fill it with people whom he could trust. There was no one in the world that he trusted more than Gerald and his sister.

"I heard Annabelle was over for dinner at your house this weekend while I was gone," Gerald said.

The sudden shift in the conversation jolted Munroe. "Yes, I had some paperwork that I needed her help with. What brought that up?"

"I was just thinking that since you're in such a deep contemplative mood, maybe you should ask yourself why you've never asked her out."

"Excuse me? Our relationship is completely professional."

Gerald laughed. "You've had a crush on her since our junior year."

"That's not true. And even if it was, she works for me. It would be completely inappropriate."

"Life's short, Deac." Gerald hesitated. "And Beth would understand. It's been a long time."

Munroe didn't respond. He pressed a button on his watch, and a mechanical voice announced the time. In a whisper, he said, "Let's see if Joey's made any progress."

~~*~~

Joey Helgeson, a master of all things technical, was on a permanent retainer with the DCIS. Although he had been part of Munroe's team for some time, he refused to officially become an employee of the government and work within an office in the Pentagon or DCIS headquarters, which had forced Munroe to call in favors to obtain and maintain Joey's security clearance. Instead, the tech guru's *command center*, as he called it, was a short walk from the Phillips Collection inside a historic home overlooking DuPont Circle. Munroe remembered the James G. Blaine mansion from before he had lost his sight. It was a beautiful four-story Queen Anne-style building with walls of dark red brick, a large porte-cochère, and a rooftop filled with intricate weathervanes. Munroe thought it a bit of a waste that Joey probably had his portion of the elegant and historic space filled with superhero memorabilia. He could always tell a lot about a person by observing the space in which they lived and worked. Even though he had been blind for over ten years now, it still bothered him that he couldn't gather such information without help.

"Where did you get this thing?" Joey asked, referring to the small flash drive that Gerald had retrieved from the battery compartment of General Easton's clock.

"Why? What did you find?"

"I couldn't access it. That's the problem." Joey's voice had a slight North Jersey accent with a nasal quality that Munroe suspected might have come from an improperly healed broken nose. His office smelled of burnt coffee, dirty dishes, and Febreze air freshener with the smallest underlying hint of marijuana residue. "This is the first example I've seen of a new system called 'Widowmaker' that the National Reconnaissance Office is developing," Joey continued. "It's protected by a sixteen-character password with a single-error shredding fail-safe. So if you enter the wrong password even one time, the entire contents of the drive get wiped beyond recovery."

"Can you crack it?"

Joey gave a throaty laugh that ended in a snort. "That's funny. There's no way to crack it. At least, not with the resources I have."

"So it's worthless."

"Not entirely. There is something strange about the way the encryption is implemented. Normally, when using a system like this, you'd encrypt the whole drive or just certain files that are sensitive. But on this baby, someone left the directory structure intact and encrypted all the files inside into a single archive. So the entire top-level structure is readable."

Munroe rubbed his temples. "Joey, what you just said makes about as much sense to me as a driver's seat on a wheelbarrow."

"Huh?"

"What does that mean? And why would it be that way?"

"I don't know why anyone would structure it that way. But what it means is that at least we have some clue about what info the drive contains." Munroe heard the clicking of Joey's keyboard. "The directory names are Compound 119, John Corrigan, Money Transfers, Site B, Trial Results, and Wyatt Randall."

Now things were starting to make sense to Munroe. Easton

wouldn't have hidden a drive for him if he couldn't learn anything from it. But the general was also probably worried about someone else finding the drive and accessing the sensitive information that it contained. The directory structure was left as a list of leads for Munroe to follow.

"That's good, Joey. I need you to find out anything and everything you can about Wyatt Randall, Compound 119, and Site B."

"What about John Corrigan?"

"I already have an idea about that one. I need you to book Gerald and me on the next flight to Leavenworth, Kansas. We're going to pay John Corrigan a visit."

Gerald said, "You know the guy?"

"I've heard of him. He's currently on death row, and I believe his execution is scheduled for sometime within the next week. So the clock is ticking."

7

Deacon Munroe had visited the United States Disciplinary Barracks many times, although his visual memories of the place were from the original facility. The stone and brick castle with its grim walls had been replaced by a new building that he had been told was indistinguishable at first glance from the campus of a high school. But the USDB that he remembered and still held in his mind was a hard place with a medieval ambience. The original had used prisoners for its construction during an age when hard labor meant exactly that.

They had called ahead and arranged a meeting with Sergeant John Corrigan, a former Recon Marine team leader awaiting execution for the murders of his wife and two children. Munroe and Gerald arrived in the visitors' area before Corrigan. Munroe could guess at the nature of his surroundings, based upon the echoes of the room and the things he could feel. A cheap plastic laminate covered the meeting table and chairs. Tiled floors. Drywall. He could tell by the way sounds carried within the space. Two vending machines hummed in one corner. The modern institutional feel of a cafeteria, nothing like the old castle that kept appearing in his mind.

He heard the rattle of wrist and ankle chains as a guard ushered Corrigan into the room and forced the prisoner into a seat across the table from the two DCIS men. "Hello, Sergeant Corrigan. My name is Deacon Munroe. I'm a special investigator with the DCIS. The gentleman with me is my partner, Agent Dixon."

"It's Inmate Corrigan now. I haven't been a Marine or a sergeant for some time." Corrigan's voice was strong and calm. He spoke quietly, without a trace of bitterness.

"Once a Marine always a Marine – or so I've heard. I've also heard that General Easton visited you recently. I'd like to know what you and the commandant discussed."

"I was very sorry to hear what happened to him. He was a good man."

"He was my friend. And I think that you may have information about who killed him."

Corrigan adjusted his chains and shifted in his seat. "I heard that he killed his wife and then himself. What could that possibly have to do with me?"

"The facts of the case are a bit blurred. Knowing the nature of your relationship to the commandant may help bring some of that into focus. So, please, what was it that you and he discussed?"

"It was a private matter."

"Regarding?"

"Things that are private."

Munroe had always excelled at questioning witnesses and suspects, but there was much to the job that depended on watching for nonverbal and subconscious clues given by the person in the hot seat. He could no longer tell whether or not Corrigan was making eye contact. Whether or not he looked away when asked about a certain subject, and in what direction he looked. There was so much to be learned from a subject's facial expressions, bodily postures, and head motions. Munroe couldn't use those things against Corrigan, but the sergeant's nervous shifting in his seat and the twisting of his chains were things that Munroe *could* hear. And they told him that this whole conversation was making Corrigan very uncomfortable.

"It just seems very strange to me, Sergeant Corrigan," Munroe said, purposely using Corrigan's old title to subconsciously prompt the former soldier's sense of duty. "Why would the highest-ranking marine in the country fly all the way out here to have a powwow with you? I've already spoken with your lawyer. He said that you've waived your rights to appeals and want the execution to move forward. He didn't know anything about these *private matters* that you were discussing with the general."

Corrigan's leg shook in a steady rhythm beneath the table. "Like I said, it was between me and the commandant."

"Did the visits concern Wyatt Randall?"

Corrigan's leg stopped shaking. "I don't know who that is."

"Of course you don't. My associate has some photos that we'd like you to look at." Munroe had discussed this part of the questioning with Gerald, and following his instructions, he heard Gerald slap the photos of Easton's crime scene in front of Corrigan one after the other, only allowing a brief second's view of each. He heard Corrigan's breathing change with each grisly image.

Then came the moment that Munroe was anticipating. Corrigan's chains rattled violently and he slammed the table, prompting the guard waiting by the door to intervene.

Gerald stopped the guard from restraining Corrigan. "It's okay. We're fine," the big black man said in his deep bass tones.

"What the hell kind of game are you playing?" Corrigan said, venom in his voice.

Munroe had purposely mixed in a photo of Corrigan's family that Annabelle had acquired for them, one displaying four smiling faces, the kind sent out as a Christmas card. Gerald pulled the pictures away and said, "Sorry. That must have gotten mixed in."

"Why would you have that picture?"

Munroe answered, "It must have come from your file. We've been looking over it. I think that these cases are related somehow. I think General Easton might have been killed because he received some information about your case. I need you to fill in the gaps and help me stop whoever did this."

"You can't make me say anything. If you have any other questions, they can go through my lawyer."

"You have nothing to lose, sergeant. Easton has kids and grandkids out there right now who are preparing to put him in the ground. It's your duty as a soldier and a fellow man to help ensure that no one else gets hurt."

"That's right. I don't want anyone else to get hurt. I've got enough blood on my hands." Munroe heard the renewed rattling of Corrigan's chains and the sliding of his chair on the tile floor as the man stood. "Guard – I'm ready to go back to my cell."

8

Four white walls, a gray concrete floor, a stainless-steel toilet/
sink/drinking fountain combination, a gray metal desk with a
built-in oval stool bolted to the wall, and a small metal cot. This
had been John Corrigan's entire world since he had been convicted
of murder and sentenced to death by lethal injection. He had
resigned himself to an almost monastic existence with only a dozen
books and a single picture occupying his cell.

The photo was the last family portrait that he had taken with
his loved ones. It matched the one that the investigator from
DCIS had showed him. His wife Debbie and their two kids,
Mark and Melissa, all wore pink in the picture. Corrigan wore
a black button-down shirt and slacks. Debbie had bought him
a pink shirt to match the clothing of the rest of the family, but
he'd refused to wear it. It wasn't some kind of macho, masculine-
insecurity thing: he just didn't like the color. At least, that was
what he had told her. As he looked at the photo now, it seemed
as if he was a darkness that had invaded the happy brightness
of their lives.

Maybe that was accurate.

His hand strayed to their faces, tracing the lines of their smiles
and the outlines of their features. Mark had Debbie's hair and
eyes and Corrigan's strong jaw and dimpled chin. Melissa had

her father's blond hair color and eyes, but her chubby cheeks and huge toothy smile didn't resemble the features of either of her parents. Maybe she was just an amalgam of both or her baby fat hadn't melted away enough to let her future looks shine through. Corrigan would never know. He often tried to imagine what the kids would have looked like if their lives hadn't been cut short and wished that he possessed some kind of artistic ability that would have allowed him to create aged versions of them. Then he could have stared at those pictures and tried to convince himself that the people from the drawings were alive in the world somewhere and would grow up happy and safe.

He had been a good father, or at least he had done his best when circumstances allowed him to be there with his children. Unfortunately, he was always off somewhere fighting in places with names that his kids couldn't even pronounce. "When will you be back from Africanastan, Daddy?" his daughter had asked him in her tiny, high-pitched voice. He had missed most of their childhoods, but before their deaths, a possible opportunity had presented itself for him to become an instructor at MCB Quantico. They could have moved to Virginia, and he would have been home and safe every night. They could have been together and happy.

The tears rained down Corrigan's cheeks, and he pressed his eyes shut. Random images of his family floated through his mind. His wife on their wedding night. His son at a soccer game. His little girl running down a hill covered with flowers on her grandparents' farm. A rainbow-colored ribbon in the girl's hair flapped in the wind and wrapped around her face as she picked one of the flowers and spun in a circle.

He opened his eyes and wiped away the tears. It was his fault that they were dead. He should have done as he was told, and then he should have kept his mouth shut. Now General Easton and his wife had suffered a similar fate, and he suspected that he might not even live long enough for the executioner to stick a needle in his arm.

No one liked loose ends, and Corrigan was a loose end that had begun to fray and unravel. The general had learned the truth and died because of it, and now this DCIS investigator might share the same fate just for speaking with him. That was if the man who had visited him was actually who he claimed to be. Corrigan was never sure who he could trust. It wouldn't have been the first time that they had tested him in order to make a point about what would happen if he talked. His wife and kids might have been gone, but he still had his parents and a younger sister. He still had more that they could take if he didn't do as he was told.

John Corrigan looked down at his hands. He couldn't see the blood, but he could still feel the stain.

9

Deacon Munroe wanted to slam his fist down on the dashboard of the Lincoln Town Car, but he restrained himself. His father, the esteemed Senator Robert Munroe, had drilled into him since he was a small child that brash displays of anger and raised voices were for the uneducated and a sign of poor breeding. Robert Munroe had practiced what he'd preached. Deacon had seldom heard his father raise his voice, despite Robert being one of the most ruthless and cruel men that Deacon had ever met.

The hum of the roadway told him that they had left the streets surrounding the USDB and were back on the highway, heading to the airport. The entire trip had been a waste. John Corrigan clearly wasn't going to talk. And how could Munroe threaten or convince a man who was days away from being executed?

"We need to find out more about Corrigan," Munroe said. "I'm betting that he has enough knowledge to blow this case wide open, but we have to find a way to get through to him. Talk to his old friends, his family. Maybe he's being threatened in some way. We could also track down the marines who served on his team. Maybe one of them would be able to convince him to open up."

"Great. More plane rides," Gerald said.

"After all these years, I figured that you'd eventually get used to flying. Statistically, it is the safest way to travel."

"For birds, maybe," Gerald said under his breath. "Deac, I wanted to apologize for mentioning Beth yesterday. I know that you don't like to talk about her."

Munroe hesitated. She'd been dead for nearly ten years, but his breath still caught in his throat when he heard her name.

"It's fine. You were right. It has been a long time since she passed. I should be able to talk about her, and she would want me to move on. She was that way, always thinking of others first. But it still doesn't feel right. Besides, next to you, Annabelle is my oldest friend. Even if things were different, I wouldn't want to screw that up. And your sister deserves better than me."

Gerald was quiet for a moment. A Led Zeppelin song came on the radio, barely audible over the rumbling of the engine and the hum of the tires. Robert Plant crooned about going to California. "You remember that time when your daddy caught Annabelle in his bedroom, trying on your mother's jewelry?" Gerald said. "He was fixin' to take a willow branch to her, but you stepped in. I thought your daddy was the scariest man alive. Could not believe that you stood up to him. I don't think he could believe it, either. Real calm, he said that you would have to take her place. And you did. You show me another guy that would do something like that for my little sister."

"I'm not that kid anymore. Haven't been for a long time. Not even half of what he was."

"Deac, let me tell you, life is—"

Something hit their car so fast and hard that Munroe felt like he had been struck by the hand of God himself. His mind didn't even register what was happening. A cacophony of sound and sensation overwhelmed him. Metal screeched and buckled. Tires squealed. Gerald screamed. The world spun upside down.

Breaking glass. The pain was everywhere, all-encompassing, consuming him. Munroe felt it deep in his bones.

When the car finally came to a stop, he found himself hanging upside down by his seat belt. Only then did he realize that they had just been in a car accident, but his thoughts were still cloudy and incoherent. He fought to get his bearings.

The next sound brought the world into focus, his primal survival instincts kicking in at the loud crack of gunfire. His hands scrambled for the belt release, and finding it, he fell against the car's roof. Glass and debris cut into his face and palms.

Large hands grabbed him, and he fought against them at first until he recognized Gerald's voice. "Come on! You have to get out of there!"

A second bullet ricocheted off the car's metal undercarriage. Gerald yanked Munroe free from the wreckage like a rag doll and shoved him violently into a sitting position next to the car. He fought to catch his breath and slow his heart. "What—"

The crack of gunshots from just over his shoulder stung his ears. "Stay down!" Gerald yelled. More shots followed the words.

Munroe felt helpless and afraid. Someone was trying to kill them, and he was nothing but dead weight. More of a hindrance than a help.

The shots came from somewhere above them, and so Munroe suspected that they had rolled down a hill of some kind, perhaps into a field or yard. His hand touched the ground, and he felt grass beneath his palms. His ears strained to hear the sound of sirens and help approaching, but he heard nothing beyond the gunfire and a high-pitched ringing. He could feel the concussion of each shot, knew from the distinctive reports that there were two attackers.

More bullets struck the car. But this time the sound had changed. Instead of the individual cracks of a pistol, Munroe heard the rat-tat-tat of a fully automatic sub-machine gun.

Gerald cried out and dropped to the ground beside him. Munroe could hear the change in Gerald's breathing. Each breath was a harsh, pain-filled gasp. His shaking hands scrambled over his friend's body. He knew that Gerald had been wounded badly even before he felt the ragged, bloody hole in his partner's chest. He applied pressure to the wound to stop the flow of blood. "What can I do?" he said.

Gerald replied with a gurgling choke, and Munroe realized that Gerald's lung had been punctured. His best friend was drowning in his own blood.

Munroe tried harder to cover the wound, but the blood flowed out around his fingers. His mind fought for a solution. How could he treat a gunshot wound that had penetrated a lung? He thought back to his training in basic first aid. He had a vague memory that something could be done with the finger of a rubber glove and a needle, but he had neither of those things.

He felt so helpless. His best friend was dying in his arms, and he could do nothing to save him. Gerald needed a hospital, an ambulance, paramedics. Munroe felt in his pockets for his cell phone but quickly realized that it must have fallen out in the crash.

He reached for Gerald's pocket to feel for his friend's phone, but the big man caught his arm and shoved a pistol into Munroe's palm. Gerald wrapped his large fingers around Munroe's hand and squeezed reassuringly, his message clear.

You can do this.

But Munroe wondered what the hell good the gun would do him. He could fire blindly, but he would never be able to hold the attackers off until help arrived. He didn't even know how many rounds were left in the weapon.

Adrenalin pounding in his ears, he placed his back against the car's door and waited. Within a few seconds, he heard the sound of cautious footsteps coming down the hill. He shifted closer to Gerald and pressed his hand against his friend's body, trying to conceal the weapon clenched in his right fist. He remained perfectly still. The footsteps circled around them from both sides, both of the assailants keeping their distance.

"Is he dead?" the first man said, his voice moving closer. "His eyes look dead, but I think he's still breathing."

"He's blind. His eyes might look like that all the time," the second attacker replied from what sounded like less than ten feet to Munroe's right.

"I've never killed a handicapped person before."

Munroe held his breath and then reacted. He needed to take out both men in one move, or he wouldn't stand a chance. He had hoped that they would approach and announce their position in some way. It was his only chance. And his wish had come true.

Picturing them in his mind, he raised the gun and squeezed off two rapid-fire shots in each man's direction. Shouts of pain followed each pair of shots, and he heard both men drop.

Jumping to his feet and screaming with rage, Munroe fired again at the sounds of movement in the grass and continued to squeeze the trigger until the slide drew back and the gun clicked empty. He listened and waited for more noises, any indication that they were still alive, but both of the gunmen were silent.

Still shaking and breathless, Munroe collapsed against the car, for once relieved that he could not see what surrounded him.

Part Two

10

Feeling with his left hand, Deacon Munroe found the edge of his sideburn and used it as a marker to start the shave. His right thumb flicked on the electric razor, and he brought the device up against his left index finger that rested against the sideburn's edge. He brought the razor down, using his guide hand in front of it to trace the contours of his face.

Even the simple act of shaving made him think of Gerald. They had learned how to shave together. Gerald's father, who had always treated Munroe like his own son, had instructed the boys in the ways of manhood, something that Munroe's own father had never even considered. He remembered teasing Gerald that he looked like a mummy from all the little pieces of toilet paper covering the shaving nicks on his smooth dark skin.

The memories overwhelmed him. He couldn't breathe. The pain and anger coursing through his blood made his whole body feel warm and cold at the same time.

He smashed the razor down against the sink, feeling the plastic pieces shatter against his palm. Screaming, he ripped the mirror down from above the vanity and smashed it against a nearby cabinet. The rest was a whirlwind of angry fists contacting any surface he could reach. He lost his bearings and stumbled into the wall. His fists kept working. He felt his hand puncture the drywall, and he slammed it through again. This time his knuckles jammed against a stud, and pain shot through his hand and forearm. He tried to lose himself in the simple pain, a pain he could quantify, understand, and overcome. He slid down the wall to the floor and could no longer hold back the tears.

The door to the bathroom swung open, and Annabelle said, "What the hell are you doing? Dammit, Deac, there's glass everywhere."

He felt her kneel down beside him and raise a hand to his cheek.

"I miss him too. But now's not the time to fall apart. He wouldn't want that."

"It's too much," Munroe whispered. "I've lost too much already. I can't imagine going on without him."

"I'm not going to listen to you feel sorry for yourself. You're better than this, stronger than this. Come on. Let's get this mess cleaned up."

Raising his hand to her face, Munroe traced the lines of Annabelle's features and stroked her thick, wavy hair. The prominent cheekbones. The soft skin. The full lips.

He had loved her for as long as he could remember. When they'd been growing up, Annabelle and Gerald had been his true brother and sister, much more so than his actual flesh-and-blood siblings. His emotions had felt strange and confusing at first. Then he had fought them out of respect for Gerald and the differences in age between Annabelle and himself. A three-year gap had seemed like a lot when he'd been seventeen. Munroe had moved on in college, found the love of his life, married, started a family. Beth had been his everything, but, through it all, his love for Annabelle had never flickered out. Even though Beth had been gone for many years, he still felt guilty for the feelings he harbored toward his best friend's sister. And now he couldn't fight them any longer.

He pulled Annabelle close and kissed her deeply and passionately. Her skin smelled like jasmine, and he tasted strawberries on her lips. The feel of her soft skin against his gave him strength and hope.

Then it was gone. She shoved him away. He could hear the tears in her voice as she whispered, "Damn you."

She stood and moved to the door. "Damn you, Deacon. How dare you?"

"Annabelle, I—"

"Don't. Do you have any idea how many years I've waited for you? And now you pull this."

"I don't understand."

"You're devastated and looking for something to hang on to, anything to make you forget. You're looking for a port in the storm, an anchor, and I just happened to be here. But I'm not going to be your painkiller. I deserve better."

"It's not like that. I—"

Annabelle slammed the bathroom door and stormed off down the hall. Munroe heard her angry footfalls moving down the stairs, his front door opening and slamming shut, and her car starting up. His hands ached from his stupid outburst, and his heart ached from her words and the pain and hurt he had heard within them. Sitting amid the broken glass and drywall dust of the ruined bathroom, Deacon Munroe felt more alone than he ever had in his life.

11

Under normal circumstances, Jonas Black would have liked his solitary-confinement cell in the Administrative Segregation building better than the communal living of the general-population dormitory. Unfortunately, the prisoner in the cell directly above his was a member of the Southern Brotherhood, and some kind of design flaw in the Ad Seg ventilation system allowed the man to piss into his vent and have it rain down right onto Black's cot. Jonas had moved his mattress to the floor, but the smell inside the tiny block-walled space was overwhelming. And the Alabama heat seemed to be multiplied twentyfold inside the walls of Ad Seg. Complaining would do him little good and only announce to the white supremacist with the overactive bladder that his attacks had succeeded. Jonas refused to give him the satisfaction.

A guard – petite, black, and female – knocked on the small glass window embedded in the cell door. Jonas couldn't imagine the kind of things that she had to put up with as a guard at Holman, and he respected her for that. "Black, you have a visitor."

"A visitor? Who?"

As the female officer unlocked the chuck hole used to insert a food tray into the cell, she said, "Do I look like your butler? They told me you have a visitor and to come get you. That's what I'm doing. Let's get cuffed up."

Jonas knew the drill. He turned around backwards and stuck his hands out through the chuck hole. The guard slapped on the restraints and called into her radio, "Open L-23."

The door slid open, and she led Jonas through the cell block past a hundred sets of eyes peering out through the tiny windows of the gray cell doors. Anything happening on the block constituted entertainment to the prisoners of Ad Seg. Jonas's tennis shoes squeaked against the concrete floor with every step. The whole block smelled faintly of sweat and excrement.

Connected to the cell block was a small room that the warden and captains often used to hold private conferences with the prisoners. An old wooden table with a scarred surface that had been spray-painted gray sat in the center of the room. Four white plastic chairs – the kind that people typically used as lawn furniture – surrounded the table.

The female guard shoved Jonas down into one of the chairs. The restraints behind his back forced him to sit uncomfortably on his hands. A man wearing expensive-looking designer sunglasses sat in one of the chairs opposite him. He guessed by the look of the quality of the man's suit that it cost more than Jonas had made from a week with hazard pay. The guy had the stink of a government agency all over him, the kind identified only by initials. Jonas Black, like many other soldiers who had witnessed first-hand the casual attitude that alphabet agencies displayed toward sending men to their deaths, was instantly distrustful of anyone representing such a bureaucracy. The woman next to the sunglasses man had skin the color of dark chocolate, wavy black hair that fell to her shoulders, and the prominent cheekbones of a model. Her eyes were red and puffy, as though she had been crying.

The man stuck his arm out over the table as if to shake Jonas's hand. Couldn't the guy see that his hands were cuffed behind his back?

The woman said, "He's restrained, Deacon."

"Apologies." The man's hand fell back under the table. "My name is Deacon Munroe. I'm a special investigator with DCIS. This is my associate, Miss Annabelle Dixon." When he spoke, the words were smooth as silk. He had a Southern accent, but it didn't have a country or redneck feel. Instead, it had a cultured quality like the voice of a professor.

Jonas sat quietly. He knew that Munroe would be expecting him to ask what interest DCIS had in him, but he had always found that silence had a strange way of establishing dominance in situations such as this.

Munroe reached up and removed the sunglasses, placing them on the table with delicate care. The man's eyes were a piercing blue, but the stare was vacant and cold like that of a dead body, gazing off into nothingness. The eyes were wide and haunting and made Jonas feel strangely uneasy.

"Do my eyes bother you, Mr. Black?"

He didn't think he had shown any reaction, especially one that a blind man could have detected. "Not nearly as much as they must bother you."

"I'm sure you're wondering about me being an investigator but also being blind. Most people do. They always ask if I have super-smelling abilities or ultrasonic hearing or things of that nature."

"An old blind man used to live next to my family in East St. Louis. The kids in the neighborhood always either treated him like he was an invalid or that he had some kind of superpowers and could hear through walls and figure out what you ate for breakfast just by smelling you. Neither of those things were true. But the bottom line is that I don't really care about your abilities one way or the other. If you don't mind, let's get to the point of why you're disturbing my rehabilitation."

"Do you have other important matters to address today, Mr. Black? Things that I'm interrupting?"

"It's meat loaf day."

"You must be a big fan."

"I hate meat loaf. I'd rather eat dirt."

Neither man spoke for a long moment. Munroe broke the silence first. "It's my understanding that you're a former Recon Marine. Is that correct?"

"Why are you here?"

Munroe slammed his fist on the table. The sudden break in the man's calm exterior startled Jonas. Munroe looked away and sighed, his jaw clenched. He looked disgusted, but Jonas got the feeling that he was more upset with himself.

"I'm here because I have a need for two things. A new bodyguard and someone who can help me get through to a man that is pivotal to my current investigation. You, Mr. Black, are in the unique position to fill both of those needs for me. I'm here to offer you a job."

Jonas laughed. "I have a pretty good career going in the prison laundry. They think I have management potential."

Munroe clenched his fists. "This is no joke. My partner and best friend was recently killed, and I *am* going to find those responsible."

The woman next to Munroe stood up and moved toward the door. Jonas saw tears forming in her eyes. "Annabelle?" Munroe said.

"I can't. I'll be outside," she said, her voice shaking.

"How long has it been since you lost your friend?" Jonas asked.

"About two days."

Jonas felt like a jerk. He supposed that a stint in prison hadn't done much for his manners. "I'm sorry. But I don't know how I could help you with anything. I have at least six months left in here. And that's if I don't get any extra time added on for an incident that I was recently involved in."

"I've already spoken to the warden, the governor, and the Alabama Board of Pardons and Paroles. Your sentence would be commuted, and you would be released into my custody. Technically, you would be an agent working within DCIS, but your only responsibility would be to aid me in this investigation."

"I don't buy it. And, even if you *could* get me out, the government doesn't hire felons. Hell, I couldn't even legally carry a firearm."

"Don't worry about that. Once we have you out, your record will be sealed and marked as classified to the highest level for reasons of national security. Only someone with very high clearance would even know that you're a felon, and they would have no reason to check."

Jonas wasn't sure what to say or believe. How could this guy have gotten all that done? And in the space of a couple of days? "Who are you?" he said.

"I've already told you that. But if you're asking how I could pull off something like this, the answer is that I've made a lot of influential friends over the years and through the course of my investigations. There are many times when the greater good can be better served by suppressing certain knowledge to keep it from public consumption. Many people appreciate me for my discretion. Plus, the chairman of the parole board is an old friend of my father."

"But why me?"

"Where I'm going, I could use a hard man like you."

"I wouldn't make a very good babysitter."

"I'm not looking for someone to wipe my ass, Mr. Black. I'm looking for someone to watch my back. And I believe that you are also perfect for this particular investigation."

"You mentioned something about getting through to someone."

"That's right. A man named John Corrigan. I believe that he was your team leader and a close friend."

"We *were* close, but I haven't spoken to John in years. I was in here when the incident happened with his family, and I haven't heard from him since all that went down. But John couldn't have done the things they said. When we were deployed, all he ever wanted was to get back to his family."

"Men who have fought together usually have a special bond that isn't easily broken. I think he'll talk to you."

"I would never do anything to betray my friend."

"I'm not asking you to betray him," Munroe said. "I'm asking you to help him. Corrigan's execution is scheduled for this weekend. I'm starting to suspect that he may be innocent. At the very least, there's a lot more to his case than meets the eye. This is a unique opportunity, Mr. Black. I'm giving you a second chance. Even when you get out of here, you'll have a difficult time finding work. People don't hire felons, as you said. Most reputable military contractors wouldn't touch you with a ten-foot pole. Your days as a soldier are over. I know a bit about your colorful past, but I also suspect that you don't want to fall back into that world. I've had two friends killed over this case, and I need your help."

Jonas still didn't trust the government man, and Munroe's comments about his *discretion* didn't help to alleviate those concerns. It sounded as if Munroe might be some kind of fixer for the DOD, someone who could make scandals go away. But Jonas knew that he wasn't in a position to judge anyone, and if he stayed in Holman, the Southern Brotherhood would eventually find a way to kill him. He might be able to hold them off for a while, but eventually, they would catch him off guard and bury a shank in his back. And if he took this opportunity for early release maybe he'd also get a chance to help Corrigan. There really wasn't much of a choice.

"Okay. When do we leave?"

12

It took a while to get Jonas Black's release processed, and once they were on the road, Munroe lay down in the back of their dark GMC Yukon to get some rest. Jonas rode up front with Annabelle. She filled him in on the details of their current case and then told him stories about her brother, who had been Munroe's partner. Jonas could tell that she was devastated by the loss, and he could empathize with how she was feeling. He had lost his brother as well, but at least she could say that hers had died a hero.

It was a long drive filled with awkward silences and bittersweet memories. But as Georgia and the Carolinas whipped by outside the window, Jonas convinced Annabelle to let him make a stop in Stafford, Virginia to pick up a few of his old things.

He had never seen the house, but he had kept tabs on its residents even from inside the walls of Holman and knew the address. It was a tiny two-bedroom ranch-style surrounded by a small lawn of dried-up brown grass. The siding was decades old but newly painted. The dark gray shingles had weathered too many storms over too many years and had begun to crack and warp. The doorbell didn't work, and so he opened the screen and knocked on an old wooden door with a small diamond-shaped window in its center.

A moment later a face appeared behind the glass. The look in the small blond woman's eyes went from shock to disgust to fury. The door opened slowly, and she stepped out onto the porch. Her breathing was fast, her jaw clenched. She looked pretty much the same as Jonas remembered. Short, blond, and beautiful. Maybe a bit heavier, a few more wrinkles around her eyes.

When she spoke, each word came slowly as if her rage could barely allow her to speak at all. "How dare you come here, Jonas."

"Hello, Stacey. I just stopped by to see if you still had my old duffle and . . . maybe see Will. Is he here?"

Stacey slapped him hard across the face and shoved him down the steps and off her porch. "Your duffle is rotting in the old shed around back. I hoped it would rot there forever, just like I hoped you'd rot in prison for the rest of your worthless life. But I guess things never work out the way you hope."

Jonas's gaze didn't waver under her hate-filled stare. "No, they don't."

"The shed's unlocked. Get your stuff and leave. If you ever come back here, I'll call the police and slap you with a restraining order."

"Listen, I realize you'll never forgive me, but I want you to know that I'm sorry for everything. I want to be part—"

Stacey turned her back on him, stormed inside the house, and slammed the door.

Jonas watched the clouds rolling through the gray sky for a moment, trying to keep the tears from falling. *Never let them see you cry.* Then he walked around the side of the small house and through the tiny backyard to an old tool shed that looked like it could fall in on itself at any moment. Inside, he found a mass of discarded junk – old children's toys, broken lawn chairs, ripped-open bags of grass seed – and stuffed into one corner was his old green duffle. He pulled it free from the rest of the junk and checked the contents. Stacey had apparently never even opened it up: a roll of old clothes still hid his MEU(SOC) pistol, just as he had left it. The big black gun was a .45-caliber based on the M1911, the standard-issue side arm for Recon. But it was also in a state of disrepair and held only seven rounds in the magazine and one in the chamber, something he had never liked about it.

He found a photo beneath the pistol. Its corners had yellowed with age and moisture. It showed him and his brother, Michael, as kids in the old neighborhood. He stuffed the photo into his pocket and packed the gun back into the duffle.

When he climbed into the Yukon, Annabelle didn't comment on the woman who had slapped him but said, "Is everything okay?"

Jonas swallowed hard and replied, "That actually went better than I was expecting."

13

Annabelle pulled the vehicle up in front of a small building built of gray weather-beaten concrete. A large display window filled with an eclectic assortment of junk occupied the building's face, and a green awning hung over the entrance with the words *Savoy & Sons Pawnbrokers* stenciled on it in three-foot block letters. A condemned building with a burned-out facade and a greasy-spoon diner flanked the pawnshop. When Jonas stepped from the Yukon, the smell of grease mixed with uncollected garbage assaulted his nostrils.

"What are we doing here?" he asked his new companions.

Munroe said, "It may take a few days for all your paperwork to go through, but you need a weapon and equipment now if you're going to act as my bodyguard. We'll get you set up with clothes and a phone after we leave here – you'll need some suits – but this is the best place to pick up a side arm without a waiting period and with no questions asked."

"A pawnshop?"

As she held open the door, Annabelle smiled and said, "Never judge a book by its cover."

The building's interior matched a thousand other pawnshops in a thousand other cities. Guitars and amps lined one wall. CDs, DVDs, and games were on another. A jewelry case. Tools.

Miscellaneous junk that some crackhead had stolen to finance his next fix. A wall behind the counter displayed a limited assortment of long guns. A small display case contained a few old handguns.

A woman with long black hair who was wearing a blue and white baseball shirt and a Washington Nationals cap stood behind the counter. She frowned at the newcomers. "You're late," she said.

Munroe replied, "It's wonderful to see you too, Tobi."

The woman stepped out from behind the counter and hugged Annabelle. Annabelle gestured at Jonas. "This is the new associate that I told you about. We need you to get him set up. Jonas Black, this is Tobi Savoy."

Jonas shook her hand and said, "You don't look like one of the '& Sons'."

Tobi rolled her eyes. "My dad doesn't have any sons. He just wishes he did." She moved toward a door in the corner with a key-code lock marked *Employees Only*. "Step into my office."

The group moved down a flight of poorly lit concrete stairs to another door at the bottom. Tobi unlocked this one with a key from her pocket and stepped inside. Jonas followed and felt the jarring sensation that he had been instantly transported to another world. Tobi Savoy's quaint little shop – named after her non-existent brothers – had enough firepower in its basement to kick-start World War Three.

The most surprising aspect, however, wasn't the guns but the atmosphere. Jonas knew that places like this existed behind the facade of normal businesses, but he had never imagined anything like this. In the movies, hidden weapons caches were, more often than not, dark and lined with steel cages and had a utilitarian feel. Savoy's hidden room reminded Jonas more of a high-end cigar shop – dark wood grains, lighted glass display cases, red leather high-back chairs, a table in the corner topped with brandy snifters and decanters filled with dark liquids.

Tobi Savoy spread her arms and looked at Jonas. "Pick your poison. You want a 9mm, a .40? Glock, SIG?"

"I hate Glocks. Their grips feel like you're holding a 2x4. And the SIG Sauer I would want doesn't have a large enough magazine capacity. What do you have in .45 ACP with a double-stack mag that holds more than ten rounds?"

"I like a customer that knows what he wants." Tobi looked at a case and tapped her fingers against her two front teeth. "Let's see. 1911s are out. No Glocks. Something with an extended mag wouldn't be good concealed under your coat. Berettas don't have the capacity you want. What about Springfield Armory?"

"Never been that impressed."

"Picky, picky. Are you familiar with Taurus?"

"I've shot some of the revolvers."

"Try this." Tobi laid a full-framed pistol with a polymer grip and stainless steel slide on the table. It reminded him of a SIG Sauer. "Tauruses are relatively inexpensive, but they have decent products that come with a lot of bells and whistles. Designed for the armed forces. External hammer. Automatic double-action re-strike. Completely ambidextrous. Safe, fire, decock. Adjustable grip with inserts to fit your hand size. Four-inch barrel. And a 12+1 mag capacity."

Annabelle said, "I thought you marines were good shots."

"We are," Jonas said with pride.

"Then why is magazine capacity such an issue? Aren't one or two shots enough to take someone down."

"Yeah, but what if there's twelve of them?" Jonas picked up the pistol and sighted down the barrel, got a feel for the weapon. The grip fit his hand like it had been tailored specifically for him. He fell in love instantly. "I'll take it. I also need a tactical knife and body armor. Actually, make that two sets of body armor, one for me and one for Munroe."

"None for me, thanks," the blind man said.

"I'm supposed to be protecting you, right? Well, this is me protecting you."

"Bullet-resistant vests are too restrictive. I have enough restrictions without adding another. You can go ahead and get it, and I'll try it. But I'm not promising I'll wear it."

After a bit more back and forth, they decided upon a vest and an open-assisted folding combat knife equipped with a tungsten-coated blade, seat-belt ripper, and glass-breaker.

Munroe said, "Okay, Tobi. What about me? What did Santa bring me for Christmas?"

Tobi placed a sealed cardboard box on the counter. "It's a bit early for Christmas, but here you go. It wasn't easy to find these. They're still in the prototyping stage."

Jonas noticed Annabelle looking strangely at Munroe, but she didn't comment. She paid their bill, and then they all headed back to the car. Annabelle carried the cardboard box under one arm and led Munroe with the other. Jonas noticed her glancing down at the package every few feet. He could tell that she was having trouble suppressing the urge to tear off the tape and discover what was inside the mysterious box. Still, she said nothing as they piled into the Yukon and headed out of DC.

14

As they entered the quaint little town of Thurmont, Maryland, a large wooden sign declared the city to be the "Gateway to the Mountains". They passed car dealerships, small diners, and other locally owned businesses. Thick patches of trees and split-rail fences surrounded several of the homes. Jonas Black noticed a few rummage sales occupying the front lawns. They opened the Yukon's windows, and the smell of burning yard waste floated in on the breeze. Bright blue skies. Rolling green mountains in the distance. Jonas had a hard time reconciling such a picturesque and serene atmosphere with the prison world to which he had become accustomed. He noticed a sign about the Catoctin Mountain Park and knew that it was the location of the famous Camp David. He understood why the President would want to visit this area to relax.

They wound down two-lane roads until they reached a rock trail hidden among the trees just north of town. A two-story colonial-revival-style home sat at the end of the lane in front of a sprawling front yard. Its gray stone facade reminded Jonas of old cobblestones. A large porch enclosed by white pillars and railings wrapped around the main structure of the house.

"This is where you live?" Jonas asked Munroe.

"You like it?"

"It's beautiful."

"Well, don't get the wrong idea. Even though we're only an hour out of DC, this place cost me less than a third of what a little condo in the city would have."

The interior stunned Jonas even more. Oak cabinets, hardwood floors, open staircase, a sun room, pocket doors, skylights, stone-accent walls, walkout basement. By his standards, it was a mansion. He felt as though he had just been adopted by Daddy Warbucks.

Once inside, Munroe navigated his way through the house like a sighted person. Apart from tripping over a basketball bag that someone had dropped in the middle of a walkway. Munroe growled and kicked it to the side. He directed Jonas and Annabelle to the kitchen table and started preparing a meal.

Munroe pulled food boxes and canned goods from the cabinet and held his phone up to each. A mechanical voice on the phone announced the name of the product. One by one, Munroe scanned the cans and packages, setting the ones he wanted aside. He grabbed measuring cups and cooking utensils marked with small Braille labels.

Munroe asked if they wanted something to drink, and Jonas watched with interest as Munroe hung a device with two extended prongs over the edges of cups and poured in the liquids they had requested. The device beeped when the liquid reached the proper level.

A door from the garage opened, and two young girls stepped into the kitchen. They both held cell phones in front of their faces, typing furiously. The older girl said to the other, "I'm telling you. He's got a horse face."

"Shut up, Mak. At least I have a boyfriend."

They both came up short at the sight of the large, dark, tattooed man sitting at their kitchen table. Before they could run screaming for the hills, Annabelle rushed over and gave each girl a hug. But they still eyed Jonas cautiously.

"This is Jonas Black," Annabelle said to the girls in her sweet Southern voice. "He's going to be working with your dad and me."

The perky younger sister stuck out her hand. She had bleach-blond hair and bright blue eyes that reminded him of Munroe's, only without the vacant stare. "I'm Chloe. The pretty one. That's Makayla. The weird one."

Jonas laughed and shook Chloe's hand. The older girl, Makayla, looked him up and down and said, "What's up." She wore ripped jeans and a Nirvana T-shirt. At first glance, Makayla seemed to be the antithesis of her sister. Reserved vs perky. Smart vs pretty. Rocker chick vs cheerleader. But Jonas sensed that Makayla carried a lot more weight on her shoulders and in her heart than her younger sister did.

He couldn't help but think of his own brother. He and Michael had also been very different. Michael had been thin and wiry. He ran from conflict, while Jonas always seemed to be fighting someone or something. One played guitar, one played football. One went to college, one went into the military.

But blood would always be thicker than differences in personal style and interests.

Munroe walked in and hugged both girls before saying, "Who dropped their bag in the middle of the hallway?"

Makayla rolled her eyes. "Take a guess."

"Chloe, you know how important it is to put your things away when living with a person who's visually impaired. A place for everything and—"

"Everything in its place," the girls finished in unison.

Munroe frowned. "Okay, smart-asses. What's been going on while I've been away?"

Jonas watched Munroe and the girls as they laughed and joked back and forth and fell into the easy rhythms of a family.

Chloe had a new boyfriend. Makayla needed help with a political-science project. Chloe wanted permission to go to a concert. Makayla needed gas money.

He guessed that Chloe was thirteen or fourteen, while Makayla was at least sixteen. With a heavy heart, Jonas thought of a boy who was about Chloe's age. His name was Will. Will Black. And unlike Munroe's daughters, Will had grown up without his father.

They all ate dinner together – the best meal Jonas had consumed in a long time – but he still felt like an outsider, even though everyone asked him questions and included him in the conversations. He remembered a *Sesame Street* song from his childhood, "One of These Things Is Not Like the Others". And that was him. He just didn't belong. Strangely enough, he felt more at home and at ease within the walls of a prison than he did sitting with a family around a dinner table.

The girls warmed to Jonas quickly, especially Chloe. She showed him a website called YouTube that he had heard about but had yet to experience for himself. "OMG, you have to see this," she said before showing him a load of funny and interesting content – a guy getting a DUI and being shot with a taser while riding a lawnmower, hilarious examples of bad lip-reading, funny real-life news footage converted into song parodies, and videos on recycling such as how to make a life vest or a raft out of empty two-liter soda bottles.

After the meal, Annabelle showed him to a guest room and then brought in some sleep clothes that she thought might fit. Her eyes moistened, and he guessed that the clothes had belonged to her brother.

Jonas lay back on the bed and stared at the ceiling. It all felt so surreal. The day before he had been sleeping on the floor of a cell in Ad Seg, and now here he was at a house in the countryside less than five miles from the President's own private retreat.

A few minutes later, the sound of arguing echoed out from one of the bedrooms down the hall, and curiosity got the better of him. He crept into the hallway so that he could hear what was being said.

15

Deacon Munroe ran his fingers over the fabric of the garments in his closet and found the suit that he wanted to wear the next day. In the past, he had tried several different organizational methods for the blind that involved marking the garments in some way or sorting them by color on the clothes rod, but those still required outside help. So when a handy device called the Bright-F became available, he jumped at the chance to own one. The gadget functioned by detecting the brightness, saturation, and hue of objects, allowing the device to determine the object's color. It had also allowed Munroe to handle his own laundry more easily. One step closer to total independence.

As he waved the flashlight-shaped scanner over his clothes and selected the proper outfit for the next day, Annabelle sat down on the bed behind him. He could feel her disapproval from across the room, but he knew that her feelings didn't relate to his wardrobe choices.

"Just say what's on your mind," Munroe said. "Your stare is burning holes in my back."

"You sure didn't waste any time."

"In what?"

"Replacing my brother."

"Jonas Black is a big dumb animal. He's hardly meant to serve as a replacement for Gerald."

"Then why?"

"You know damn well why."

"This investigation already took my brother. I don't want to lose you too. Just let it go, Deac. Let NCIS handle it."

Munroe walked over and sat next to Annabelle on the bed. He wanted to take her hand but wasn't sure how she would react. They had yet to speak of their kiss and her abrupt exit. She seemed content to pretend that it had never happened. "NCIS doesn't have both oars in the water on this one," he said. "I owe it to your brother to find the people responsible."

"You've never been a crusader."

"Maybe now's a good time to start."

"By bringing a murderer into the house where your daughters sleep?"

Munroe shook his head and gave a dismissive laugh. "You read his file. Black's a soldier and a trained killer, but he's not a murderer. Not really. He had less than six months left on his sentence."

"I know. He seems like a good man, but—"

"I'm not running from this fight, and, make no mistake, it will be a fight. Good old-fashioned, down and dirty. Jonas Black is an attack dog. And when I find the people to blame for this mess, I'm going to let that dog off his leash."

16

Wyatt Randall might have been some kind of scientific genius, but he wasn't good enough at being on the run to hide from Antonio de Almeida forever. Randall had phoned his mother to let her know that he was okay, and the considerate act had been his downfall. Almeida easily tracked back the call to a small rented house in the countryside near Annapolis, Maryland that Randall had paid for with cash. Almeida found it terribly convenient that Randall had chosen a place with no immediate neighbors to hear the scientist's screams.

Now Almeida stared down at Randall's unconscious form. After knocking the man out, he had placed him in the small home's bathtub and prepared him for the interrogation to come. Before beginning, Almeida took a moment to pray for Wyatt Randall's soul and for God to open the man's heart and mind so that he would answer his questions without suffering needlessly.

With a wave of smelling salts beneath his nose, Randall's eyes fluttered open. His gaze darted around his surroundings with animal-like fear. The rest of his body didn't move.

"Hello, Wyatt," Almeida said. "Don't bother trying to move your arms or legs. I've injected lidocaine into your brachial plexus nerves and the subarachnoid block, essentially paralyzing your extremities."

"What the— Please . . . You can't kill me. Lennix needs me."

Almeida shrugged. "I think that like many Americans you overestimate your own worth." He moved to the edge of the tub and leaned down close to Randall. "When I was a boy in Colombia, I was stolen from my family and forced to work as slave labor in the coca fields. This was years before I met Ramon Castillo, and the man in charge of the fields showed no such compassion to me as Ramon did. They encouraged us to chew on the coca leaves while we worked. It gave us more energy, and as we became addicted, we grew more dependent on our captors. The leaves had a strong tea-like odor and a pungent taste. I can still feel the texture on my tongue. One night, a group of Colombian and American soldiers raided the camp, and during the fight, the building where the children were held caught fire. Almost all my friends were burned alive. Only myself and a few others, who had been selected to work that night, survived the battle. In the confusion, I ran into the jungle and hid beneath an outcropping along the bank of the river. But the mud there was like quicksand. My feet sank down, and I was not strong enough to pull them out."

"Please, I—"

"Shhh." Almeida hushed Randall gently like a mother comforting her child. "It started to rain, and the waters of the river slowly rose around me. Creeping up my body as though some great beast was devouring me, like the way an anaconda feeds. I learned that day how frightened and helpless it can make a person feel to see his or her own death slowly approaching. I have never felt fear like that again. I would have given anything to hold back the waters. Luckily, God answered my prayers, and I learned something from that experience. I learned much about myself, but also about the nature of fear and our primitive survival instincts. Later on, I put this knowledge into practice when I went to work for the Castillo Cartel."

"You'll never find anything if you kill me."

Almeida ignored the comment, his calm and smooth demeanor never cracking. "Today, Wyatt, you will feel what I felt as the waters slowly consumed me. I'm going to turn on the faucet here in the tub, just a slow stream, and your paralyzed body will be unable to escape it. I will not stop the flow until you've told me all that I want to know. Please do not test my resolve on this. You will tell me where to find the stolen files or you will die. But first, you will learn the true power of fear."

17

When deciding on a design for the organization's new corporate headquarters, Brendan Lennix had wanted something that would make headlines. He wanted to show the world that the company's previous financial challenges were over, that they were now one of the premier pharmaceutical research powers in the world. The Lennix Building twisted into the sky like a natural honeycomb spire. Complex lattice bracings clad in panels of white Corian – a substance normally found in kitchen countertops, bathroom vanities, and showers – surrounded a concrete core. The unique building had graced the covers of several newspapers and architectural magazines, just as Brendan had hoped. To the outside world, Lennix Pharmaceuticals was at the top of its game.

Brendan's penthouse office occupied the entire fifteenth floor. And why not? It was called the Lennix Building, after all. He stared out over the city of Bethesda like a king admiring his domain. He sipped a glass of Macallan 1939, a ten-thousand-dollar-a-bottle Scotch, and wondered where everything had gone wrong.

The situation was way out of control. Brendan Lennix had never wanted anyone to get hurt. In fact, his goal had always been to help people, to make the world a better place – while turning a large profit for the company that his father had founded, of course. Unfortunately, since his father's death and

Brendan's rise to the seat of power, he had made a long string of bad business decisions that had sent that company teetering on the verge of bankruptcy.

It was at that point that he had sold his soul to the devil.

It had seemed so perfect at the time, so serendipitous. His chief of security, a former Spec Ops soldier turned mercenary named Oliver Pike, had offered him a way to pull the business back from the edge of oblivion. Pike had done some work for a wealthy organization in Mexico that then invested the money necessary to keep Lennix Pharmaceuticals afloat. Then fate had dropped Wyatt Randall into his lap with a breakthrough that could literally change the world.

They had immediately approached the Defense Department about financing the drug, and they would eventually have the rights to release it to the general public. They would make billions upon billions. But that was when everything had started to unravel.

Lennix's phone vibrated in the holster on his belt. Recognizing Almeida's burner cell-phone number, he said, "Tell me you have good news."

"I have news. I'll let you decide how you feel about it. I've found Randall. He's told me everything. He gave the stolen files to General Easton."

Lennix threw the glass of Macallan 1939 across the room. The shards rained down on the dark hardwood floor, and the exorbitantly priced liquid slid down the wall. "You said that you and Pike searched his files and questioned Easton about this."

"The missing files were not on his computer nor in his office. He must have hidden them or given them to someone else. As I've told you, we didn't have time for a proper interrogation, and the commandant was not a man who frightened easily. He was a soldier. Like me."

"You're not a soldier, Almeida. You're just a psychopath with delusions of grandeur. Normally, I wouldn't care about that, but since you seem unable to do your job, it's becoming a problem."

"Mr. Lennix, I understand that you are under a terrible amount of stress and so I will not hold your comments against you. But insulting me serves little purpose."

Almeida's calm tone and measured reply made Lennix's blood boil even more fiercely. He fought to maintain his composure. After a moment, Lennix said, "I do have one idea about who Easton might have given the files to. A DCIS investigator named Deacon Munroe showed up to pay a visit to John Corrigan. He was also at Easton's crime scene. I ordered the two men stationed in Leavenworth to eliminate him. They killed his partner, but Munroe himself survived."

"That was very stupid," Almeida said. "If this Deacon Munroe really did have full access to the files, he wouldn't be visiting Corrigan. He'd be taking this to the DOD, and they'd be busting your door down. And Corrigan probably didn't share anything with him. It might have ended there. The trail might have dried up. Munroe might have let the investigation drop. But now that you've attacked him and killed his partner, he'll keep pushing. Once again, I will need to step in and clean up your mess, Mr. Lennix."

"My mess! Why, you son of a—"

"I don't have time to contend with your ignorance. Tell me everything that you know about Deacon Munroe."

"I know that one of the people on his team has been asking around about Wyatt Randall. So apparently he knows more than you think."

"Perhaps. Either way, we can use his knowledge of Wyatt Randall to our advantage. Do you have anything else that you'd like me to ask Mr. Randall or anything that you'd like me to tell him?"

"Why?"

"Because, unfortunately, I'm going to have to kill him now."

18

The Washington, DC NCIS field office resided inside the Forge Building at the back of the Washington Navy Yard. Munroe had crossed paths and swords with the NCIS on many occasions. It was often difficult enough for governmental organizations to establish who had jurisdiction on cases. FBI, NCIS, Homeland Security, and others were always fighting for control when the lines blurred. Then there was Deacon Munroe, the resident wild card. His cases often intruded into the territories of other agencies, but there was little they could do since he was typically acting on special orders from the Joint Chiefs or DOD. In this instance, however, he was on his own. Luckily, NCIS Special Agent Dean Markham knew that, in the same way that normal people had hobbies or collected knick-knacks, Deacon Munroe collected favors. Markham was a practical man and realized that it was far simpler to give Munroe limited access rather than fight him on the issue. When they arrived, Markham led Munroe and Jonas Black past the buzz of cubicles to a bank of elevators leading to the autopsy room.

The NCIS medical examiner's space had a cold sterile feel. The hum of refrigeration units and an industrial-strength ventilation system filled the space, reverberating off the tiles of the floor and the stainless steel of the examination tables. Contrary to popular belief, a properly run autopsy room didn't smell of rotting flesh or decay. The staff washed it thoroughly and meticulously and systems were in place to keep the odors of death at bay. Still, beneath it all, Munroe could detect a hint of the wet and almost sickeningly sweet smell of human remains.

"Dr. Stapleton," Munroe said, extending his right hand, "Wonderful to see you again. I trust that you are as lovely as ever."

She took his hand, and as he typically did, he wrapped his left hand around her forearm. With this light touch he could feel the rough, wrinkled skin, but he could also tell that she had kept her figure. The wrists and forearms were thin and muscular. Munroe had known Dr. Terry Stapleton for a long time, and he also knew that she was past the age of retirement and had been fighting against being put out to pasture for the past year.

Stapleton laughed. "Deacon, I appreciate the flattery, but it almost hurts my feelings that the only one I hear things like that from these days is a blind man."

"All the others are just too intimidated to speak in the presence of such radiance."

This earned him another chuckle. But then, after a moment of silence, her voice grew solemn. "I heard about Gerald. I'm really sorry."

Munroe suppressed his feelings and replied, "I'm sorry as well, but where are my manners? This is Jonas Black. He's going to be assisting me on this case."

"Pleasure to meet you."

"Ma'am," Jonas said in his deep gravelly voice.

"How's Annabelle holding up?" Stapleton asked, but Munroe heard Markham sigh.

All business, Special Agent Markham said, "I'm sorry, Dr. Stapleton, Agent Munroe, but I do have other matters to attend to. Can we go ahead and get started?"

"Of course," Stapleton said, switching into professional mode. "I'll cut to the chase. I'm sure that you were hoping for something more, Deacon, but I haven't found anything unusual with the bodies. The wife died of blunt-force trauma to the face and head. The wound patterns are consistent with the husband's fists. Lacerations on General Easton's face and neck match the size of the wife's fingernails, and I found his DNA beneath her nails. Based on the powder burns on his temple and GSR on his hands, I can say almost certainly that he held the gun and shot himself."

"Could someone have forced him to do it?"

"Physically, I don't think so. He was still in great shape for his age, and there was no bruising on the limbs to indicate that he was restrained in any way. I hate to say it, Deacon, but it certainly looks like he beat her to death and then shot himself."

"What about the toxicology report?" Munroe asked.

"All negative. The only odd thing we found was elevated levels of certain monatomic metals."

"Could that have caused some kind of hysteria?"

"No, there are several supplements on the market that contain monatomic metals and that make all kinds of wild claims. Nothing really substantiated, but they're readily available. My guess is that the general was trying one of those supplements. Either way, the metals are inert. Their presence wouldn't cause any adverse effects. Certainly nothing that would cause a sane man to go crazy."

"Markham, have your techs found anything else out of the ordinary at the scene? Any trace evidence that's out of place?"

"No, nothing concrete. There wasn't any blood on the gun case or shell casings, but we're operating under the assumption that he loaded the gun before he killed her."

"Then why not just shoot her?"

"We don't know. Maybe he was going to kill himself, and she walked in and tried to stop him."

"But why would a man like Easton kill himself?"

"Why do people do anything? We did pull traces of . . ." Munroe heard the shuffling of more papers and guessed that Markham was checking the file. "Marine clay, brick dust, plaster, insulation, and glass particles from the floor. We also found traces of . . . chlorpyrifos. But all that could have been tracked in by anyone."

Munroe asked, "And what exactly is chlorpyrifos?"

"Says here that it's a pesticide. EPA banned it in 2000 for household use, but it is still commonly used on golf courses, treated wood, and for agriculture. Easton was a golfer, so that's probably where it came from."

"In what part of the room were those traces found?"

"Along the periphery. Maybe from some subordinate."

"What about his computer files, phone records, financial statements?"

Markham sighed. "You're welcome to *look* . . . I mean, *go through* everything yourself, but trust me, my people have been over it all. There's nothing there. Sometimes people just do things that can't be explained. I know he was your friend, but people surprise me every day."

"What about the men that killed Gerald and attacked me? I suppose that's just a coincidence? They were mercenaries."

"Yeah, mercenaries with long criminal records. We've followed up on that, too. But, as I'm sure you've found as well, there's no link between them and General Easton. Let's face it. The list of people who wouldn't mind if you ended up dead is not a short one. It's probably a grudge from one of your old cases. Someone could have hired them from prison. Who knows? Just let it go."

Munroe's hand snapped out to where he estimated Markham's

tie to be. He overshot and grabbed a handful of his shirt instead. Jerking Markham close, Munroe said through gritted teeth, "Let it go? My best friend is dead, and I'm going to find out why if I have to turn over every rock in this city and step on whatever slithers out."

19

The disappointment in himself still stung like a thorn in Munroe's mind. He had always been able to keep his emotions in check. When other people became flustered and flew off the handle, he took pride in maintaining his composure and his dignity. But whenever he thought of Gerald, the anger was more than he could contain. He was intimately familiar with the five stages of grief – denial, anger, bargaining, depression, and acceptance. He had suffered through the stages after losing his sight and essentially dealing with the death of the man he had been, the death of his old way of life. He had endured them again when his wife had passed away.

The thing that people often misunderstood was that there wasn't a clear-cut transition between each step. He didn't just reach acceptance and stay there. He bounced around between all the different phases, sometimes experiencing every step in the same day. But more than anything else right now he felt anger, and he was going to harness that fury and guide it like a missile toward the people responsible for Gerald's death.

Jonas led him clumsily to a booth at a local restaurant. With Gerald, he had never needed to use his collapsible white guide cane. Gerald had known how to use small movements of his arm to alert Munroe when steps or obstacles were in their path.

They had an almost psychic symbiosis that made Munroe feel as though he could actually see the path in front of him. Jonas was still struggling with the basic concepts, and so Munroe had broken his old guide cane out of retirement to use it in tandem with the big man's arm. Once they'd found the booth, he collapsed the cane and placed it on the tabletop.

On their way back, he had told Jonas to choose a place for lunch. Judging by the strong smell of grease mixed with body odor and the sizzling of burners, his new partner had chosen some hole-in-the-wall greasy-spoon diner. The customers were loud, and the place was abuzz with conversation and the clattering of silverware on plates.

A waitress said, "Hey, sweetie. Can I get you handsome men something to drink? Oh . . . I'm sorry. What does your friend want?" She whispered the question to Jonas.

She had obviously just noticed the cane and dark glasses. Munroe wasn't in the mood. Normally, he took such moments in his stride, with a calm smile. After all, people were just trying to be considerate in their own misguided way. But he wasn't sure if he would be able to suffer the indignity in his present state of mind.

Jonas replied, "I don't know. Why don't you ask him?"

Munroe could feel the woman lean down in his face. She smelled of too much hairspray and had bathed in perfume. He recognized the scent. It was an expensive brand. With her voice raised nearly to the level of a shout, she said, "WHAT WOULD YOU LIKE TO DRINK?"

Putting on his best smile, he said, "May I see your left hand, ma'am?"

She paused a moment, clearly wondering if this was some weird blind thing. "Umm, okay," she replied.

Munroe opened his palm, and she placed her hand on top of his. He ran his fingers over her ring finger and asked, "You've been having problems in your marriage lately, haven't you? Is your husband cheating?"

"Excuse me?"

"I just noticed the way that you're being overly flirtatious with your customers. You've also spent a lot of time on your hair. I can smell the hairspray from here. Your perfume is a rather expensive brand, which doesn't make sense when you're working in a place like this where the smell of grease will soon overpower that scent. I doubt that you could afford to use that perfume daily for an extended period, so your marital issues must be fairly recent. Then there's your wedding ring. You removed it right before your shift. The skin is soft there and still indented from where the ring was. Maybe you just wanted to keep it from getting dirty, but considering all the factors as a whole, I suspect that your husband has been cheating, and now you're either looking for a new man or a way to get back at him."

Munroe let the waitress's shocked silence hang in the air for a moment.

"And I'll have coffee. Thank you. Two sugars."

He heard her gasp and scurry off. Jonas said, "I could have just punched her in the gut for you."

"I'll keep that in mind for next time."

He felt his phone vibrate against his thigh. The accompanying ringtone told him that it was Joey. "What have you found?" he said into the phone.

"I just got a major hit on the name Wyatt Randall, but you're not going to like it."

"Something is always better than nothing."

"Police in Annapolis found a body at a small house in the country earlier today. But the weird thing is that someone called 911 from the house and told the cops where to find the body and who the dead guy was."

"Let me guess: Wyatt Randall."

"Does that make any sense to you?"

"No, Joey, it does not. I need you to contact the detective in charge. Have him meet me at the scene in an hour. Tell him that it's regarding national security – that always gets the locals moving. Then find out everything you can about the recently deceased Mr. Randall."

20

Munroe barely spoke to Jonas during the hour-long drive into the countryside around Annapolis. He didn't want to be bothered with idle chit-chat while focusing on the case. Jonas, to his credit, didn't attempt any kind of small talk to fill the silence. Joey called to inform them that the techs had finished processing the crime scene but the local detective was waiting there for them.

When they pulled up, Munroe stopped Jonas from exiting the vehicle and said, "Describe the scene to me."

"What do you want to know?"

"What does the house look like? Neighbors around? Just paint me a picture."

"Okay, it's a small bluish-colored house, probably two bedrooms tops. It looks like one of those modular homes. We're at the end of a long lane. No neighbors that I can see, but the place is surrounded by trees. Two cars in the driveway. A one-car detached garage."

"That's enough. Anything else that stands out beyond the obvious?"

Black paused for a long moment. "I don't know. I don't think so."

"Okay, let's go meet the detective."

The local cop stepped slowly and reluctantly out of his

still-running vehicle. Munroe heard the car's air-conditioner churning at full blast. With a yawn, the man introduced himself as Hank Cullins. Munroe shook Cullins's hand with both of his, feeling the wrist and forearm to guess at overall body shape, and instinctively leaned forward enough to catch the man's scent. He could tell that Cullins was heavyset but not overly so and smelled of baby powder. The cop probably had a young child at home. Maybe the baby had been keeping him up at night.

Once inside, Cullins said, "We found him in the bathtub."

"Cause of death?"

"ME's initial thought is that he drowned."

"Were there signs of a struggle? Did someone hold him under the water?"

"Nothing. And he was fully clothed. It's like he just laid there and let it happen."

"But someone called it in and even gave you his name. So you know that there was another person involved."

"Right, but we don't know how they were involved. I have my doubts that someone could hold themselves under the water like that. So my guess is that he was drugged. But whether or not he and a friend were getting high and it went bad or somebody did this on purpose, I don't know."

"Did you find any drugs or anything else at the scene?"

"No, but they would have had time to clean that up. There's barely anything in the fridge and only a couple changes of clothes. We spoke to the owner of the property, and the victim's the one that rented the place. He paid cash and has only been here a couple of days."

"Prints?"

"Just the vic's. We did find a shoe print that doesn't match and some tire tracks outside that we're testing for a make. We also pulled some trace from the shoe print. The full tests aren't back yet, but our guys thought it looked like plaster, fiberglass insulation, and clay. Like maybe from a construction site."

"Marine clay?"

"Don't know. Is that important?"

"Not yet. Thank you, detective. You've done good work."

"Do you want to tell me how this guy relates to national security?"

"Soon. Let's see the bathroom."

By the cop's hesitation, Munroe knew that Cullins had stumbled over his use of the word *see*, but the man recovered quickly and led them to the bathroom. Once inside the small space, Munroe groped for the toilet and sat down. The bathtub was to his immediate right. He tried to connect the dots of what had happened here. If this was the correct Wyatt Randall, and there was no reason to assume otherwise, then why had he been killed – and how? He suspected that Randall had been tortured for information, but then why would the killer report the crime and even give the police the man's name? Judging by Black's description of the property, it could have taken weeks for the crime to be discovered. The obvious conclusion was that someone wanted the body to be found. But why? Was it a message? And if so, a message for whom?

21

As they continued down the cream-colored corridor and passed the turn toward his cell block, John Corrigan stopped and turned to the guard. The man was in his early twenties, with freckles and youthful features. "Where are you taking me?"

The guard responded by shoving Corrigan forward. He stumbled and tripped over his shackled feet, the restraints barely giving him room to move, but the guard caught him by the back of his dark blue jumpsuit and dragged him down the hall to the prison laundry.

Silence filled the large space. The machines were quiet. The only light came from two windows in the double doors leading back into the corridor. Three of his fellow prisoners stepped from the shadows. Each brandished a metal pipe, holding it like a club.

Corrigan's heart throbbed against his ribcage. He clenched and unclenched his fists. He had known this day would come, but that knowledge still hadn't prepared him for the sudden realization that he was about to leave this world.

The guard said, "Okay, make it look good, but not *too* good." He bent forward, gritted his teeth, and clamped his eyes shut. Then one of the inmates, a wiry black man who had been an Army Ranger in a former life, stepped forward and struck the side of the guard's face with the pipe. The guard cursed, blood running down his face, and told the inmate to hit him again. The former ranger complied, and the guard dropped to the concrete floor with the second blow.

The former ranger then turned to Corrigan. "I'm sorry," he said. "You deserve better than this."

Corrigan shook his head and closed his eyes. "No, I don't. Let's get it over with."

22

Joey Helgeson placed the last of his new action figures on the shelf. He already had the entire carded set of the Kenner Super Powers collection, but he had only recently acquired these special figures that came on smaller cards and were part of a promotion offered by Shell gas stations in Canada. He admired the entire set of eight heroes which included Superman, Batman, Robin, Wonder Woman, Green Lantern, Firestorm, Red Tornado, and Martian Manhunter. They weren't terribly rare or expensive, but Joey found it too easy and convenient to purchase new additions to his collection on sites like eBay. He preferred to scour the convention scene and antique shops. After all, the hunt and the story was a big part of the fun in collecting. And he was a collector at heart with tastes that ranged from superhero memorabilia to restoring vintage muscle cars. His current project was a black 1969 GTO Judge convertible.

As a young boy, he had suffered from Gorham's disease, an affliction also known as phantom bone disease, which was characterized by gradual bone loss. The condition affected his pelvis, and although he had gone into spontaneous remission – a common occurrence with the rare disorder – he still walked with a limp and lived in fear that the disease would come back and this time affect his chest or upper spine, which could prove fatal.

Joey's action figures rested inside antique barrister bookcases that lined his apartment inside the historic James G. Blaine mansion. The cases had been included with the rental, left by the previous tenant, and it was easier for him to leave the heavy shelves and adapt them to his purposes than to cart them out. The dark hardwood floors made from heart pine, the antique wrought-iron light fixtures, and the intricate woodwork weren't really his style, but he loved the location and the beautiful view overlooking DuPont Circle. He spent almost all his time inside this apartment, and so a window with a view was a necessity.

Gazing out of his window, Joey tried to see over the top of the local branch of PNC Bank to the building that housed the closest Starbucks. He had become infatuated with one of the baristas there and had been trying to work up the nerve to ask her out. He still wasn't sure why he was so reluctant to do so. There was another Starbucks only a block away in the opposite direction. Worst-case scenario was that he would be forced to walk a bit farther to get his coffee. Glancing back at the faces of his heroes as they watched him through the glass of the bookcases, he tried to absorb some strength from them. After all, when he had been bedridden as a boy, these heroes and their stories of overcoming adversity were what had given him the strength to get better. Maybe they could come through for him again.

A muffled thud sounded from the front room, and Joey thought that he heard the sound of his front door closing.

"Hello?"

Surely he was imagining things. This was a decent neighborhood. People didn't just walk in and rob you. But maybe a homeless person or a drug addict . . .

Had he locked the front door? He was sure that he had.

Joey grabbed a stapler from his desk and held it up like a weapon. "I'm armed," he said into the silence of the apartment.

He waited, listened. His pounding heart and labored breathing were the only sounds beyond the ambient bustle of the city outside the window. Trying to convince himself that he was being paranoid, he sat back down at his desk. But a strange sensation of being watched crawled over him. He wouldn't be able to get any work done until he checked.

Opting for a better weapon than a stapler, Joey hefted a metal bust of the Green Lantern from his desktop and went to search the apartment.

The front room was empty, the door still shut and locked. Nothing had fallen off a shelf or been knocked over. Nothing out of the ordinary. He continued on to the bathroom and bedroom. The bed was still unmade, but he pulled off the covers and looked beneath it from a distance. No one was hiding underneath. No one inside the shower stall. No one in the closet.

It was just his imagination.

Joey moved back toward his office by way of the kitchen in order to pick up a drink and a snack. But when he entered the room, he cried out and dropped the bust of the Green Lantern to the floor. It struck the hardwood with a clang.

A large man sat at his kitchen table. The intruder wore a dark pinstriped suit. Shiny black hair was swept back from a dark bronze face. A black pistol with a long suppressor attached to its muzzle rested in his right hand.

The bronze man gestured toward another chair at the table. "Please forgive the intrusion, Mr. Helgeson."

Joey opened his mouth, but nothing came out. His brain told his legs to run for the front door, but they refused to listen.

The man raised the gun higher and said, "Have a seat, and I'll explain. Don't force me to hurt you."

Joey fought to maintain control of his faculties, but he had never been so terrified in his life. Could he make it out of the room before the man shot him? Stay or go. Run or surrender. What would his heroes do?

The bronze man fired once into the wall beside Joey, and he immediately shuffled to one of the chairs as he fought to maintain control of his bladder.

"What do you want with me?"

The man's bronze features were completely placid. No sign of anger or malice. "You work for a man named Deacon Munroe, handling his technical operations. He's currently investigating the death of the commandant of the Marine Corps. I want you to tell me everything you know about this investigation. I want to know what Munroe knows."

The thought of resisting or lying entered Joey's mind for a split second, but he dismissed it almost as quickly. He wasn't some kind of trained soldier or operative. If this guy pushed him with violence, he would topple like a house of cards. Might as well save himself some pain and skip the torture part. He opened his mouth, and the information flooded out in a tidal wave of words. He told the bronze man about the flash drive, John Corrigan, Wyatt Randall, and everything else that he knew. When the flood subsided, he just sat there, shaking and breathing hard.

The bronze man smiled and said, "Thank you for your honesty, Mr. Helgeson. I truly appreciate you being so forthcoming without forcing me to resort to certain unpleasantries. Where is the flash drive now?"

"I don't know. Munroe took it back. I assume that he has it with him."

The bronze man slid a phone across the table. Joey recognized it as his own. "Please call him and find out for sure. Try to make it seem natural and use the speaker function so that I can hear."

Joey complied and tapped in Munroe's number. Munroe answered on the second ring, his Southern baritone made tinny by the phone's speaker. "What do you have for me, Joey?"

"Umm, nothing yet. But I have another idea about that flash drive. Where is it?"

"I have it with me. Should I bring it to you or is it something you can do remotely?"

"I'll need—"

The bronze man hung up the phone and ended the conversation. Then he produced his own phone and made a call. "He has the drive with him. Eliminate them, but make sure that you retrieve it intact."

On the word *eliminate*, Joey knew that he was going to die and decided that he had to do something. In that split second, he summoned all the courage from every comic book that he had ever read and dove toward the door.

But the bronze man was quick. He kicked Joey's legs out from beneath him.

Joey toppled forward, and his head slammed against the corner of his stainless steel refrigerator. The pain lanced through his skull, but he pressed on, crawling toward the front door on his hands and knees.

The bronze man placed the heel of his shoe in the center of Joey's back and pressed him to the floor. The black abyss of the gun barrel loomed over the back of Joey's head.

The bronze man said, "Our business is now concluded, Mr. Helgeson."

23

Jonas Black watched the worry lines crease across Munroe's forehead as the blind man placed the phone back in the pants pocket of his dark tailored suit. Jonas tugged against the collar of his own suit and said, "Is everything okay?"

"No, Mr. Black, something is very wrong with this whole situation." Munroe pulled a small device from his pocket and rolled it through his fingers. "I think we may have walked into a trap."

"What do you mean?"

Several objects bursting through the windows of the small dwelling answered his question. Jonas immediately recognized the metal cylinders rolling across the floor and spewing white smoke as tear-gas canisters.

Training kicked in, took over.

Assess the situation.

Their enemy's tactic was clear. The strike team outside had filled the space with tear gas, making it impossible to stay inside. The enemy would expect them to rush from the building where they would be mown down by gunfire or could be easily subdued and captured.

The gas quickly filled the space, stealing all the breathable air.

Munroe and the local detective, Cullins, hacked and coughed

and tried to cover their faces with their shirts. It wouldn't help, only prolong the inevitable. Cullins stumbled toward the front door, but Jonas stopped him and said, "We can't go that way or out the back. They'll be waiting."

Clear liquid dripped down the detective's face as he said, "We can't stay here!"

Jonas's eyes, nose, and throat burned as the gas attacked mucous membranes in those areas, but this wasn't his first experience with tear gas. In Recon training, one of the final exercises had required him to carry a fallen comrade through miles of rough terrain while his instructors shot tear gas into his path. It didn't come close to making him immune to the effects of the gas, but it had showed him how to push through the pain and disorientation in order to achieve his mission. In Recon, the mission always came first, long before concerns over a soldier's own safety or personal comfort. And today, his mission was to protect Deacon Munroe.

"Come on!" he said as he dragged the other two men into the home's tiny kitchen. If they couldn't use the current exits, the only other option was to make one of their own.

Jonas raised his PT845 and fired a full magazine of .45-caliber slugs to form a circle in the linoleum of the kitchen floor. Then he used his considerable weight to stomp through the flooring and plywood sheeting into the home's crawl space.

Unfortunately, the strike team outside either thought that he had opened fire on them or realized what he was attempting. Bullets shredded the modular building's walls to pieces and turned the air into a maelstrom of drywall dust, pink insulation, and shards of broken glass.

Jonas dropped to the floor, hauling the dead weight of Munroe and Cullins with him. Then he violently shoved the crying and gasping pair into the hole he had created. The two men fought for air as they rolled in the dirt and spider webs beneath the house.

He pushed Cullins clear of the opening and dropped in behind them as the barrage of gunfire subsided above. Wasting no time, he scrambled through the dirt as he struggled to pull his sizeable bulk through the tight space toward an access panel at the rear of the house. With barely enough room to maneuver and with his back scraping against the floor joists, he finally reached the panel. The view through the louvered opening showed a large Hispanic man wearing a bulletproof vest over street clothes. An MP5 sub-machine gun was held tight against the man's shoulder as he crept toward the house with an economy of movement that spoke of training and skill.

Wiping the sleeve of his new suit over his eyes, Jonas cleared the tear gas away as best he could and prepared for combat. With his right hand, he readied the PT845 while his left prepared to push out the panel. Taking three sharp breaths, he lunged forward and tore the panel from its housing. It flew into the backyard and struck a nearby tree trunk with a loud crash.

The gunman spun toward the sound but had enough discipline not to fire blindly. His enemy less than ten feet away, Jonas easily dropped the man with a well-placed shot to the head. The gunman crumpled in on himself as a red mist filled the air.

Over the ringing in his ears, Jonas could hear two sets of running footsteps. One coming from each side of the building. If he stayed in the crawl space, he knew that he'd be a sitting duck. The only option was to meet the attackers head-on. He ripped himself from the tiny opening and tried to gain his feet. The suit jacket caught on a nail, and the material tore away.

Jonas didn't hesitate.

He sprinted toward the left side of the house. As the gunman came around the corner, the man's eyes went wide at the sight of Jonas bearing down on him. The man raised his weapon, but Jonas batted it aside. Without slowing, he lowered his shoulder like a linebacker going for a tackle on the other team's quarterback. He caught the smaller man low, spinning him end over end. As he landed on his back, the man wheezed and gasped violently.

Jonas spun on his heels and jerked the disoriented attacker from the ground like a rag doll. Grabbing the gunman by the back of his bulletproof vest, Jonas held him out as a human shield and rushed toward the third attacker, who was coming around the opposite corner of the house.

The third man didn't hesitate to sacrifice his comrade as his MP5 spat fire at Jonas. His human shield shook with each impact as Jonas rushed forward. But he didn't halt his forward progress until he was within fifteen feet of his opponent. Then, without warning and in one fluid movement, he dropped his human shield, raised the PT845, and fell to one knee in a shooting stance. Sighting down the barrel, he squeezed the trigger three times.

The first two rounds caught the third gunman in the chest, rocking him back on his heels. The final shot caught him in the face.

Wasting no time, Jonas grabbed up one of the MP5s, checked the magazine, and methodically secured the perimeter. He saw no signs of more assailants but did hear a vehicle pulling away in the distance beyond the trees.

When he returned to the rear of the small house, he found that Cullins had helped Munroe out from the crawl space. Doubled over with their hands on their knees, the two men coughed and hacked out the remnants of the tear gas. Cullins rubbed furiously at his eye sockets as he growled in pain.

Jonas knew better than to ask if they were okay. Instead, he said to Munroe, "This is why I told you to wear that damn Kevlar vest I got you. Are you hurt?"

In a harsh whisper, Munroe said, "I'm fine, but we need to send help for Joey. I suspect he may be in worse trouble than us."

24

Annabelle Dixon had come to think of Joey Helgeson like a younger brother. Joey excelled to the point of genius in some areas, and yet in many situations, he was clueless. During the previous week, she had spent two hours on the phone discussing ways for Joey to ask out some girl who worked at the local Starbucks. They hadn't made much headway, but at least she had dissuaded him from enacting an elaborate plan involving origami and Hershey's Kisses. As she sped down New Hampshire Avenue NW toward Joey's apartment, she couldn't dispel a twisting fear in her guts, a fear of losing yet another brother.

Police cars surrounded the building and officers had erected barricades on the sidewalks. Annabelle pushed through the crowd of onlookers and flashed her DCIS credentials at the officers to gain access. The interior of the building smelled of old wood and the white vinegar used for cleaning it. She bounded up the dark wood stairs to Joey's apartment. Ghastly images flashed before her eyes. She expected to see her friend's lifeless form covered with a white sheet, blood soaking through its surface.

Instead, she found Joey in his office being questioned by the DC police. He noticed her and stood. The churning knots in her stomach untied, and relief overwhelmed her. She rushed forward and embraced him. "I thought you were dead," she said in a choked whisper.

Joey returned the hug and said, "I won't sleep for a year, and I may have ruined a good pair of Superman undies, but other than that I'm fine."

"What the hell happened?"

He described the intruder and his requests and then added, "The guy said that he only takes life when it's absolutely necessary and that my death wasn't required for the completion of his mission. He said it just like that. No emotion. Just facts."

"You're lucky to be alive." Annabelle turned to the officer who had been questioning Joey. "Sorry to have interrupted."

The handsome cop gave her a large smile and said, "No problem. I have everything I need. Mr. Helgeson, if we have any more questions someone will be in contact." He stood and headed for the door.

Annabelle said, "Deacon will want to know that you're okay." She dialed Munroe, who answered before the second ring. She and Joey explained the events that had transpired. Munroe expressed his relief and informed them that he and Jonas Black were still answering questions in Annapolis but would be done soon.

"I need you to book the two of us on the next flight to Leavenworth, Kansas," Munroe said. "It's time for Jonas Black to pay a visit to his old friend John Corrigan and get us some answers."

Annabelle hesitated. Munroe had requested to be informed if Corrigan had any visitors and so the warden at the USDB had felt that Munroe would also want to know about an incident that had taken place in the prison's laundry room. She had received the call not long before hearing of Joey's situation.

"Speaking to Corrigan is going to be a problem, Deac."

Silence filled the line for a moment, and Annabelle knew that Munroe could sense her unease. "Why is that?" he said slowly.

"Because some inmates attacked Corrigan and one of the guards. The guard's fine, but Corrigan suffered a lot of damage. He's in a medically induced coma."

25

An investigation could often seem like a house of cards that would topple if one lead or piece of evidence was moved or shifted or fell through. The investigator's job was to make the house of cards stand on its own despite what sometimes felt like a million remorseless forces pressing against it. Normally, this process didn't frustrate Munroe. But most cases didn't lead back to the people responsible for his best friend's death.

In this instance, the loss of whatever information John Corrigan might have possessed devastated him. Munroe tried to ignore it and move forward to the next lead, but he couldn't shake the feeling that he would never learn the truth. The people who wanted this case buried obviously held positions of power within the government, and despite the favors owed to him by those in the upper echelons, he was still just a DCIS investigator.

Such thoughts still weighed on him even as Jonas Black led him into the office of Dr. Phillip Karnowski, one of Wyatt Randall's former colleagues. Randall had been a chemistry professor at Georgetown University before abruptly abandoning his tenure and dropping off the grid. Joey had contacted the university, tracked down the person with the most knowledge of Randall's work, and arranged a meeting.

Dr. Karnowski greeted them at his office, a small room within

Georgetown's Reiss Science Building. He had a firm handshake and thick hairy forearms. Munroe gripped the man's arm with both hands and could estimate Karnowski's height relative to his own from the angle at which the forearm sloped upward or downward. Karnowski was a short man.

Fluorescent lights hummed overhead, and the stink of dry erase markers hung in the air. Munroe bumped his shin against something hard as Jonas Black shoved him roughly into a padded office chair. Munroe had explained to Black that the proper procedure was to guide Munroe's hand to the back of the chair and let him find his own seat, but apparently the big man wasn't a quick study, another stinging reminder of Gerald's absence.

"So how can I help? Your associate didn't give me much information over the phone," Karnowski said. He had the booming voice of a professional lecturer.

Munroe replied, "We're here to get more information about Wyatt Randall and his work. I understand that the two of you were friends?"

"I suppose you could say that. We weren't close, but we went out for drinks a few times and consulted with each other."

"So you were aware of what Randall was working on?"

"Yes, officially he was interested in the stereodynamic chemistry of chiral compounds and the development of new antimalarial drugs."

Munroe raised an eyebrow. "And unofficially?"

Karnowski tapped a finger against the surface of his desk and took a deep breath. "The truth of the matter is that I never thought much of Wyatt or his work. He was sloppy and prone to fantastical thinking. Don't get me wrong: I respect visionaries, but Wyatt didn't have the brains to back it up. He was coming dangerously close to losing all his funding, and honestly, the money would have been better off going to someone else."

"But he had some kind of pet project that showed promise?"

Karnowski laughed. "Oh, he had a pet project, but I wouldn't refer to it as promising. Randall's father had died from some degenerative brain disease. After that, Wyatt went on a bit of a personal crusade to find a treatment for such conditions."

"Sounds like a noble cause."

"Yes, but unfortunately, his passion led him into areas that I would consider pseudoscience at best. He became obsessed with m-state metals."

Munroe felt his excitement rise as things started to click into place. Dr. Stapleton's words floated through his mind from her report on General Easton's death and her discovery of *elevated levels of certain monatomic metals.*

"Monatomic metals?"

"Yes – are you familiar with the concept?"

"Only on a surface level."

Karnowski shifted into lecture mode. "The center of the periodic chart of elements consists of what are known as the transition elements, meaning that they can transit from metallic to monatomic or diatomic via chemical treatment or through other means. Because they are chemically inert, they can be ingested."

Munroe had already heard from Stapleton that certain supplements on the market contained monatomic metals, but he played dumb. "Eat metal? Why would someone do that?"

"Well, not only do our cells communicate via chemicals and electricity in our nervous system, they also communicate intercellularly through the exchange of photons or light particles and other processes as well. The human body is a marvelous bioelectric machine, and all its processes depend on the clear and ideally unimpeded conduction of electrical messages. Light, as proven by fiber optics, can carry more information with less interference. It's a purer form of transmission. The theory behind ingesting m-state metals is that it's like transforming the body's wiring from simple copper cable to fiber optics, where the same wiring is able to carry much more processing information. There are supplements available that claim to have this ability, but while the properties of m-state metals are fascinating, most reputable scientists don't believe in such effects, and there isn't any real scientific evidence that I've seen to support these claims."

"But Randall thought that, by boosting people's brains with monatomics, he could repair the damaged pathways?"

"That and more. But, as I said, it's a pseudoscience at best, and in my opinion, many of its proponents aren't scientists but new-age scam artists. Despite my objections, Wyatt claimed that he had found a way to combine m-state metals with an Ampakine and a revolutionary nanobot delivery system that provides the user with more energy, concentration, a quicker reaction time, and even increased intelligence, essentially allowing him or her to operate at their fullest potential even with very little sleep or rest."

"Did you see any of his results from this? Anything to back up his claims?"

"No. Shortly after he told me about his supposed break-through, he resigned his post and left the university. He didn't tell me why he was leaving or even that he was leaving. I heard about it second-hand after he was gone. I suspect that it was more of a *breakdown* than a *breakthrough*."

"And you haven't heard anything from or about him since?"

"I heard a rumor that he was working with an old friend to bring his discovery to the market, but I don't put much stock in that."

Munroe stood. "Thank you, Dr. Karnowski. We appreciate your time, and you've been most helpful."

He shook hands with the professor and left a card in case Karnowski remembered anything else. Then Jonas Black led him out of the office and down the hall. The tiles squeaked beneath

Jonas's thick-soled shoes. The former soldier had refused to wear dress shoes with his new suit, quoting something about tactical concerns and opting instead for black steel-toed boots.

Jonas said, "We're coming up on the stairs."

"Okay, walk in front of me a bit, and I'll feel your body shift as you step down."

It was around dinner time, and most of the students and faculty had abandoned the halls. This made the quick footsteps of two people behind them seem all the more out of place. Munroe was about to tell Jonas to check who was coming up on them so quickly when a man at their backs said, "If you move or turn around, I'll shoot you."

26

During his time as an Army Ranger, Oliver Pike had worked as his unit's marksman or sniper, and he had always found the traditional military rifle systems to be too cumbersome. For this reason, once he became a mercenary and could afford to use whatever equipment he wished regardless of price, he had instantly fallen in love with the Stealth Recon Scout made by Desert Tactical Arms. The bolt-action sniper rifle fired a .308 round from a bullpup design, which meant that the feeding mechanism was positioned behind the grip and the trigger. This allowed the Recon Scout to be one of the shortest, most portable, and most effective sniper rifles on the market.

On the roof of the brownstone opposite his target, he flipped down the rifle's bipod and calculated the variables – distance, bearing, wind speed, barometric pressure, ammo temperature, air temperature. Most of the calculations and factors were overkill in this situation. It was an easy shot, but he still liked to be thorough – and it was good to stay in practice.

The target sat alone at the sidewalk cafe across the street, eating her salad and tapping keys on the laptop that occupied the rest of the surface of the small circular table. The conditions couldn't have been more ideal if he'd designed them himself: a stationary target in the open for a measurable period of time directly opposite an easily concealed vantage point from which it was easy to escape. Perfect. The surge of anticipation and adrenalin he felt was better than sex. He didn't believe in God, but staring down the scope, he estimated that he was closer to a supreme being than any of the maggots below would ever come.

"Are you ready?" Almeida said over his shoulder.

Pike placed his scope's cross hairs directly over Annabelle Dixon's skull and said, "Just say the word."

27

At the order of the mysterious gunman, Jonas Black raised his hands while weighing his options. Without looking over his shoulder, he couldn't even tell precisely where the speaker stood in the hall, whether a gun was pointed at his back, nor if the attacker was unarmed and alone. In a voice so deep that it was difficult to understand, the man said, "Up the stairs."

Jonas complied and led Munroe up a metal stairwell to the roof, while constantly scanning for a way to turn the tables on the aggressor. He saw none that wouldn't probably result in a tragic ending. The door to the roof was unlocked and opened onto a metal catwalk leading down to an area of weather-worn concrete tiles. A brick dividing wall surrounded this portion of the roof, and a greenhouse occupied the space. No one else was around.

The gunman told them to stop in the empty space between the access door and the greenhouse. The glass front of the greenhouse showed the reflections of the two men behind them. Both had swarthy bronze complexions. The speaker stood with his arms at his sides, while his companion held a Glock pistol at his hip, pointing the gun lazily at their backs. It shocked Jonas to see that the first man was a bona fide giant, and to Jonas Black, that description wasn't one that was thrown around lightly. The stranger towered well over seven feet tall and had a wide flat face and shoulder-length black hair. He wore a long trench coat with what could have been an MP5 sub-machine gun concealed beneath the folds of the material.

The giant's phone rang, and he handed it to Jonas. The voice on the other end told him to put the phone on speaker so that Munroe could hear as well.

"Mr. Munroe," the man on the phone said in a Hispanic accent. "I figured it was time that we discuss the current situation like gentlemen. You have something that belongs to my employer. A small flash drive. I find it unfortunate that people have been harmed because of something so small and inconsequential. I do not wish further hostilities, and I've been told that you are a reasonable man. I have a simple request. Give me the drive and you and your large friend may go."

"And if I don't?"

"We'll kill you and take it. And, in case you're considering something rash, you should know that another of my associates is currently looking down the scope of a sniper rifle at your friend Ms. Dixon."

Munroe's jaw muscles tightened and his fists balled up. Through clenched teeth, he said, "I'm going to reach into my jacket pocket."

"Slowly," the dark-skinned giant said.

Munroe's hand came out of his pocket with a small gray device that Jonas assumed to be the flash drive. He passed the drive to the giant. "I gave it to your man," Munroe said to the phone. "You going to kill us now like you did Gerald and General Easton?"

"The death of your friend was unfortunate, and I apologize for that. It was not by my orders. I'm afraid it was the action of overzealous private contractors. But you shouldn't live in the past, Mr. Munroe. Try to focus on the present and live in the moment."

"You work for Ramon Castillo, don't you?"

The man on the other end of the line hesitated just long enough to show his surprise, and Munroe continued. "I have a friend who works on the FBI's task force on organized crime. We had dinner a few weeks back, and he told me about how the Castillo Cartel out of Mexico has been worming their way into legitimate US companies that have fallen on hard times. He said that the cartels were a hundred times more dangerous than any group we've faced here in the US. Fortunately, the Senate is preparing to ratify a new bill that would declare the cartels as terrorist organizations, which means that the government can grab any holdings or companies linked to them. It would be terribly incon-venient if any evidence surfaced that showed such a link between the cartels and a large US corporation, especially one with a lucrative military contract. I wonder if that's what's contained in the directory on the drive marked as *Money Transfers*."

"You're a clever man. Unfortunately, without the drive, you have nothing. I hope you're clever enough to realize that this situation has escalated out of your control. This is your one chance to walk away. Give the phone back to my associates, and they will leave you in peace. But if you continue down this path, you will leave me with no choice but to engage in certain activ-ities that I find . . . distasteful. Goodbye, Mr. Munroe."

Jonas handed back the phone without turning around. In the reflection on the greenhouse, he saw the giant place the phone into a pocket. Then he watched each of the men carefully, expecting one of them to raise a weapon. And if either of them did so, he was ready to make a move. Jonas Black didn't intend to go down without a fight.

But neither of them made an aggressive gesture. They simply started backing toward the exit. The giant said, "Don't move or turn around. And don't try to follow us. If we don't call in again in five minutes, the sniper will kill your friend."

Jonas couldn't believe it. The man on the phone had been telling the truth. They were leaving them alive. He felt the terrible weight of fear and uncertainty lifting as hope that he would live to see another day crept into its place.

And then Munroe shattered that hope as he said, "Wait. You're forgetting something."

28

Munroe knew how lucky he had been to survive the confrontation with the men who had killed Gerald. Repeat the same scenario one hundred times, and he would be able to make those shots only a quarter of the time, probably less. That realization bred fear and doubt, and the helplessness he experienced led him to devise a method by which to defend himself. Tobi Savoy had provided the tools necessary to level the playing field and give him an option if attacked, an option for a situation exactly like the one in which he now found himself.

"What are we forgetting?" the giant Hispanic man said behind him.

"The key-code for the drive."

"What key-code?"

Munroe tried to fake exasperation. "I would have just kept it, but since you're actually going to let us live, I don't want this coming back on me later. I want to put this whole mess behind me."

He heard the giant step closer. "Then give me the key-code."

"I'm going to reach into my other pocket and retrieve it."

Munroe lowered his hands and reached toward his jacket with slow and non-threatening movements. His hand slipped inside the pocket and gripped a small device that resembled a hockey puck. Fingers danced over the detonator, and then he dropped the grenade down the back of his jacket, letting it hit the ground and roll toward their attackers.

~~*~~

Jonas Black wasn't sure what Munroe was up to, but he was positive he wouldn't like it. The black circular device that fell from beneath Munroe's jacket confirmed that suspicion. He managed to look away, but it wasn't enough.

A blinding flash and deafening explosion seared Jonas's senses. He had experienced the sensation many times before – the detonation of a flash-bang grenade – but there was no defense against the attack, no way to get used to it or fight through the pain.

He felt hands wrap around his bicep and urge him to move. He stumbled in the direction in which the hands led him. His vision had gone white, and a high-pitched ringing beat against his eardrums. The PT845 pistol rested in his right hand, but he wasn't sure how it had gotten there. The hands pulled him down into a crouch. He smelled something moist. Vegetation. Fertilizer. The greenhouse?

Finally, the white dots started to clear from his vision, at least enough so that he could see his surroundings. Munroe crouched beside him in the greenhouse. Apparently, the blind man had set off the flash-bang, covered his own ears, and then dragged Jonas to cover with him.

Munroe's lips moved frantically, but Jonas couldn't understand the words. The ringing in his ears blocked all other sounds.

In what seemed like slow motion, the greenhouse exploded all around them. Shards of glass flew everywhere, filling the air, as the gunmen opened fire from outside. On instinct, Jonas pulled Munroe down and close to him. The plants disintegrated under the barrage. Soil and mulch and water droplets mixed with the glass shards in a hurricane of debris.

The translucent glass had kept the gunmen from getting a clear bead on their targets, but now the panes had been destroyed in several places. Jonas saw a face appear in one of the openings. The man who had held the gun on them. The man's head pulled back from the opening, but Jonas could still see the man's shadowy frame reflected in the adjoining pane of glass.

He raised his gun and squeezed the trigger several times in quick succession. The ringing in his ears had decreased slightly, and he heard the man cry out in pain and fall.

One down, but the giant was still out there.

Staying in a low crouch, Jonas moved back to the greenhouse's entrance. Upon reaching the door, he used the frame as a pivot to scan the area beyond. No sign of the large Hispanic man. Maybe he had fled with the flash drive.

Jonas knew that the force of the shock wave had pushed the little hairs in his inner eat flat, causing the ringing sound. But the effect had begun to wear off, and another noise registered over the high-pitched tone. His senses still disoriented, it took a second for the source and direction of the new sound to register.

When it did, he wheeled around in time to see the giant bearing down on him, the huge man's dark face contorted in pain and rage.

~~*~~

Munroe knew that he could do little to help Jonas Black, but he could save another member of his team. If their attackers were to be believed, at that moment, a sniper's cross hairs were centered on Annabelle.

He pulled out his phone and issued a voice command to dial

her number. With each unanswered ring, his despair grew. Finally, after five rings, she picked up.

"Hello?"

"Don't show any reaction or surprise. Act as if this is just any other phone call. Listen to me carefully. I'm told that you're at a sidewalk cafe. Is this correct?"

"Yes."

"I'm also told that a sniper is watching you right now, but we're going to deal with that. Are there any cars parked nearby?"

"There's one right across from me."

"Good. When I tell you, I want you to hang up the phone, set it down casually, and act as if nothing is out of the ordinary. Then count to ten and dive toward the car. Get underneath it and stay there. Do you understand?"

"Yes."

"I'm going to call the police. You stay under that car and wait for them to arrive. I'll call you back in a minute. Okay?"

"Not really."

"You're going to be fine."

"Deacon, I—"

"No time for that. Hang up now and start counting."

~~*~~

Annabelle placed the phone down on the circular patio table and pushed her salad away. As she counted down from ten, she tried to look around casually at the other people in the restaurant. She didn't want the sniper to sense that anything was wrong.

Nine. Eight.

She watched a young couple laughing in the corner. The man's hand rested lovingly over his companion's.

Seven. Six.

The waitress approached and asked if she needed more water. She smiled and said, "No, thank you."

Where was she? Three? Two?

Annabelle supposed it didn't really matter. Moment of truth.

Trying her best not to betray her intentions, she tensed her trembling muscles, ready to spring from the chair. She realized that this could be her last moment on Earth, and the thought froze her in place. So much life left to live. So much that she still wanted to do. So many missed opportunities.

But she wasn't dead yet. She tried to focus on that and forget all the rest.

And then she dove toward the car.

~~*~~

The huge Hispanic man struck Jonas Black with the force of a freight train. His feet lifted off the concrete, and he struck the reinforced frame of the greenhouse door. Pain shot down his spine and through his legs.

The giant grabbed a handful of Jonas's shirt and threw him onto a raised metal shelf that held potted plants. The huge man ran him down its length, the clay pots shattering against his skull.

When they reached the end, the giant let Jonas fall to the glass-covered ground and then smashed his face against the concrete. He felt the loose shards of broken glass slice into his forehead, and blood ran into his eyes.

He fought against the giant's grip, but the stranglehold of the man's huge hands was impossibly strong.

The giant jerked Jonas from the ground, and arms like tree trunks wrapped around his chest and squeezed. He couldn't breathe. He felt his ribs flex and pop. With his arms still free, he slammed both fists against the giant's head and neck, but the crushing embrace didn't loosen.

Spots filled Jonas's vision once more, this time from lack of oxygen. His fingers groped over the giant's flat face and found the eye sockets. With one hand on each side of the broad face, he drove his thumbs into the giant's eyes.

A roar of agony escaped the big Hispanic's mouth, and the pressure around Jonas Black's midsection eased. He continued to press his thumbs into the man's skull, but the giant shoved his arms up between Jonas's and knocked them away.

The eye trauma would have disabled most men, but instead of halting the giant's attack, it only served to enrage him further. The huge man was like a snarling animal, full of fury and an all-consuming desire to kill.

He fell on Jonas with all his strength and weight. Meaty fingers wrapped around Jonas's neck, and the giant's weight drove him back to the concrete.

He kicked and punched the giant's side and rammed his fists against the man's head, but, screaming in agony and insanity, the giant didn't even register the blows.

Unable to breathe. Throat crushed. Fingers scrambling, searching. Pain everywhere. Terrible relentless pressure. Vision growing lighter and then darker. World fading.

In a mad rush, Jonas's fingers slid over something sharp. Frantically closing his fist around it he pulled the shard of glass closer. Its sharp edges sliced into the meat of his fingers, but he barely noticed, just one more pain in a world of agony.

With his last reserve of strength, his arm shot upward and jammed the glass into the giant's neck.

The huge man fell back. His fingers clawing at his throat as blood spurted onto the concrete. The giant's body convulsed for a moment and then fell still.

Jonas wanted nothing more than to just lie back and rest. He wiped blood from his face. The taste of copper and stomach acid filled his aching throat.

Then he remembered Annabelle.

He pulled himself up and searched the ruined greenhouse for Munroe. The blind man was still crouching near where he had left him. "Annabelle?" Jonas said in a harsh croak.

Munroe's sunglasses had fallen off at some point, exposing his dead blue eyes. Tears ran down his cheeks.

"We need to get help for Annabelle!" Jonas repeated.

Munroe nodded. His voice cracked as he said, "I just spoke to her. She's safe."

Jonas Black bent over with his hands on his knees and said, "Have you reconsidered that body armor yet?"

29

Munroe still remembered his office at the Pentagon fondly, even though it had been over ten years since he had actually *seen* it. He could have used his influence to requisition a larger and more luxurious space, one with a private office for him, but he liked the communal feel of the room. He called it his *War Room* – and they were most assuredly at war. The twenty-by-twenty space held three matching walnut desks, all facing each other, and, thanks to Annabelle, always smelled like vanilla or cinnamon or whatever fragrance had most recently piqued her interest. His desk sat at the back of the room against the outer window with Annabelle and Gerald's desks flanking his in a U shape. He remembered the way in which the yellow-tinted bullet- and blast-resistant glass of the Pentagon had cast an unusual pallor onto everything in the room. Munroe had heard rumors that the Secretary of Defense had paid out of his own pocket to have the glass replaced with a more expensive crystal-clear variety, but he had never asked the Secretary if the rumors were true. At one time, Munroe had filled the rest of the room with cork boards and dry-erase boards displaying pictures and bits of information pertinent to cases, but now all that had to be done in his head.

Jonas Black had barely said a word to Munroe since the attack at Georgetown the previous evening. He tapped a finger on his desk and could feel Black's hard stare burning holes in him.

"You don't agree with the way that I handled the situation at the university?" Munroe finally said.

"We were lucky. You almost got us both killed. And Annabelle. Is that drive really worth all our lives? Most operators would have shot us both in the back of the head and searched the corpses for the intel."

"This man isn't most operators."

"What was all that about Ramon Castillo?"

"Castillo is the leader of one of the largest cartels in Mexico, and many believe him to be one of the most dangerous men in the world."

"But how did you connect him to all this?"

"An educated guess that our Hispanic friend confirmed for us. I was telling the truth when I said that a friend at the FBI had described the Castillo Cartel's business dealings here in the US. It made sense that the cartel could be connected. Any other questions?"

Jonas Black released a long disgusted breath but said nothing. Munroe could feel the heat coming off the big man in the silence that followed. The ringing of Munroe's cell phone cut through the tension. "What did you find, Joey?" he said into the phone.

"You were right to have me look through the photos of people associated with the Castillo Cartel. I found the guy that broke into my apartment. His name is Antonio de Almeida. He's a Colombian who rose through the ranks to become one of the group's top enforcers. It's rumored that Almeida's become Ramon Castillo's right-hand man since Castillo's son was killed in a recent attempt to take down Ramon himself."

"Good work. What about Wyatt Randall's financials?"

"Nothing unusual there. If he was getting paid from

somewhere, the money wasn't going into his bank account. Which means no paper trail. But I did get a pretty big hit on people from Randall's past. Apparently he went to college with Brendan Lennix."

"The president of Lennix Pharmaceuticals?"

"Right, and word is that Lennix has been working on some highly classified project for DARPA and the DOD. Pretty good for a company that was almost bankrupt."

"I can take a guess on who helped Lennix overcome his financial troubles. Keep digging. See if you can find out anything else about Lennix's mystery project. What about Randall and General Easton? Did you find any connection there?"

"Easton's son attended Georgetown during the same time Randall taught there. Annabelle's verifying it, but we think he might have been one of Randall's students. If so, we're going to track him down and find out if he put Randall in touch with his father."

"Don't bother. Verify the records, but don't contact Easton's son. That family's been through enough. I don't want him to feel somehow responsible."

Munroe said goodbye, hung up the phone, and leaned back in his chair, organizing the various strands in his mind. Things were starting to make sense. Wyatt Randall had taken his discovery to Brendan Lennix. Randall then learned that Lennix had borrowed money from the cartels and had stolen evidence to give to General Easton. But that still didn't explain how Corrigan tied into everything and why the disgraced soldier was so important. Munroe guessed that Corrigan was linked to Wyatt Randall's so-called miracle drug somehow, but he had no evidence. The dots were there, but he had yet to connect them all, and he couldn't prove any of it. But maybe he could at least verify some of his suspicions.

Munroe stood up from the desk and said, "Mr. Black, let's take a walk."

"Where are we going?"

"I thought maybe we'd drop in unannounced over at the executive wing."

30

By floor area, the Pentagon was the world's largest office building. The iconic headquarters took up around six and a half million square feet, and over thirty thousand people went to work there every day. It was the nerve center of the American military, and a self-contained city in its own right. A worker at the Pentagon never had to leave during the day. The building housed dentists, doctors, myriad retail stores, a fitness center, and just about everything else in between. But Damian Lightoller, the Under Secretary of Defense for Acquisition, Technology, and Logistics, appreciated the food choices the most. Lightoller was not a small man and had always enjoyed food. He hated eating the same thing day in and day out. Variety was the spice of life, after all. Luckily, the Pentagon provided as much variety for food choices as any shopping center the world over – everything from Subway to McDonald's, Pizza Hut to Panda Express. And most importantly for those that burned the midnight oil in defense of the nation's freedom: Starbucks and Dunkin' Donuts.

Lightoller had tried just about every diet on the market, and he had no trouble finding the discipline to lose weight in the short term. It was sticking with it that posed the problem. Fortunately, a low-carb diet (with the weekends off, of course) seemed to suit him fairly well. So, keeping with the diet, he sat at his desk and sipped a sugar-free vanilla latte made with whipping cream. When the door of his office opened without any warning from his secretary, Lightoller nearly spilled the latte down the front of his Brooks Brothers suit.

"Mr. Lightoller, I tried to stop them," his secretary said from the next room.

"Hello, Damian. I need a word. National security and all that," Deacon Munroe said from the doorway. A large stern-looking man stood next to the DCIS agent. The big guy radiated an aura of physical confidence, like a bouncer at a strip club, though Lightoller sensed the big man's intimidating stance was more than just bravado.

"It's okay, Becky," he said as he stood and offered his hand. Munroe didn't reach out for it, and Lightoller experienced a moment of guilt when he realized that Munroe couldn't see the proffered greeting. "Please, have a seat."

"Thank you," Munroe said. The big man pushed Munroe roughly into a chair, earning him a look of annoyance from the blind man.

"So what can I do for you, Special Agent Munroe? I'm afraid that I'm leaving for an appointment soon."

The big guy took up position to Munroe's left but remained standing. Munroe adjusted his dark sunglasses and said, "I won't take up much of your time, and since you have other engagements, I'll get right to the point. What can you tell me about Lennix Pharmaceuticals?"

Lightoller swallowed hard. "I've heard of them, but that's about as far as my knowledge goes. Just what I've seen in the papers."

Munroe's head tilted to one side. "Really? That's very odd."

"I don't know what you mean."

"I just find it strange that the man in charge of acquisition, technology, and logistics isn't familiar with a company that's in bed with the DOD and DARPA."

Ethan Cross

Lightoller leaned back in his chair. "I'm sorry, Deacon. Yes, we do have a contract with them, but you know that I can't discuss the details of classified projects."

"It's on a need-to-know basis?"

"That's right."

"Well, I need to know. All this ties back to the reason why General Easton was murdered and to a marine that's about to be executed."

"I thought Easton committed suicide."

Munroe smiled. "If you buy that story, then your elevator's stuck between floors."

"I still don't see how I can help."

"You know, this whole thing started a couple years back with the marine. John Corrigan. You were sitting in that same chair at that time, and I figure that means there's a pretty good chance you were involved in whatever cover-up went down."

"First of all, I don't appreciate you barging into my office. You want to speak to me, make an appointment. Second, if you intend to make wild accusations, you had better come to me with more than a three-hundred-pound gorilla at your side. You had better have some proof."

The big man's eyes narrowed, and he cracked his knuckles. Lightoller immediately regretted the gorilla comment, but it was too late to back down now. He said, "Your time's up, Munroe. See yourself out."

Instead of getting up, Munroe leaned back in the chair and crossed his legs. In a calm, friendly voice, the blind man said, "Did you know that I lost my wife to cancer within only two years of losing my sight? That was a difficult time. A very dark time for me that was filled with a lot of anger and confusion. When I learned that my wife had only a few months to live, I couldn't deal with it. I called a taxi and checked in to a hotel. To this day I can't explain exactly why I did it. It was probably the most cowardly thing that a man could do in that situation, but I suppose that I just couldn't deal with losing her and sitting idly by as she withered away."

Munroe turned toward the far wall as if he were reliving the moment. Then he lowered his head and intertwined his fingers as if in prayer. Lightoller said, "I'm very sorry to hear all that, but—"

"It took less than a day for me to come to my senses," Munroe interrupted. "My wife wasn't even angry. She seemed to understand that it was because of how deeply I loved her that I felt I had to leave. But I was angry enough with myself for the both of us. I still think about the time that I missed by leaving. Even though it was only a few hours, I would give anything to have those moments back. To have the opportunity to spend them with her now."

Munroe stood up, placed his hands atop the desk, and leaned toward Lightoller. "After that moment, I vowed I would never run from a fight again as long as I lived. I've lost two friends over this, one of them the oldest and dearest friend I had in this world. There's no force in Heaven or Earth that will stop me from seeing it through. I'm going to find those responsible, and I'm going to burn them down. Make no mistake about that."

The big man gave Lightoller one last contemptuous glare and then led Munroe from the room. After they had gone, Lightoller just sat there for a moment, trying to calm his thundering heart and plan his next move carefully. Then he picked up his desk phone, tapped one of its many buttons, and said, "Becky, get me Brendan Lennix on the line immediately."

31

The Pentagon had always reminded Jonas Black more of a shopping mall or a hospital than a military complex. Wide corridors, off-whites, a maze of halls – he could have been magically transported to any large medical center and not known the difference between the two, except that the other people filling the halls would have worn scrubs and white jackets instead of suits and military uniforms.

Munroe was quiet at his side, and Jonas wondered if his new boss's thoughts still dwelled on old memories. "Lightoller was lying," Jonas said.

"About Lennix? Obviously."

"Not just about that. I got the distinct impression he knew that Easton was murdered and that Lennix was connected to it."

"What makes you say that?"

Jonas debated on how much of his own story to share, but Munroe had already referenced his checkered past when they'd first met so it probably wouldn't be a surprise to him. He said, "Have you ever seen a movie where a group of Mafia types have someone tied to a chair and one guy is asking questions and another guy is beating the piss out of the dude in the chair?"

"I suppose so."

"Before I became a marine, that's pretty much what I did for a living."

"You were an interrogator?"

"No, I was the guy that gave the beatings. But you do enough of those and you start to develop a sense of when the person is lying or telling the truth."

"Hmm," Munroe said, "It sounds like you developed a talent for kinesics."

"What does that mean?"

"Take the next right."

Jonas cocked an eyebrow at his companion. "You know where we are?"

"I always try to have a general sense of my location relative to my surroundings, especially in places with which I'm intimately acquainted." Jonas took the next turn, and Munroe continued, "And kinesics, for future reference, is the science of observing and analyzing the body language and verbal behavior of witnesses and suspects. Certain people have a natural talent for it. You're probably subconsciously picking up on those types of cues. People with a natural aptitude toward it make the best kinesic interrogators. Maybe that's a skill you should consider developing."

"Does that mean you're getting used to having me around?"

Munroe ignored the question. "I believe we've arrived."

Jonas glanced around the hall. The sign by the closest door read *The Reflection Room*. "Arrived where?"

"This used to be a storage closet, but after 9/11, this place became known as *The Reflection Room*. It's dedicated to those from the Navy family who lost their lives here and on the aircraft during the attack."

Jonas opened the door and led Munroe inside. The room didn't contain an elaborate memorial or intricate adornments. The walls were the same off-white and the floor the same dark blue marble as in the corridor leading to the space. A simple stone tablet containing a list of names flanked by the American and Navy flags rested in a niche along one wall. Stone benches sat in the room's center. The lights had been dimmed, and the room was currently unoccupied. Jonas felt an inexplicable weight fall upon him when he entered – a power or resonance that nearly brought him to tears.

Munroe sat down on the bench facing the list of names.

"Were you here when the attack happened?" Jonas asked.

Swallowing hard, Munroe replied, "I'd like to be alone, Mr. Black. Grab us some coffee and then come back for me. Take your time."

32

The attacks of September 2001 still weighed on Jonas Black's mind, and so he decided to pay a visit to the interior portion of the Pentagon 9/11 memorial. He wandered the hall until he reached the space designated for those who had senselessly lost their lives that day. The walls were some type of brushed metal, and obsidian displays lined the room. Over the center display, large black lettering read *America's Heroes*. Beneath that was a seal embossed with an eagle and the words "A Grateful Nation Remembers."

Jonas would certainly never forget where he had been that Tuesday. Home on leave, he had been visiting his brother. Michael went to work, and Jonas had driven to a local shopping mall to pick up a gift for his nephew. On the drive there, he remembered the disc jockeys joking that some idiot had apparently flown a Cessna into a building in New York. He hadn't thought much of it, but within a few moments, the radio personalities apologized and gave more details. When Jonas arrived at the mall, he and a group of other people stood in front of an electronics store and watched the attack replaying on twenty different screens of various sizes. The smell of cinnamon rolls and donuts hung heavy in the air from a nearby Dunkin' Donuts as he watched the destruction. It was a good thing that he had never been partial to sweets, since the mental association forged that day had forever turned his stomach against any fresh-baked donut, roll, or pastry.

As the day progressed and more attacks occurred, Jonas remembered feeling distinctly that it was the end of the world or, at least, the end of life as most Americans knew it.

Munroe had told him to take his time, and so he padded slowly back and forth across the dark gray carpet, examining each obsidian slab with care. A table attached to the center display held binders detailing the biographies of all those who had died. Jonas skimmed through it, examining each smiling face. The binders also listed the names of those military personnel awarded the Purple Heart from that day and the select civilian DOD employees who had received the Defense of Freedom medal.

As Jonas glanced through the lists, his gaze caught one name – one of those DOD employees awarded the Defense of Freedom medal. Printed in small black lettering on the page was the name *Deacon Munroe*.

33

Munroe's thoughts swam in a maelstrom of pain, anger, and confusion. He thought of all that he had lost. His sight. His wife. His best friend. Not for the first time, he considered how much easier it would be to just lie down and die, to give up, save himself from the burden of living and the pain of remembering. But one name that he knew was etched into the simple plaque in to in front of him kept him from giving in to the darkness. It was the name of a Navy officer who had saved his life on September 11 2001. He owed it to that man to live, to do something worthwhile with the life that a brave soldier had exchanged for his own.

The door opened, and Munroe thought at first that Jonas Black had returned. But the footfalls and cologne didn't match the big man. It was probably just another pilgrim paying homage. He didn't say anything to the newcomer. This was a place for quiet contemplation, not idle chit-chat. The person moved up behind him, and he shifted to the edge of the bench to allow room for the stranger to sit.

The attack occurred so swiftly and expertly that Munroe barely reacted. The stranger's hand slid over Munroe's nose and mouth and a piercing pain shot up his left side. Cold tendrils of agony and then numbness swept over him.

He tried to move his limbs, to fight back somehow, but the shock was too great. His strength left him. He clawed feebly at the stranger's hand over his face.

Keeping the hand over Munroe's nose and mouth, the stranger laid him back on the bench. Munroe felt the blood pumping out of his body through the wound in his side. Nausea. Fear. Confusion. Cold chills. A desire to fight but no strength to do so.

The stranger searched through Munroe's pockets and pulled something out. The flash drive.

The sound of retreating footsteps. The door closing. Munroe tried to call for help, but his scream came out as a wheeze. Laying his head back against the bench and accepting his fate, he turned to the memorial and thought of the name etched there, the name of the man who had saved his life.

Munroe felt guilty for wanting to give up and apologized to the Navy officer. And then darkness surrounded him, embraced him, devoured him.

Part Three

Part Three

34

At a makeshift airfield located in Alexandria, Virginia that was little more than a long strip of grass, Antonio de Almeida watched the Cessna Corvalis TTX make its approach. The sleek little single-engine plane looked more like a private jet with its smooth, aerodynamic lines and rounded cockpit. Despite the uneven terrain, the pilot put the plane down gently and maneuvered it to a gradual stop between the white pines and hickories that bordered the runway. The doors on both sides of the Cessna opened, and the pilot and two large Hispanic men hopped down from the craft. The protectors scanned the area and gave Almeida a nod. Then they assisted the plane's final occupant to the ground.

Ramon Castillo's black pinstriped suit didn't even look wrinkled from the flight. The cartel boss wore a silver shirt, no tie, and wire-framed spectacles. Black hair, streaked with gray, swept back from a bearded, handsome face that had only recently begun to show the signs of age. Ramon was a third-generation cartel leader, but this hadn't caused him to become decadent or spoiled. The people called him Vaquero, meaning cowboy, because a rumor had spread that Castillo had descended from the original herdsmen who first came to California with the Jesuit priest Eusebio Kino in 1687 and were the first cowboys to visit the region. Unlike many of the other cartel bosses, the people loved Ramon as well as fearing him. He had a reputation for only being ruthless when necessary and only toward those who stood against him. To the people of the regions he controlled, he had always shown compassion and mercy and had actually greatly improved their standards of living.

Almeida approached Castillo with open arms, and the cartel leader embraced him firmly. "It's good to see you, Vaquero," Almeida said.

"And you, my son." They walked toward a black Mercedes GL550, and Castillo growled as he slid in a patch of blue-gray mud. "Dammit, I should have just landed right on the fairway instead of all the way over here."

Almeida laughed. "The guests at the country club might have noticed, Vaquero."

A pair of businesses camouflaged the Castillo Cartel's base of operations in Virginia. One was the Hill Crest Landfill, and the other was the Hill Crest Golf Course and Resort. The landfill site housed mostly construction and demolition debris, while the resort catered to the rich and famous.

Castillo asked, "Has Mr. Lennix calmed down yet?"

Almeida shrugged. "He is a difficult man, not built for this kind of conflict."

"Did you acquire the drive?"

"I'm afraid not. One of our men took a drive from Munroe, but it was a fake, just a decoy. Munroe must have hidden the real drive somewhere."

Castillo swore under his breath. "But he can't access it?"

"No, he doesn't know anything about what we're planning or the weapon. He's put some of it together, but not nearly enough to cause us problems."

"Is he still alive?"

"I'm not sure. Our man stabbed him, but they rushed him to

the hospital for treatment. I haven't heard beyond that. I'm sorry, Vaquero. I should have had him killed instantly at Georgetown, but I thought that perhaps I could reason with him."

Castillo smiled and clasped Almeida's shoulder. "That's why I love you so much, Antonio. Many of the men who gravitate toward our profession are borderline sociopaths. They don't care who they hurt and actually enjoy the killing. But not you. You realize that even a soldier must maintain honor and keep a clean soul. It's about business and raising our people out of the gutter, not about causing pain. But sometimes even that is necessary. Think of the wars that King David fought in defense of his people, and he was a man after God's own heart."

"You're right, as always, Vaquero," Almeida said, nodding. "We'll find Munroe and get the drive back."

"I know you will, my friend. When I found you on the streets of Bogota living like an animal, even then, I could see greatness in your eyes. I know you won't disappoint me."

Almeida thought back on his early years in Bogota, all the things he had done to survive. He had sold his innocence to perverted old men in exchange for food. Sometimes he still woke in the night thinking that he could feel their hot breath on his neck and the stink of cigar smoke and aguardiente in his nostrils. He had stolen food from the mouths of other children. Once another boy, who was only six years old, had managed to pinch a muffin topped with arequipe. Almeida bludgeoned the boy to death and took the sweet confection for himself. And then one day he stole the wallet of a young man in a fine suit. The man caught him, and young Antonio thought his life was over – not that it was much of a life, anyway. But instead the young man, named Ramon Castillo, saw something in him and gave him a life and a purpose. From that day forward, Castillo took Almeida under his wing and treated him like a son.

They climbed into the Mercedes and headed off in

the direction of the resort. In a few moments, the lights of the clubhouse came into view. The forty-five-thousand-square-foot facility featured an elegant ballroom, a restaurant, a tavern, and a well-stocked golf shop. A red-roofed dining terrace supported by massive stone columns wrapped around the front of the impressive structure.

As they approached, Castillo spoke in a voice so low that Almeida could barely hear him over the hum of the engine and the car's air conditioner. "These American politicians think that we are nothing but cockroaches, Antonio. Their corruption and greed and hypocrisy make me sick. They stand on pedestals and spew lies about their ideological and moral superiority, while all the time they're abusing every ounce of power they have in shady back-room deals while snorting our cocaine off an underage prostitute's backside. They talk about their Geneva convention, about human rights and due process while they send their black-ops assassins to murder my family. But they will pay for their transgressions. Just as God himself struck down Sodom and Gomorrah for their sins, we're going to burn Washington, DC to the ground."

35

As the last shackles of sleep and disorientation fell away, reality took hold, and Deacon Munroe remembered the stabbing and the theft of his decoy flash drive. After the encounter at Georgetown, he had switched the real drive with one from his office so that, if anyone else tried to take the drive from him, he could provide them with a fake instead.

He tried to sit up, but the movement tugged against the needles in his arms and the monitors attached to his body. On his right side, his youngest daughter, Chloe, said, "Mak! I think he's awake."

Footsteps sounded from his left, and he felt Makayla's soft fingers intertwine with his own. "Dad? Do you know where you are?" she said.

Munroe opened his mouth to speak, but the words came out as a dry crackling like the crunching of dead leaves. "Here, take a drink," Chloe said.

After letting the cool liquid slide down his throat, he said, "How bad?"

"You're lucky," Makayla replied. "You probably would have died if you had a kidney on your left side."

Munroe had lost his left kidney and a piece of his liver at the same time he had lost his sight, and now that old injury had apparently saved his life. "Where's Black?"

At the foot of the bed, another voice answered, "He's in the hallway. Do you want me to fetch him?" He hadn't realized that Annabelle was also keeping vigil by his bedside.

"Yes, thank you."

"You shouldn't be worrying about the case. It's over now. Fuller wants you in protective custody and says to let NCIS handle the investigation." Their supervisor, Jack Fuller, was an intelligent and forward-thinking man and mostly stayed out of Munroe's way, but he also had his own career to consider.

"Did you tell him about the flash drive?"

"No, but you should. I'll be right back."

Munroe heard Annabelle's footsteps move away from the bed and toward the door. Chloe stroked his hair and said in a strained voice, "We thought we'd lost you."

He squeezed her hand and said, "I'm much too ornery to die, darling."

"It's not funny. Black told me about the other attempts on your life. I know you're doing this because of Uncle Gerald, but it's not worth losing you too. You think that—"

"We can talk about that later," Makayla interrupted. "He's barely even awake."

Chloe shot back, "Somebody needs to talk about it *now*."

"I said that's enough."

"You're not in charge here, Mak. I can say whatever I want to *my* father."

"You are such a brat. Dad doesn't need this right now."

"Girls, please. Both of you. I'm fine. I'm going to continue to be fine."

Chloe began to cry. "I just don't want to lose you, too."

Munroe placed an arm around her and pulled her close. She had always been the sensitive one. She was the daughter who rescued stray animals, who nursed birds with broken wings back to health, and who had been strongly considering a vegetarian lifestyle after seeing a video at school about the poor treatment of livestock. Her nature reminded him of her mother's. Makayla, on the other hand, was analytical and practical and took more after him. He wanted to comfort Chloe by saying that he would let the case go, but he also didn't want to lie to her.

Makayla gasped as heavy footsteps pounded in from the hall. "You need stitches," she said to Jonas Black. "How did that happen?"

"What, this?" Munroe couldn't tell to which part of his body Jonas had pointed. "Just a souvenir from the attack at Georgetown. You should see the other guy."

"You realize that you're in a hospital? You should get that looked at."

"I don't like doctors. I'm damn near immune to anesthesia. It takes about six times as much to have the proper effect, and by the time I get stuck with that many needles, most of the time it's easier to just get whatever it is done without being numb. It made going to the dentist a ton of fun when I was a kid."

Interrupting the conversation, Munroe said, "Girls, can you give me a few minutes alone with Mr. Black? Maybe fetch my doctor. I'd like to know when I can get out of here."

"They want to keep you for at least a few days," Makayla said.

Chloe sighed. "You're not a doctor, Mak."

As their voices moved toward the hall and faded away, he heard Makayla reply, "And you're not a baby, but you whine like one."

On Munroe's left, a chair scraped across the floor and creaked under Jonas's weight. Light feminine footsteps entered the room, and the door closed behind them. The scent of jasmine grew stronger as Annabelle took up position next to him. "They're worried about you," she said.

"They're smart girls. They should be worried. We've stumbled into something big here. Whatever is on that drive is worth a whole heap of trouble."

"And now they've got it back," Jonas said.

"No, they took a fake. I hid the real one somewhere safe after Georgetown. Did they find the man that attacked me?"

Annabelle replied, "He got away. They have camera footage but, so far, no hits from facial recognition."

"It sounds as if I'll be laid up for at least a couple days, but we can't afford to let things settle that long. The case needs to continue forward. By the time the docs clear me, it could be too late."

"Fuller gave me specific orders that we were not to pursue this case any further," Annabelle said. "He even went as far as saying that the orders came from above, so there was no point in you trying to call in a favor and go over his head. It wasn't supposed to be our investigation in the first place."

"Normally, I have no problem following orders, but not this time."

"Dammit, Deac. I miss Gerald too, but this has gone far enough. Nothing you do will bring him back, especially getting yourself killed."

"I'm not just going to roll over on this. And it's bigger than just Gerald. General Easton and Wyatt Randall were murdered. Corrigan's about to be executed. Who knows how many more people have died or will die over whatever the hell is being covered up here? You think everything'll be fine if we just stop making waves?"

"It's not our problem! Someone else can handle it."

"Easton contacted me because he didn't know who else to trust. And neither do we. Once we have the big picture and some usable evidence, we'll take it up the food chain and get help. But right now, it's on us."

Annabelle stood and stormed toward the door. "You stubborn bastard," she said under her breath.

Munroe closed his eyes and gritted his teeth. "What about you, Mr. Black? Are you ready to let it go?"

"I don't have anything better to do."

"So you agree with me?"

Jonas seemed to consider the question carefully. "I honestly don't know, but I owe it to you to see it through."

"Good enough."

"What's our next step?"

Munroe was quiet for a moment as he weighed their options. Then he said, "I'm going to recover, and while I'm doing that, you're going to be my eyes and ears out on the street. You're going back to the beginning, Mr. Black. You're going to find out how John Corrigan's family really died."

"I'm not an investigator."

"A fact of which I am most certainly aware. But I think I know who may be able to lend you a hand."

36

Katherine O'Connell had been fifteen years old when her family had immigrated from Ireland, and she had never been able to lose the accent. As if she didn't have enough obstacles to overcome simply by being a woman, she also had to deal with the issues that accompanied her status as an obvious immigrant. In most lines of work, such things wouldn't matter, but as an agent within the Naval Criminal Investigative Service, she had to deal with soldiers every day. They tended to treat her like some spy from a foreign intelligence agency. She had to work twice as hard as a male agent in order to gain their trust and respect and then she had to fight against the stigma of not being a natural-born citizen. At least she didn't trace her origins to a country hostile to the US, otherwise she would never have been able to insert herself into the military culture.

But sometimes her long red hair and Irish accent gave her an advantage. Feminine charm could often break down the barricades erected by even the hardest soldier. In those instances, the men would glance hungrily at her body in much the same way as the man who was currently sitting in her office.

Jonas Black had demanded to speak with her and, after showing DCIS credentials and being allowed access, had started fiddling with an iPad, trying to bring up some type of video

146

call. She wondered if a gorilla would be making more progress. "You need a bit of help with that?" she asked for the third time.

"No, I think I've got it." He turned the device to face her and the image of another man sitting in what appeared to be a hospital bed loaded onto the screen.

"Hello, Agent O'Connell," the man on the screen said. "My name is Deacon Munroe. I'm a special investigator with DCIS. I would have preferred to greet you in person, but circumstances dictated that our first encounter be facilitated through the miracles of technology."

"Let's not muck about, Munroe. What are you after?"

"Straight to the point. I like that. My associate Mr. Black and I need your assistance with a case on which you were the lead investigator."

"Why?"

"Because I believe it to be tied to my current investigation."

"In what way?"

"Do you remember the case involving Sergeant John Corrigan?"

"The man I put on death row? Yeah, it rings a bell or two. Corrigan waved all rights to appeals and confessed to the crimes. Why would DCIS show such a sudden interest in a closed case?"

"We believe that his confession might have been coerced."

Katherine sat forward. "That confession was handled by the book. I did nothing—"

"I'm sorry, Agent O'Connell. I didn't mean to imply any impropriety on your part. I believe that he might have been coerced by influences outside of the investigation."

Munroe started at the beginning and laid out the information they'd uncovered to that point. Although Katherine didn't like the implications, she couldn't fault most of his conclusions. Plus, the Corrigan case had never added up to her. The evidence had been overwhelming, and Corrigan had confessed, but her gut told her that some aspect of the case had gone unnoticed.

She held her comments until Munroe had completed his story, and then she leaned back in her desk chair and steepled her fingers, mentally processing the new information. After a moment, she said, "So if I'm reading you right, you want me to drop everything, go back on a case I worked in which a Marine was sentenced to death, and check everything out again. A case, I might add, where the suspect confessed and the evidence overwhelmingly indicated his guilt."

The corners of Munroe's mouth curled up into a large grin. "That seems to be the long and short of it."

37

Although Katherine hated taking the time away from her current caseload, she also didn't want it to come back on her if something had been missed during Corrigan's original investigation. A few hours reviewing evidence was better than spending days having her every move dissected and second-guessed by some oversight committee. Plus, if there was even a small chance that Corrigan was innocent or that others were involved, she wanted to know. She had the files delivered to one of the conference rooms, and she and Jonas Black began the arduous process of laying out the documents across the surface of the twenty-foot maple conference table. The files carried a musty acidic odor that was at odds with the leather-and-vanilla scent of the meeting space. She dropped a file on the table and then washed down a king-sized Snickers bar with hefty gulps from a two-liter bottle of Mountain Dew. Jonas Black hadn't said much, but she noticed him examining her from the corner of his eye more than once.

Finally she said, "So what's your story, Black? I haven't seen a lot of DCIS agents with tattoos on their knuckles."

He shrugged. "I like to defy expectation."

"*LIFE* and *PAIN*. Life is pain. Kind of a pessimistic and depressing thing to tattoo across your digits, don't you think?"

Without looking up from the file he was reading, he said, "You're reading it wrong."

"How so?"

"You have it backwards. It doesn't say, 'Life is pain.' It says, 'Pain is life.'"

"What's the difference?"

Jonas placed the file down on the table and met her gaze. "It's a reminder that, no matter how bad things may seem, I'm still kicking. Every moment you can say that is a gift. You have to take the good with the bad. And sometimes it's those moments of pain that shape who we are and give us the strength to face what comes next. Like most everything else in life, it's all in how you look at it."

He returned to the files, but Katherine stared at him for a moment longer, noticing for the first time how attractive he was with his dark complexion and muscular frame. She realized that she had made the same mistake with Jonas Black that every male chauvinist made when assuming that a woman couldn't do anything that a man could. She had taken one look at his size, muscles, and rough exterior and assumed that being big and being dumb were synonymous. The guilt over that stereotypical assumption forced her to see him in a different light. And a part of her had to admit that what she saw intrigued her.

Jonas's phone rang. He put it on speaker and set it in the center of the table. "Okay," Munroe said from the other end of the line. "Let's run this thing down. Give me the details."

"Corrigan was found cradling his family and crying while covered in their blood," Katherine said. "His DNA was collected from beneath his wife's fingernails, and the scratches on his neck matched up. Corrigan claimed that he had blacked out and couldn't remember the actual murders. Psych evals showed that he wasn't suffering from any form of psychosis or PTSD that could have explained the blackout or the violence. The face of Corrigan's watch was smashed and pieces of the glass were retrieved from his daughter's cheek where he had backhanded her. Bite impressions on his wife matched Corrigan's teeth. His tox screens showed no drugs or illegal substances. Financials are all clear."

"Did the blood tests show any presence of monatomic metals?" Munroe asked.

"Hold on." Katherine flipped through some of the files and said, "I don't see anything on it, but they may not have tested for that."

"Perhaps. What about motive?"

"We questioned everyone associated with Corrigan and the family. No indications as to why he would have done it. That was the one thing about the case that didn't add up. According to everything we found, Corrigan was a loving husband and father."

Jonas Black said, "Yeah, he was. When we were deployed, getting back to his family was all he talked about."

"Hold on," Katherine said. "You served with Corrigan?"

"That's right. He was my team leader in Recon."

Her eyes narrowed. "So this is personal?"

Jonas's gaze didn't falter beneath her harsh stare. "It's always personal to someone. If you're asking if I care whether or not my old friend gets a needle in his arm and if I would stop that from happening if I could, then yeah, I guess it's personal."

"Let's keep to the facts," Munroe said, trying to defuse the tension of the interaction. "Maybe we're looking at things all wrong. Reviewing evidence is like staring through a kaleidoscope. You have to twist everything up from time to time."

Katherine said, "Okay, what do you want to *twist up*?"

"We need to stop wondering *if* he did it or *why* he did it and start asking what could have *made* him do it. What would cause a man who by all accounts is a loving husband and father to suddenly snap and murder the people he loved most in the world? What did he see? What did he experience? What was he exposed to? Was the military experimenting on him in any way?"

"I don't see anything like that in his file," Katherine said.

"What was he doing when it happened?" Munroe said. "Where was he stationed?"

"At the time of the murders, Corrigan and a small group of Spec Ops soldiers from all the various branches were staying in temporary housing at Fort Meade in Maryland. Corrigan had traveled back to Camp Pendleton in California for the weekend, specifically for his daughter's birthday."

"Fort Meade?" Jonas said. "That doesn't seem right. Meade is an Army base. I've never heard of Recon Marines being stationed or training there."

"They surely participate in cross-training programs among the different branches?" Munroe asked.

"Absolutely. Marines attend the US Army Airborne Course, Jump Master, HALO, SCUBA school, and a bunch of others. But there's nothing like that at Meade."

Katherine remembered reading something about the program at Fort Meade in one of the files. She rifled through the stacks and pulled out the folder she wanted. "It says here that they were at Fort Meade taking classes at the Army's Defense Information School."

Jonas shook his head. "That school's for public relations and journalism. Why would a bunch of Spec Ops soldiers need that kind of training?"

"It was a course in handling cultural issues."

Munroe asked Katherine, "Were all the other members of the class questioned?"

"They were, but we didn't focus on the actual training that was taking place. Our inquiries mainly dealt with Corrigan and his state of mind."

"Then that's where we start. We need to find out exactly what those soldiers were doing at Fort Meade."

Katherine leaned back in her chair and ran her hands through her long red hair. "Those men are probably spread all over the world by now. If you think I'm going to drop everything and go hoofing around the globe because you said so, then you're daft."

Jonas Black held up the file displaying the names of the other soldiers who had participated in the so-called cultural relations class. "You won't need your passport," he said. "I know one of these guys, and he's less than an hour away."

38

MCB Quantico was built on nearly one hundred square miles of land and had become known as the crossroads of the Marine Corps. It housed the Corps's Combat Development Command, the Marine Corps Officer Candidates School, the Marine Corps Research Center, and the Marine Corps Brig as well as the famed FBI Academy. Jonas Black remembered the first time he had visited Quantico. He had expected something more urban, simply based on depictions he had seen on TV, but in actuality, the area was very rural and had a small-town feel to it. Daryl Gelman, the man they were coming to see, worked for Combat Development Command along with twelve thousand other military and civilian personnel living on the base.

As they drove beneath the red-brick archway and sign marked with the Marine Corps seal, Jonas watched intently as Katherine O'Connell chugged the last of another two-liter bottle of Mountain Dew and tossed it into the back of her black Dodge Charger. He turned to the back seat and stared down at the enormous collection of candy wrappers and soda bottles that filled the space. Then his gaze traveled back to Katherine's slender form.

"What are you gawking at?" Katherine said.

"I'm just wondering how you eat like that and stay so thin."

"High metabolism and exercise, I suppose. I try to run ten miles a day."

"You eat a lot of junk food."

Katherine drummed her fingers on the steering wheel in time with the song on the radio. "I'm a bit partial to my afters. You aren't one of those health nuts, are you?"

"I don't think so, but I also don't think I've consumed as much sugar in my life as you have in the time I've known you."

"What about when you were a boy?"

"We didn't have sweets."

"Were your parents communists?"

Jonas said, "Parent, singular. My mom. But no, we were just poor."

"Candy bars and soda pop ain't that expensive. Poor people enjoy them all the time. Someone should have called family services on your mum. I think that's one of the things a parent is required to provide: shelter, running water, and dessert."

Jonas grinned. "I admire your passion on the subject."

"Hey, what the hell's the point in living if you don't stop to have a piece of cake now and then?"

"I prefer a big steak myself."

Katherine looked him up and down. "I can see that."

They passed through the security checkpoint, and Jonas read off the directions that they had been given. Soldiers marched along concrete paths, and trees encircled nondescript brick buildings. Jonas Black considered that if you replaced the soldiers with back-pack-carrying kids, the base would have been indistinguishable from a college campus. The car windows were open, and the breeze carried the smells of nature – with an underlying hint of spent ammunition and burnt gunpowder.

"So how do you know this guy?" Katherine asked. "Was he on the same team with you and Corrigan?"

"No, we were on base together in Afghanistan. We both grew

up in the St. Louis area, and so we knew a lot of the same places. It helps to be able to talk about home with someone. Of course, he was from a nice neighborhood in St. Charles, and I grew up in the hood in East St. Louis. He went to a private school, and I was the only white kid in my class."

"It's not fun being different. Being the outsider."

Jonas sensed that she was speaking from experience but didn't ask. "It made me tough. I learned how to stand up for myself. Of course, that also led down some bad roads."

Katherine was quiet for a moment as they wound slowly through the base, but then she said, "Can I ask you something? Something personal."

"Since when are you shy?"

"What is it like over there? Being in combat."

"It's hard to describe. Why do you ask?"

Katherine twisted her hands on the wheel and chewed on her lower lip. "My baby brother's currently deployed to Afghanistan."

"What branch?"

"He's part of the 1st Cavalry Division out of Fort Hood."

"That's a good unit. Did you know that Oliver Stone is a veteran of the 1st Cavalry Division?"

"You're avoiding my question."

Jonas took a deep breath. "You want the truth?"

"I think so."

"I sort of feel like I've been in combat in one way or another my whole life, and so my experience may be different from someone who dropped in from the burbs. But descriptions ranging from boring to exciting and gratifying to depressing all seem to apply. It's a rollercoaster."

He was quiet for a moment as he thought back on his time overseas and tried to put a name to his emotions. Eventually, he said, "Honestly, if I had to sum it up in one word, it would be loneliness. That was the only emotion that remained constant – for me, anyway. As a soldier, you have to accept that it doesn't matter how good you are or think you are. You could be the bravest, most disciplined man on the battlefield and still get smoked. That's just the way it is. You roll the dice and hope they don't come up snake eyes. Facing your own mortality in that kind of unforgiving environment gives you a certain perspective on things, and you realize that no one back home will ever understand what that's like. It separates you from them. Separates you from the person you were before."

Katherine pulled the car into the parking lot and turned off the engine. Jonas turned to her and saw tears forming in her eyes. "I'm sorry. I shouldn't have—"

"No," she interrupted and touched his arm. "Don't apologize. I appreciate your honesty." She wiped her eyes and added, "Let's go talk to your friend."

39

Captain Daryl Gelman was waiting for them in the lobby. The space was better designed than Jonas Black had expected. Tall ceilings. Sandstone textured walls. Silver accents. Polished floors. Wrap-around windows. Not the type of minimalistic facility that he recalled from his own time in the Corps. Gelman had also changed. A bit heavier. A bit more comfortable in his own skin. Gelman held out a hand and gave an inviting smile. A long nose sat over a thick black mustache on the captain's face, hiding the cherub-like features that Jonas remembered from Afghanistan.

"Corporal Black!" Gelman said. "It's been a long time."

"Yes, it has. And I guess it's Agent Black now." Jonas still didn't feel comfortable presenting himself in such a way. It felt like a lie, but Gelman didn't need to know that. "And congrats to you on the captain's bars."

"Thank you." Gelman gave him a strange look. "I heard some rumors . . ."

Jonas looked at Katherine, not wanting her to hear about his checkered past. To Gelman, he replied, "Tales of my demise have been greatly exaggerated."

Gelman laughed. "Good to hear it. Good to see you. I'm told you have some questions for me. It's a beautiful day, and I have an appointment coming up across base. Why don't we take a walk?"

The captain led them out of the building and down a path that cut through a swath of trees. The area was alive with birdsong and the chatter of squirrels. Jonas nodded at Katherine. Now that the ice had been broken, it was time for a professional to take over. She removed a notebook from her pocket, and in her lilting Irish accent, she said, "We're here, Captain Gelman, to discuss the period when you were stationed temporarily at Fort Meade."

Gelman nodded thoughtfully, but Jonas couldn't help but notice his old friend's gaze dart around as if searching for any other listeners. "What would you like to know?"

"What you were doing there?"

"I was participating in a training program on cultural relations designed to help us know how to interact with local populations around the world."

"And where was this class taking place?"

"At Fort Meade, as you said."

"Fort Meade's a big place. Where on base?"

"At the Defense Information School."

"I thought that was for journalists."

"In part. Besides, we were just using their facilities."

"I see. What did you think of those facilities?"

"Umm . . . they were fine, I suppose. This is about the facilities at the DINFOS?"

"No." Katherine let a silence hang in the air as they continued up the path. Gunfire sounded somewhere far in the distance, but the birds above their heads continued their singing, accustomed to the chattering of automatic weapons.

As Jonas suspected was Katherine's intention, Gelman felt the need to fill the silence. "I don't really remember much from my training at Fort Meade. It was pretty boring and straightforward. Common-sense stuff."

"You were in a class with Sergeant John Corrigan, is that correct?"

159

"Yes, I was." Gelman looked at Black and then at the ground. "I remember he was your friend. It was a terrible thing."

Katherine continued. "Do you recall anything strange that might have happened while you were at Fort Meade that could help to explain the incident with Sergeant Corrigan?"

"No – like I said, it was boring." Some other officers and a man in a suit passed them on the path. Gelman glanced at them warily.

"The military didn't do anything or give you anything that could have caused Sergeant Corrigan's behavior?"

Gelman halted briefly and then continued walking. "Of course not."

"What about—"

Jonas interrupted Katherine's question and said, "I think that's all we needed, Darryl. But hey, we're going to have dinner at the Globe and Laurel tonight before heading back. I've always wanted to check that place out. Why don't you meet us there? My treat. What time does Uncle Sam let you out of your cage?"

Gelman looked around again and said, "Sure. Is seven too late?"

"That's perfect. We'll let you get to your appointment, but I really look forward to catching up later tonight. If you remember anything else about your time at Fort Meade, you can let us know then."

They shook hands and separated. As she and Jonas headed toward the car, Katherine said, "What the hell was that about? He was obviously holding something back, and you let him off the hook."

"That was going nowhere. He seemed uncomfortable talking here. Gelman's a good man. He'll think about things, and then tonight, maybe we can get him alone and he'll open up."

She checked her watch. "You had better be right, Black. Or this whole day will have been a waste of my time."

40

With their plans growing closer to fruition but still missing the crucial catalyst that would set all the other events in motion, Antonio de Almeida decided that he would handle Munroe and his large friend personally. Sitting in a generic navy blue Ford Taurus, he watched as the NCIS agent and Jonas Black met with Captain Gelman. He listened in using a sophisticated directional microphone attached to a small parabolic reflector. Shame filled him at the prospect of what would have to come next, but he was too close to completion of his mission and had come too far already to allow doubt to derail his efforts.

Jonas Black and Katherine O'Connell climbed into the Dodge Charger, to which Almeida had attached a discreet tracking device, and pulled out of the lot. He watched them go, intending to catch up with them later. Then he stepped out of the Taurus and stood for a moment in the sun.

Saying a quick prayer, Almeida checked the items he would need and set off with a renewed sense of purpose.

41

Located alongside the Jefferson Davis Highway, the Globe and Laurel was one part restaurant and one part makeshift museum. Rick Spooner, a retired USMC Major, and his wife Gloria had wanted their restaurant to honor all the men and women who served their country and community, whether in the military or in any law-enforcement agency, by putting the proud histories of such patriots on display. The restaurant's many rooms contained military memorabilia from before the Civil War, displays tracing the evolution of the US Marine emblem, a donated Medal of Honor, Marine insignia displays, one of the largest collections of law-enforcement shoulder patches – it covered the ceilings of the quaint establishment (a tradition dating back to the opening of the FBI Academy in 1972) – and much more.

It wasn't a unique concept for a restaurant to have a theme or to display old collections or memorabilia of one type or another, but Jonas Black felt that there was more to the Globe and Laurel than just an attempt to create an atmosphere. The history within its walls resonated with him. The restaurant projected a certain honesty and dignity, as though the pride of patriots and heroes from many generations was converging in one spot. Maybe it was simply because of his status as a former

Marine, but he felt at home and experienced a sense of belonging and safety in the place, despite never having been there before.

He and Katherine requested a secluded table where they could discuss the case without worrying about someone overhearing their conversation. Then Jonas called Munroe at the hospital and put the phone on speaker. He imagined the blind man was chewing his fingers off in anticipation of their report. Munroe struck him as someone who had to be in control and didn't trust anyone else to do their jobs properly.

"What did you learn?" Munroe said without preamble.

"Just the official line," Katherine said, "but I got the distinct impression that he wasn't telling us everything. Unfortunately, someone stopped me from pushing him."

"Who?"

Jonas shook his head and shot her a dirty look. "He was freaked out, Munroe. I didn't think he would ever open up while we were in the middle of the base, and so I asked him to come out to dinner with us tonight. He should be here in just a few minutes."

He half-expected Munroe to berate him worse than Katherine had, but instead the blind man said, "Sounds like a good idea. Remind him that his fellow Marines are dying because of this mess, and he can help put a stop to it. What about Corrigan's financials, Katherine?"

"I already told you that we checked all that."

"Did you just look at his bank and credit card statements or did you check the actual leave and earnings statements he received from the government?"

Katherine rolled her eyes. "Oh, of course not, we were just foostering about. It's not like I know how to do my damn job or anything." She reached across the table and killed the call. To Jonas she said, "Is your boss always such a wanker?"

He thought of Munroe's name in small black letters inside the binder at the Pentagon Memorial. "He's been through a lot, but I don't really know him very well. I've only been working with him for a few days."

"What did you do before DCIS?"

"This and that."

The waitress arrived and asked to take their orders. She was pretty, with long black hair done up in a French braid and dimples in her cheeks. Another waitress walked by with a large strip steak on a tray, and as the smell of sizzling meat wafted past, Jonas realized how hungry he was. He checked the time on his phone. Gelman would be arriving in about half an hour. "We have someone else coming in a few minutes," he said to the young brunette.

"But I'll have one of your ice-cream sundaes while we're waiting," Katherine added.

The waitress gave them a nod and a smile and headed toward the kitchen. Jonas said, "What are you, like five years old? You're going to spoil your dinner."

"Thanks, mum, but it's more important to me to make sure that I have room for dessert." Then Katherine's smile faded abruptly, and her demeanor turned cold. "Who are you really?"

"I don't know what you mean."

"I tried to pull your file. Apparently, it's classified. Are you like some sort of CIA assassin?"

"Not that I recall, but maybe they erased my memory. You were checking up on me?"

Katherine leaned back in her chair and crossed her arms. A cold silence stretched between them. They sat and stared at each other for a few moments. Jonas cracked first. "Okay, you win. Up until a few days ago, I was in prison."

Her expression told him that she had considered a lot of scenarios, but that had not been one of them. "And now you're a federal agent?"

"Sort of, I guess. I don't think Munroe likes to color within the lines, and apparently, he's pretty well connected. Plus, I had less than six months left on my sentence. It's not like he sprung Charlie Manson. He needed me to convince Corrigan to talk to him, but now Corrigan's not talking to anyone."

"Wow." Katherine's head seemed to be swimming with the implications. "What were you in for?"

"I killed my brother."

Her eyes went wide. "I think I'm going to need a wee bit more explanation than that."

Jonas Black hadn't discussed that night with anyone for years, not since the trial. The guilt and pain were always there at the edge of his thoughts like a ghost watching him from the shadows, but discussing such things had never helped. He'd visited several counselors, both after his time in the war and after his brother's death. But some scars never healed, no matter how many times people with good intentions forced him to tear the wounds back open. Talking about the past didn't change it or make it easier to live with his choices. But something disarming in Katherine's gaze made him want to open up. So he took a long drink of water and then told her everything.

42

As he told his story, Jonas Black watched Katherine closely, but she didn't speak or show much reaction. She didn't try to counsel him or comfort him. She offered no absolution for his sins. Nodding, she said simply, "That's horrible. I'm sorry."

"So am I," he muttered, not knowing what else to say.

"Did your brother have a family?"

"Yeah, a wife and a little boy. Will and Stacey. But they won't have anything to do with me. Stacey hates me, and it's been over five years since I've seen my nephew. He was only eight when it happened. He probably doesn't even remember me . . . or his dad."

Katherine didn't say anything, just gave another almost imperceptible nod. Jonas imagined that she didn't know what to say beyond the standard *I'm sorry* that she had already used once. Her discomfort with the situation was clearly visible, but he appreciated the fact that she didn't try to offer hollow words of consolation.

The ringing of her phone saved them both from the awkwardness of the moment. Jonas listened to the one-sided conversation and could see by her expression that something bad had happened. Signing off with "Thank you," she said, "That was NCIS headquarters. They knew I came out here to speak to

Gelman. And they just got a call that he fell down the stairs at his office building and snapped his neck."

Jonas cracked his knuckles and, his jaw clenched, said, "Which means he was murdered. Because of us. We got him killed." He slammed his fist down on the table.

Katherine reached across and squeezed his hand. "You had better call Munroe," she said softly.

With the phone on speaker, he dialed and Munroe answered almost instantly. "Well?"

"Gelman's dead."

"What? How?"

"They say he fell down the stairs and broke his neck."

"Dammit, they'll probably figure out that it was murder when the ME gets a hold of him, but that still doesn't help us. Listen, I had Joey look up the leave and earnings statements—"

Katherine shook her head dismissively. "You have to be kidding me. I told you multiple times that we looked through all that."

"Yes, you examined the records for Corrigan, which could have been tampered with."

"So whose records did you pull?" she asked.

"Darryl Gelman's."

"And?"

"Nothing."

"I told you."

"That's not what I mean. I mean there were no records on file for him during that time period."

"He had to have gotten paid. What about the actual paper records?"

"They don't exist. Everything's digital now. Any records are destroyed after the daily batch of updates is made in the database."

"So it's a dead end."

Jonas thought back on his friendship with Gelman in Afghanistan, the hours on base trying to pass the time, talking about family back home. "Wait a second," he said. "Gelman would have received a copy of any of those records, right?"

"I suppose so," Katherine said.

"Gelman always talked about how much of a pack rat his wife was. Said she kept everything. She probably still has a copy of those statements somewhere."

Munroe's laugh sounded tinny over the speakerphone. "That's good thinking, Mr. Black. If you can get me those records, then we'll actually have some hard evidence to support our theories. With that in hand, I may be able to go to the Secretary of Defense and get to the bottom of this mess."

43

By the time they arrived at her home, Eileen Gelman was bordering on hysteria. Confusion showed in her beet-red face, and she seemed to Jonas Black like a woman stumbling half-coherent through a waking nightmare. When they questioned her about the leave and earnings statements, Jonas felt like an ambulance-chasing vulture preying on a defenseless and fragile woman on the worst day of her life. But his assumption had proved correct. She kept the files at a self-storage yard in Montclair, Virginia. They stressed the importance of the documents and cajoled her into handing over the keys. She mumbled something about putting everything back the way they found it just before another bout of sobbing racked her body. They left the new widow in the care of a sister, but Jonas knew that in reality she was alone with her grief, no matter how many people were by her side. The whole exchange left him feeling dirty.

The storage yard resembled a thousand other such facilities that dotted the nation – a standard collection of corrugated metal containers strung together on the edge of town. Katherine pulled up to the gate and entered a code that Eileen had provided into a hooded keypad attached to a white metal pipe. Upon completion of the code, the facility's black rod-iron gate slid aside with a high-pitched metallic scrape and a loud buzz.

The yard had both indoor and outdoor containers, and Jonas was happy to see that Eileen had opted for the indoor unit. Rain slapped against the Charger's roof, and a dense fog had settled over the entire area. Visibility had dropped to zero, and he didn't want to be outside in the rain more than necessary.

Inside the building, a narrow maze of walkways led to the various storage units. Fluorescent lighting hummed in exposed metal beams overhead and reflected off the polished concrete floor. A roll-up metal door and a padlock sealed each container. After a bit of wandering, they found Unit 318, designated by faded numbers applied in green paint, and Katherine used the key to undo the lock. Black pulled up the door to reveal a twelve-by-twelve space stacked from floor to ceiling with all manner of junk – boxes, totes, old furniture, a fake potted tree, children's toys, an ugly 1970s-style floor lamp, a rack of old clothes, old bikes, unused exercise equipment, a big black stereo, and what seemed like a million other objects. The space smelled faintly of mothballs and old varnish.

Katherine pulled her long red hair back in a ponytail as she said, "You sure know how to show a girl a good time."

Jonas sighed and threw his jacket over a stack of totes. "Where did Mrs. Gelman say the file was?"

"A file box marked *Military Records*."

As they started checking boxes and rummaging through the junk, Jonas said, "Sorry to have kept you out so late. I'm sure your boyfriend is pissed."

Katherine smiled. "Try not to be so obvious. And no, I don't have anyone waiting up for me."

"That's good. I mean, it's not good, but . . ."

"I know what you meant. I was in a pretty serious relationship up until a few weeks ago, but it didn't keep."

"What happened?"

"You ask a lot of questions," she said. "Pull your socks up and find that file. I don't want to be here all night."

After a few more minutes, Jonas moved aside a box marked with a bright green Christmas-tree sticker and found what they were searching for, a large translucent plastic file box with *Military Records* written on its top in blue permanent marker.

"This is it." He pulled out the tote and added, "You're the professional. I'll let you do the honors."

"What a gentleman."

Katherine flipped up the box's hinged top and sifted through the records. At last, she found the right dates and pulled the papers free. She scanned the numbers and information and said, "I'll be damned."

"Don't keep me in suspense."

She showed Jonas the paper held in her left hand and gestured to a few of the dates and numbers. "Gelman was getting paid quadruple hazard pay. Four times what he would have received for being in a war zone, even though he was stateside in Maryland and supposedly participating in a cultural-relations class. This is proof that there was a hell of a lot more going on than teaching troops how to be more sensitive to the locals."

"Yeah, the military was conducting some kind of experiments, and these poor bastards volunteered to be the crash-test dummies."

"And you think that whatever they did to him caused John Corrigan to kill his family?"

Jonas nodded. "And now we have the proof."

"Not so fast there, cowboy. This proves that Gelman was involved in something at Fort Meade that was dangerous enough for him to get paid four times hazard pay, but that's it. Anything beyond that is speculation."

"Maybe, but you heard Munroe. With this, he can force the brass to come clean. Or at least get some more info on what really happened."

Katherine shrugged. "We'll see. Since you have so much energy, why don't you put all this junk back so we can get out of here? I'm going to have a cigarette."

"You smoke too?"

Rolling her eyes and heading for the entrance, she said, "Don't start."

Jonas watched her slender form move down the narrow row. She looked over her shoulder at him once and smiled, and then she turned the corner and was out of sight. He started placing the collection of boxes and junk back in the order in which it had come out.

He had only just begun the tedious process when the overhead lights blinked out and total darkness closed in all around him.

44

Jonas Black was no stranger to night-time operations executed in total darkness, but in almost all those situations, he'd been the guy wearing night-vision goggles and carrying out the assault. In this case, he had a bad feeling that the roles had been reversed. The lights going out could have had a very simple explanation. Even then, he heard the rain pinging off the building's metal roof, but he hadn't seen any lightning or detected any thunder.

Jonas resisted the urge to immediately retrieve the cell phone from his pocket to use as a light source. First, he listened and analyzed the situation. If they were under attack, which seemed like a definite possibility considering the events of the past few days, he needed to keep his head, think of how the assault team would react, and do something that they wouldn't expect.

The sound of the rain, his own breathing, and the pounding of his heart seemed to be the only sounds. But then Jonas heard something else in the distance, echoing off the concrete.

Cautious footsteps? The rustle of fabric? A slight rattle of tactical assault gear? Was it Katherine?

If he called out to her, he would reveal his exact position, and the sound he had heard seemed to come from the direction opposite to that in which she had been heading.

No matter what was out there in the darkness, even if it was nothing but Jonas's own imagination or Katherine making her way back to him, he couldn't simply wait for something to happen. Being passive got you killed. Being proactive saved your life.

Risking turning on the phone to get some light, he shone the device's screen into the open storage unit. Then he quickly unscrewed three light bulbs from an ugly old floor lamp resting along one wall and ripped a T-shirt from a rack of clothing. He wrapped the bulbs in the T-shirt and, making as little noise as possible, crunched them into small shards of glass. The faint sound he had heard seemed to have come from the building's west corner. The building contained multiple rows, and an attack could come from almost anywhere, but Jonas guessed that an assault team would move straight to Gelman's storage unit and then fan out from there. And so he sprinkled the broken glass of the light bulbs on the paths leading out from that area. Then he moved east to the end of his row, squatted down, pulled his PT845 pistol, and waited.

If someone came down one of the marked paths, night-vision goggles or not, Jonas would hear them coming before they stepped around the corner and saw him. That would give him the extra second of tactical advantage that made all the difference in a firefight.

~~*~~

Katherine was five feet from the storage building's exit when all the lights went out. The sudden onset of darkness made it feel like the floor had fallen out from beneath her feet. She shuddered, and her stomach crawled into her throat. The sensation lasted only a second before she realized that it was probably nothing more than a power outage. But still, what if it was more than that?

She considered calling out for Jonas or using her phone as a light, but would that alert anyone approaching in the darkness to her position? The exit lay just ahead, and the parking lot was well lit. The open space of the lot seemed like the best option at that moment, and so she decided to simply push forward to the exit and worry about everything else once she was outside and free of the darkness that seemed to be physically pressing down on her from all sides.

Katherine covered the final five feet and groped for the door's handle. It felt like an eternity before she could locate it, but she tried to tell herself that there was nothing to fear. Finally, she found the handle, pushed down on it, and shoved.

It wouldn't budge.

A terrible sensation of claustrophobia flooded over her.

Someone had blocked the exit. She was trapped.

Locked inside with an unknown number of killers converging on her from all directions.

Right behind her. Warm breath on her neck.

Calm down, she told herself. She forced her mind to focus and almost immediately recognized her mistake. The realization made her feel like a silly little girl, a child that needed a parent to check under her bed and who believed that pulling the covers over her head would protect her from monsters.

Katherine growled at her own stupidity. *The door opens inward, you eejit*, she reminded herself. Yanking back on the handle, she stepped outside and moved toward the car.

The glove box contained a flashlight, and once she was out of the rain, she would call Jonas and tell him that she was coming back inside with the light. After all, he and Munroe had been attacked recently, which would set anyone on edge. She didn't relish the idea of a friendly-fire incident and wanted to give him a heads-up.

She unlocked the door of the Charger, climbed inside, and retrieved the phone from her pocket. Then she dialed the number that she had programmed earlier for Jonas Black.

~~*~~

Waiting in the darkness with his sight stolen from him, forced to rely on other senses, Jonas felt very alone and very helpless. He had never considered how much reliance he placed upon his ability to see his surroundings. Operating in total darkness felt like someone had tied his hands behind his back and then told him to clean and fieldstrip an M16 assault rifle using only his teeth. It was truly paralyzing and made him respect Munroe's perseverance all the more.

He squeezed the grip of his Taurus PT845 pistol and tried his best to quiet his breathing. He held the gun in his right hand and the phone in his left. When the time was right, he would need the light from the phone's display to illuminate his target.

Then he heard it.

The crunching of broken glass beneath someone's foot.

Then nothing.

His enemy must have realized that they had given themselves away and were waiting for Jonas to make a move. But war was a game of wills. In a combat situation such as this, the most patient and disciplined soldier won the day.

His antagonists couldn't see Jonas hiding behind the corner. They would have to choose whether to move forward or back. He imagined them second-guessing and worrying and trying to predict his tactics just as he had done with them. He had turned the tables on the predator and now he would—

The phone vibrated in his left hand, and the display lit up.

It startled him and forced a split second's hesitation.

And then the enemy converged on him with swift and violent determination.

~~*~~

Katherine frowned as she reached Jonas Black's voicemail. Why hadn't he answered? Were they really under attack? Or was she just acting like a child again?

She opened the glove box and pulled out the flashlight. If Jonas was in trouble, she had to help him. And if not, it was time that they took the evidence and left. They could worry about repacking the storage unit in the morning.

Then she realized with a start that the lights of the parking lot were still burning brightly. If it really was nothing more than a power outage, she reasoned, then all the lights would have been extinguished.

Katherine grabbed her phone in order to call for backup. She briefly considered calling her office but decided that a simple 911 call would bring help much faster.

Her finger had pressed the nine and was moving toward the one when a hand wrapped around her mouth and an arm snaked around her chest, crushing her against the seat.

Someone in the back of the car. Someone trying to kill her.

She tried to scream, but a gag muffled the sound. No, not a gag. A piece of cloth. A cloth drenched in the sweet chemical scent of chloroform.

Katherine struggled against the strong arm choking the life from her. Clawing, scratching. She reached for her Glock, managed to pull it from the holster – and then fell into sleep.

~~*~~

In the dim light of the phone's display, the first man threw off his NVGs and used his whole body as a weapon to ram Jonas like a charging rhino. The squat black-skinned attacker couldn't match Jonas in size, but the man was thickly muscled and clearly knew how to use a lower center of gravity against a larger opponent. Jonas rocked back on his heels, arms flailing. Then the man focused on Jonas's right hand, knocking the pistol free. It clattered across the smooth concrete floor.

The second man kept his distance but took aim with a strange-looking sub-machine gun. Then he pulled off his own NVGs and flipped on a tactical light located at the end of his weapon.

Analyzing the situation within an instant and letting the pain and adrenalin fuel his attack, Jonas regained his footing and deflected the black man's next blow. Then he followed through with a swift and violent strike of his own.

An open palm was often thought of as a less effective bludgeon than a traditional closed-fist punch. But, in reality, an open-palmed blow could be very damaging when a fighter applied enough force behind it. The palm covered a wide area, almost the entire side of a man's face, even more so when the palms concerned were the size of Jonas Black's. Plus, a closed-fist punch could inflict almost as much damage on the attacker's hand as on the receiver's face, while an open palm could administer just as much force with less risk of injury to the striker.

Knowing this through instinct and training, Jonas slapped both his palms against the black man's ears and temples. Then he chopped him in the neck and thrust one palm up beneath his chin. As the man's head flew back, Jonas's fingers closed over the attacker's face and found the eye sockets. Instinctively attacking the weakest areas of his opponent's body, Jonas pressed his index and ring fingers into the man's eyes. The black man screamed in agony, and Jonas shoved him back toward his companion.

But the second man was ready. This attacker, a stocky Hispanic man with a shaved head and thick mustache, had kept his distance. He sidestepped his companion and opened fire.

Jonas tried to dive away, but he couldn't react in time. He screamed in agony as he felt the rounds tear into the muscles of his thighs. A cold fire rippled out from the impacts, and he fought to stay upright.

But the trauma was too much for his body, and despite his best efforts, he fell back against the concrete, the impact driving the air from his lungs. He couldn't breathe, and his legs tingled with a strange numbness that seemed to be spreading throughout the rest of his body.

Jonas frantically scanned the floor for his gun and caught sight of it a few feet away. Scrambling painfully on hands and knees, he inched toward the weapon.

But the Hispanic man didn't let up. Jonas felt the same cold fire strike his shoulders and arms. More rounds from the strange sub-machine gun tearing into his flesh.

Dizziness. Disorientation. Confusion.

The world pulsed and spun end over end.

Jonas felt nauseated. So sleepy. He just wanted to lay his head against the concrete and forget about everything. Forget about Corrigan and Munroe, and the case, and Katherine, and his nephew and sister-in-law. Just give up and let it end. Let it finally end.

He wrestled against the sudden desire to sleep but was no match for it. He felt cold and tingly all over. So weak. So tired.

Then calm acceptance and warmth flooded his consciousness and blocked out the rest of the world.

He wondered absently as he slipped away if this was what it felt like to die.

45

Standing atop a secluded bluff overlooking the Potomac River, Antonio de Almeida summoned up his resolve for what would come next. The smell of ozone and pollen from the recent summer storm filled the air. The rain had dissipated, but the fog still clung to the landscape like a blanket. Almeida couldn't even see the river through the mist, but he could hear the slapping of water against the base of the precipice below. He waved smelling salts beneath the noses of Jonas Black and Katherine O'Connell. The pair sat inside Katherine's Dodge Charger. Almeida and his men had driven them up to the edge of the bluff and placed Katherine behind the wheel with Jonas occupying the passenger seat. As the salts took effect, the captives jolted to life, but only their eyes moved, frantically scanning the car's interior.

"What the hell?" Jonas muttered in a tired whisper.

Almeida leaned down into the open driver's side window. "My men shot you with a tranquilizer gun, and we brought you here. But don't bother trying to move your arms or legs. I've paralyzed your limbs by injecting a local anesthetic called lidocaine into your brachial plexus nerves and subarachnoid block."

"What do you want from us?" Katherine said.

"I want you to tell me where Munroe has hidden the flash drive."

180

Jonas said, "You're wasting your time. We don't know where it is."

"Perhaps. Perhaps not. I suppose it doesn't really matter, anyway. My associate will have Munroe in custody shortly, and I know for certain that he can tell me its whereabouts. But still, you could save your friend a lot of unnecessary pain if you told me now."

"We don't know."

"What about Corrigan and Gelman? What information have they shared? I, of course, have the earnings statement that you retrieved from the storage unit, and we took all the other files just to be safe. But it would be helpful if I knew how much Munroe knows as well."

"Corrigan wouldn't talk and neither did Gelman. But it doesn't really matter what I tell you, does it? You're going to kill us either way."

Almeida laid a hand on Jonas's shoulder and nodded thoughtfully. "It brings me no pleasure to do so, but it's a necessary evil. I've given you and Munroe ample opportunity to walk away, but you kept pushing. We're soldiers, Mr. Black, and war has its casualties."

"You're not a soldier, and this isn't a war."

"I'm afraid that it is, whether you know it or not, and one that your government has declared on us. Twelve months ago a group of US black-ops commandos similar to yourself infiltrated one of our compounds in Mexico in an attempt to assassinate our leader. Luckily, Vaquero wasn't there. Instead, they killed his wife, three sons, and his daughter. I was the godfather of the two youngest. Of course, your government denies responsibility, claiming that it was a rival organization that carried out the killings. And now your masters intend to pass a law declaring us terrorists. They come into our country and murder our families and then call *us* terrorists."

"You kidnap tourists, sell drugs to kids, murder anyone who gets in your way, and lord knows what else. You may not be Al Qaeda, but you're close enough for me. You're criminals, not revolutionaries. Just a pack of killers and thieves."

"I know that I'm a sinner, and I ask for forgiveness every day. But you're a soldier just like me, and unlike most normal people, you and I will do what is necessary to win the war. That's what I'm doing, Mr. Black. The leaders of your country are a pack of bullies who think that they know what's best for the rest of the world. But soon they will be forced to reconsider their positions on many things. Unfortunately, you and your companions are collateral damage in that fight. For that, I am sorry. I will pray for you. And I suggest that you spend the next few moments asking for forgiveness of your own."

Then Almeida reached up to the steering column, put the car in neutral, and started them rolling toward the edge of the bluff.

46

Jonas Black didn't spend his last moments praying. Instead, he tensed and untensed all his muscles in an attempt to wake them from their chemically induced sleep. Moving only his eyes, he looked over at Katherine. Tears dampened her cheeks. She breathed in quick, short gasps. But she wasn't screaming or displaying any other hysterics. Her eyes darted back and forth, scanning for a way out.

Jonas continued to tense and untense, willing his muscles to break free of the bonds and move. For his entire life, an overly high tolerance for painkillers and anesthetics had plagued him. Now he hoped that it could save their lives.

Still, he couldn't be sure that his tolerance applied to the drug Almeida had administered. And maybe the Colombian had increased the dosage to account for Jonas's large size.

The car's roll toward the edge started slowly. Then momentum built, and their speed increased.

If he could just move his foot enough to hit the brake . . .

Jonas felt his toes twitch. Adrenalin pumped harder through his veins as death approached. Fingers flexed. His hand opened slightly. If he could raise his arm and throw the vehicle into park, it would at least stop their slide toward the edge. Almeida

Ethan Cross

would see that they had stopped, but Jonas needed to focus on one problem at a time.

He fought to bring up his arm or foot, and with every second, some movement returned. But with every tick of the clock, they also inched closer to the edge of the bluff and the cold waters below.

Then it was too late.

Jonas's stomach jumped into his throat as the ground gave way to open air and the Charger shot toward the river.

The thick fog obscured their view to the point that the water below wasn't visible. They plunged through the mist as if falling into nothingness. It could have been ten feet or a thousand miles, and they wouldn't have known the difference.

Katherine screamed.

Jonas closed his eyes and braced for impact.

The collision with the river felt like they had hit a brick wall. Their heads jerked forward, but the seat belts that Almeida had strapped around them kept their bodies from flying out of the vehicle.

The cold water of the Potomac flooded in immediately. Jonas had seen a car hit the water before and knew that, unlike in the movies, it could take a few minutes for a vehicle to completely submerge and fill with water, depending on a lot of factors. He also knew that the open driver-side window would cause them to fill up faster.

Either way, he still had time.

As death grew closer, his resolve strengthened. He refused to die. It wasn't just that he didn't want it to happen, he rejected the possibility. He projected himself into the future, using his inner resources. It wasn't *if* they survived, it was *how* they would survive. The solutions were present. He just needed to identify them.

Jonas heard Katherine praying, but he ignored her. He would

not accept death. He lived a life of war, and he had no intention of losing the battle.

"We're going to get out of this," he said to Katherine. "Just stay calm."

She didn't respond.

The water soaked through his shoes and pants. The level rose with every passing second. The cold of the river felt like death's fingers wrapping around his ankle to drag him to the deep.

The water reached his knees.

Then Jonas broke through some interior biological wall, and his arm moved. His movements were sluggish, and his limbs felt like dead weights, but he could move nonetheless.

Still, his current state prevented him from swimming to safety by himself, let alone carrying a grown woman with him.

He frantically scanned the car's interior for something to help them.

The glove box wouldn't contain anything helpful. Unlike the cushions in planes, the car's seats couldn't be used as flotation devices. The back seat contained only trash – candy-bar wrappers and old . . . two-liter soda bottles.

One of the recycling videos that Chloe had showed him on YouTube came to mind – old soda bottles repurposed as rafts and life vests. The air trapped inside the empty bottles made them perfect flotation devices.

The chilling water passed Jonas's waist, but at least it served to shock his system and wake his sleeping muscles even further.

With great effort, he forced his heavy arms to grab the empty bottles from the back seat and floorboards. Then he started to shove them beneath Katherine's black button-down dress shirt.

"What are you doing?" she said, her voice trembling.

"Saving your ass."

The water reached their chests, and it took all Jonas's strength to push the air-filled bottles beneath the surface and under their shirts. He held his breath and went under. Then he quickly tucked Katherine's shirt into her pants and repeated the procedure with himself.

He looked up to see Katherine's face submerged just above his own. Pure terror showed in her eyes, but he also detected a measure of hope and trust in them.

Her seat belt came off easily, and he pulled her from the Charger as it fell into the river's depths. The bottles popped her to the surface, but her face still rested beneath the water.

Jonas had placed most of the bottles beneath Katherine's shirt, and the ones under his own didn't provide nearly as much support as he would have liked. Still, he was able to flip her over and pull her toward the shore.

But the river didn't want to give up its prize, and the strong current and dead weight of his limbs fought against his forward progress. Unable to fight the forces pulling him down, he fell below the surface.

47

It would have been so much easier to give up, just let the waves take him down and the river consume him. Jonas Black's whole life had been a battle and that showed no signs of changing. The fatigue drained his will. Did it really matter if he made it to the shore? What did he have to look forward to?

But he also knew that Katherine would never make it out of the river without him, not in her present condition. Unlike him, someone out there loved her. A family. Parents. A brother. They would mourn her passing.

He willed his tingling, numb legs to kick and push. He focused on small movements, on the next kick, the next breath. It seemed like an eternity. Kicking, pulling Katherine along, gasping for breath, taking in huge mouthfuls of water. But then they reached sanctuary. The sand and rocks of the shore surrounded them as he pulled Katherine from the water and then fell back onto the beach.

Katherine coughed up a torrent of brown water, but she was alive.

He lay back and closed his eyes. He just wanted to sleep.

Almeida's words floated back to him like something from a dream. *Munroe.* The Colombian had said that one of his associates would have Munroe soon. Jonas had to send a warning before it was too late.

He checked his pocket but found that his cell phone was gone.

His legs trembled as he pulled himself up from the sand. He managed to lurch upright but then stumbled forward onto a patch of grass and rocks. Pain lanced through his arms and chest, but pain was good. Pain was life.

Tired, numb, dizzy, and shaking, Jonas tapped an extra reserve of strength hidden somewhere deep inside himself and pushed his aching body upright again. This time he managed three steps forward before falling back to the ground.

48

Deacon Munroe hung up the phone and growled at the receiver. He didn't have time for this. When John Corrigan had gone into the hospital, Munroe had asked to be notified if his condition changed in any way. Corrigan's doctor had called a few minutes ago and told him that, if things went as planned, they would be ready to wake the disgraced soldier in two days. Munroe wanted to be there when Corrigan's eyes opened, but unfortunately, Jonas Black hadn't answered any of Munroe's five phone calls.

His own doctors would protest at his early departure, but he didn't care. His side still ached and pains shot through him if he moved, but he could walk, which meant that he was well enough to get out of the damn hospital. This investigation wouldn't wait for his body to heal, and he suspected that another *accident* would be arranged for Corrigan soon. This time they'd ensure that they finished the job.

Munroe had already dressed and contacted Annabelle to ask her to pick him up, and Joey had booked two seats on the next flight to Leavenworth.

But where the hell was Jonas Black?

49

The decorative get-well-soon flower arrangement and brightly colored Mylar balloon that he was carrying helped Oliver Pike to blend in and hide his face from the cameras. But it didn't really matter if the police later identified him, since he'd be out of the country once he'd completed the mission anyway. He had studied the hospital's floor plan and quickly found Munroe's room. He made a quick pass-by to assess the situation discreetly, and then he moved to the nurse's station and played the part of a confused visitor.

He asked animatedly for directions to an area of the hospital that was back the way he had already come. This would give him the opportunity to pass the guard again without raising suspicion. The federal agent sat in a chair next to Munroe's door. Two additional agents had previously been stationed there, but Almeida had arranged for the other men to be called back to headquarters, leaving only one obstacle between Pike and Munroe.

Palming a small injection device in his right hand, Pike moved back down the hall. The fluorescent lights reflected off the overly polished floors, and despite the strong odor of disinfectant, the slight smell of death and sickness permeated the air and made him uncomfortable. The guard watched him carefully as he approached, and Pike tried not to notice.

Then he made a show of tripping and stumbling into the agent. The man's right hand immediately went to his gun, and he grabbed Pike with the left in a defensive move that would allow for a quick takedown. Pike recovered almost immediately from the fall, displayed an awkward and disarming smile, and apologized for his clumsiness.

He lowered his shoulders in a non-threatening way and backed away from the agent. The tension released from the man's stance, and, sitting back down, he said, "No problem."

Pike felt the agent's suspicious stare still upon him as he walked away, but he had executed the maneuver flawlessly. When he had stumbled against the guard, he'd stabbed the needle into the agent's right arm in such a quick and fluid movement that only the keenest observer would even have registered the attack.

The powerful sedative would take effect within a few moments, and then Pike could stroll into Munroe's room, drug the blind man in the same way, and take him out of the building in a wheelchair, just like any other recovering patient on his or her way home.

50

As Oliver Pike roamed through the hospital corridors, nodding thoughtfully and smiling to the hospital staff and visitors whom he passed along the way, he thought of the games played by the military's bureaucracy. Little had changed in the world since they had run him out of the service for being a homosexual. The men in his unit, those who had fought with him, had been completely accepting, and they knew his preferences, even though he had always followed the *Don't Ask, Don't Tell* policy. He found the military's position on the matter to be a joke, but he was also a good soldier and followed orders.

But when a newbie lieutenant started harassing him and dropping comments – probably to make himself feel big like the bullies Pike had faced down in the schoolyard back in Connecticut – Pike decided that his time in the military was over. When his contract was up, he chose not to re-enlist.

He could have fought back like Margaret Witt, the Air Force major who had battled prejudice and won, laying the foundation for the 2010 repeal of *Don't Ask, Don't Tell*. But Pike wasn't a social activist, and it made more sense for him to just leave quietly and join the private sector. He could make more money there, anyway. As it turned out, his ideas about the moneymaking potential of being a mercenary and hired killer had proven to be conservative estimates, and his new position with the Castillo Cartel would make this a banner year.

Back in front of Munroe's room, he could see the guard's head slumping to the side, but Pike still approached cautiously. After casually checking the rest of the hallway, he opened Munroe's door and stepped inside, turning back to lock it behind him.

It was a single-occupancy room, and a privacy curtain concealed the bed. A cheerful blue covered the walls, and the place smelled like a scented candle. Pike couldn't fault Munroe for wanting to block out that antiseptic hospital smell.

"Mr. Munroe? I'm Nurse Zachary. I'm here to check on how you're doing. Is everything okay?"

Pike pulled the curtain back gently. But the bed was empty.

51

Deacon Munroe slid his feet along the narrow concrete ledge outside his window and tried not to think about what he was actually doing. He couldn't see the drop to the ground, but he could sense the deadly chasm that loomed in front of him. It seemed to him even more frightening to stand on the edge and *not* be able to look down.

He wondered, not for the first time, what the hell he had been thinking. When he had received the frantic call from Jonas Black telling him that someone was coming for him, the first thing that Deacon did was to try and inform his protectors. When he found the agent unconscious, he knew that he didn't have long and that his attacker might even have seen him enter the hallway. For all he knew, his enemy had been right next to the door, watching him with some kind of psychopathic pleasure.

His mind had then run down the list of other possibilities and exits. He could have called hospital security, but he doubted they would arrive in time or that he even had time to make the call. He considered simply locking the door but knew that would provide little protection against a professional killer. With his back against the wall, he decided that his only viable course of action was to climb out the window and shimmy his way along the ledge and across to the next room. From there, he could call hospital security, hide, and wait for help. And if push came to shove, he would not be without some defenses.

It had seemed like a good idea in the comfort and safety of his room, but once Munroe sensed the giant empty space looming in front of him and felt his heart pounding against his ribcage, he realized the flaws in his plan. He considered that the next room's window could be locked, but then he remembered that someone was occupying the room. He had heard the sound of a television and the noise of anxious movements throughout the day. But he hadn't heard anything recently. He hoped that the room's occupant was merely sleeping and could be woken, otherwise he would be trapped clinging to the ledge like an overgrown – and flightless – pigeon.

That was if he made it over to the window without falling. And if the ledge reached all the way to the next window.

As the different dangers and possibilities flew through his mind, Munroe considered turning back, but then told himself that he had already come this far. He focused on moving one step at a time toward his destination.

Progress was slow. He crept along the ledge, bombarded by strong winds carrying the smell of exhaust fumes and a million noises that echoed up from the ground below and indicated just how far he had to fall. Tires on gravel. Horns honking. People moving away from the hospital. He had learned to judge distances by sound, but at that moment, he wished that he could turn the ability off, like flipping a switch in his head.

His right hand gripped the wall to give him an anchor and a bearing, and now that hand felt an opening in the brick surface. A recess that Munroe prayed housed the window of the next room.

As he turned the corner, a bird took flight from its perch beside the window and startled him.

He lost his balance, felt himself falling back. His arms wheeled as he struggled to regain his footing. Throwing his body weight forward, his left foot slipped from the ledge and into open air. But he managed to stumble into the recess, and his face struck against the cool glass of the window.

His heart blasted out an unhealthy allegro rhythm as he took a second to get his bearings and calm down. He had made it. He was safe.

Keeping one hand against the window for balance, Munroe stooped down and pounded on the glass. He strained to hear any movement inside the room, but he detected none. He pounded again, with more force this time. Still nothing. The room was empty, and he was trapped.

52

Pike thoroughly checked everywhere in the hospital room – the closet, bathroom, under the bed. Many of Munroe's things remained, but there was no Munroe. The blind man couldn't have just left with the guard stationed out front, and if he had, the guard wouldn't have remained at his post. Unless it was a decoy of some kind. Or perhaps Munroe had realized that the guard was unconscious and had left the room?

The mercenary cursed and slammed his hand down on the bedrail.

Deciding to search the hallways, he moved toward the door. Then he heard something. A whistling sound. Wind. The window was open, just a crack. He checked it and found that the frame would open just enough for someone to climb out. But surely the blind man hadn't gone out the window? Then again, Munroe had proven his resourcefulness in the past, and Pike had no intention of underestimating him again.

Pike opened the window further and leaned out. Then he heard another sound. A knocking. Someone pounding on the window of the next room.

He had to smile. Munroe had balls, and as a former Spec Ops soldier, Pike admired that bravery. Plus, this could work out just as well for him.

He moved back into the hall and went to the neighboring room, opening its door and then locking it behind him. He could still hear Munroe pounding frantically on the glass. Opening the window just a crack and acting surprised, he told Munroe to step back and that he'd help him inside. Remembering at the last second that he was wearing black leather gloves, Pike ripped them off before offering his hand to Munroe and pulling him into the room.

"What were you doing out there?" Pike said, playing the part of a patient or member of the hospital staff.

Munroe gulped in greedy lungfuls of air and leaned over a table that sat beneath the television on the room's far side. "You saved me, friend. I don't know what I would have done if you hadn't showed up. Listen, I need you to call hospital security. Someone's after me."

Pike pulled a second injector from his leather jacket and stepped toward Munroe. He visualized the attack. Munroe had his back to him. *Grasp the forehead with the left hand, pull back the head, needle goes into the neck on the right side, and then lights out. Simple.*

"Don't worry," Pike said as he continued to move forward. "We'll get help and sort this whole thing out."

53

When the man had first helped him inside, Munroe could think only of being safe and free from the ledge. But, when he heard the stranger move, he knew that something was wrong. Whenever a person moved, they made distinct sounds based on the intricacies of their individual body and the clothes they wore. Most people never detected such subtle tones, but those tiny details built the world in which Munroe lived.

And this man's details didn't match up.

A hospital patient would have been barefoot or in socks or slippers, and a staff member would have worn comfortable tennis shoes, but Munroe could hear this stranger's heavy combat boots. Particular fabrics made distinctive sounds. A hospital gown or scrubs made from light materials would clothe a patient or nurse, but when the stranger moved Munroe heard the tell-tale creak of a leather jacket.

He supposed that his savior could be a visitor who had just happened to be walking past and had heard his knocking, but something in the man's demeanor and the facts of the situation told him that wasn't the case. No help would come. If he was going to escape the hospital, he would have to do it himself.

Trying not to betray his movements, Munroe's hand snaked inside his jacket and grasped the item that Annabelle had smuggled into the hospital at his request. Tobi Savoy had provided him with a box of the wonderful little devices, and they had saved him once already.

He heard the stranger move closer. Perhaps the man planned to sedate him in the same manner in which he had made the agent in the hall unconscious. Munroe didn't plan to wait and find out.

He laid the flash-bang grenade on the table and pressed a button to activate it. Different than the standard M84 stun grenade, this prototype device had a programmable timer, a more easily concealed shape and size, and a whole load of other bells and whistles. Munroe suspected, however, that it would never see actual combat. This type of grenade was too expensive for wide-spread military usage, especially considering its fire-and-forget purpose.

He counted to two, and then he jumped away from the table in the direction of the door. His hands cupped his ears tightly, and he bent forward while opening his mouth slightly to help absorb the coming shock wave. The stranger would have no time for such reactions.

Even with his hands over his ears, the magnesium-based pyrotechnic charge deafened him when it went off. The stranger screamed and cursed and knocked over chairs and other objects in the room as he stumbled about.

The air smelled like burning metal. Munroe's head throbbed from the concussion wave. He could barely hear the stranger thrashing about over the ringing in his own ears, but he knew the effect was already wearing off.

Munroe groped for the door, found the handle, and pushed. But it was locked. He searched for the locking mechanism, deactivated it and then stumbled into the hall, not caring what or who he ran into as he did so.

He found the far wall and, using it as his marker, moved away from the attacker as fast as he could. Running footsteps and concerned voices echoed up and down the hall as the hospital staff scrambled to work out what had just happened.

Someone grabbed him and said, "Are you okay?" A female voice, young, probably a nurse.

"I was in protective custody down the hall and was just attacked by a professional killer. I need you to get me out of here. Call the police."

"Okay, sir, stay calm. Come with me."

The nurse guided him farther down the maze of halls, away from the room in which he had left the killer. He couldn't make out what was happening around them because of the flood of sounds reverberating off the laminate floors.

Then a shrill scream cut through the rest of the noise. The distinctive pop of a gunshot followed.

"We need to get out of here – now," Munroe said.

"We're at the elevator." He heard a rapid clicking as the nurse tapped the call button. The whirring of motors and a pulley system sounded as the elevator rose toward them, but he could tell that it wasn't close enough.

Munroe heard the sound of running feet, but the pitch of the noise was different than before. These weren't the padded footfalls of hospital staff coming to help. This sound came from the hard treads of combat boots.

Another loud pop and a scream.

The pop originated from down the hall. The scream came from the mouth of the woman beside him.

Munroe felt her falling back. Her fingers clawed at his shirt, seeking help, and she dragged him to the floor with her.

She tried to speak, but she lacked the strength for the words to carry from her throat. He felt blood spatter on his face. He ran his hands over her body to find the wound, but all he could feel was the warm liquid that seemed to be coming from everywhere. The sweet metallic smell of blood surrounded him.

Munroe couldn't help her. She was dying, and he was all alone in a world of darkness.

Where could he go? How could he escape from this alien place with a killer on his heels?

The elevator bell dinged as the doors behind him slid open.

He crawled over the dead nurse's body toward the opening, the poor woman's blood soaking through his clothes. His head throbbed. He felt dizzy and couldn't breathe.

Finally, he fell in a heap on the floor of the elevator and reached up to tap a staccato rhythm on the buttons of the control panel. He didn't care where it took him, just as long as it was away from here.

The pounding of the combat boots grew louder and closer.

Then the metallic scrape of the elevator doors signified that they were sliding shut. Munroe could sense the change in pressure and sound as they connected and sealed out the rest of the world.

A loud bang shook the doors as the killer slammed against them, but the stranger was too late. The elevator car began its descent, and Munroe ran his fingers over the Braille plates below each button on the control panel until he found the one for the underground parking area.

Part Four

Part Four

54

Annabelle had only been a few blocks from the hospital on her way to pick up Munroe when she received his frantic phone call. She found him hiding in the parking garage. He looked like one of the living dead, white from fear and adrenalin and covered in blood. He immediately called their supervisor, Jack Fuller, and told him about the attacks. Fuller wanted them to come in, but Munroe refused. All he requested from Fuller was to put Makayla and Chloe into protective custody. Then he hung up on his superior.

"We should listen to Jack and come in," Annabelle said. "You have friends in the FBI and other agencies that would let us use a safe house. Or, hell, we could just find a cheap motel and hide out there until all this dies down."

"Have you heard anything from Black?" he said.

"He called me right after he called to warn you. I sent Joey down to pick them up."

"Good. You were right about finding a place to lie low, but we're not going to hide there. I'm not running or hiding. We're going to regroup and plan how to strike back."

~~*~~

Twenty minutes north of DC, the Motel 6 in Frederick, Maryland was the perfect place for the group to meet. It wasn't cheap or dirty enough to make anyone's skin crawl, and it wasn't fancy enough to draw any attention or raise questions when they paid for two adjoining rooms with cash.

As they waited for the others to arrive, Deacon Munroe sat on one of the beds without speaking or moving. He entered completely into his own mind as if the rest of the world no longer existed. Annabelle lay down on the room's other bed and watched him think.

When she'd been a girl, Deacon Munroe had been her guardian angel. Although he had always played it off as no big thing, he had looked out for her on more than one occasion. Once, he stood up to his father and took a beating that should have been hers. On another occasion, when they were in junior high, a boy from his class named Ricky Ross had started teasing her and hurling racially charged insults at her nearly every day. Deacon hadn't walked up and punched the boy in the face or threatened him physically like her brother or Jonas Black probably would have done. Instead, he picked the lock on the boy's PE locker and replaced Ricky's gym clothes with lacy women's underwear. Once Ricky's anger from the humiliation had died down, Deacon approached him with Annabelle in tow. The young Deacon Munroe told Ricky in a calm conversational tone that if he so much as looked at Annabelle with unkind eyes, then next time it would be much worse. Next time, Deacon would steal the answers to a test from a teacher's desk and make sure that Ricky was caught with them. Or perhaps he would stash a bag of weed in Ricky's locker and get him expelled outright. Ricky had blustered and threatened, but the icy determination in Deacon's eyes had ensured that Ricky didn't attempt any retaliation and never spoke ill of Annabelle again.

Deacon had once told Annabelle that he believed *justice* to be a myth, but he definitely believed in *balance*. And that was the kind of thinking that shaped his life.

They had gone their separate ways after school. Annabelle had become an investigator at an expensive law firm in Baltimore and had married a cruel and distant man who worked out of the District Attorney's office. She had wanted children, but he had refused. He seemed to hate children, and half the time she felt that he hated her as well. Deacon, on the other hand, had married a kind and quiet woman with whom Annabelle became fast friends. After Beth died and Annabelle's divorce became finalized, Annabelle had often considered pursuing a relationship with Deacon, and she knew that he harbored feelings for her as well. But she worried that it would feel like a betrayal of Beth or that it would ruin the close relationship that they already had. Perhaps their own histories together were too much to overcome, and they'd both be better off meeting someone with whom they could start fresh.

Aunabelle really didn't know what to think about Deacon anymore or where things would go between them. But she knew that she loved him and never wanted to see him get hurt.

An hour later, Jonas Black and Joey arrived and introduced her to Katherine O'Connell, the NCIS agent who had worked Corrigan's original case. The beautiful young redhead seemed confident and competent and had no problem holding her own with the men in the room. Katherine and Jonas told the others about the attempt on their lives and what they had learned from the records contained in Gelman's storage unit.

Munroe said, "As long as his condition doesn't deteriorate, the doctors in Leavenworth plan to wake Corrigan from his coma the day after tomorrow. He's apparently recovering well."

"Great," Jonas said. "Just in time for his execution."

Annabelle nodded in agreement. "If he lives that long. They may try to finish what they started and arrange another accident for him. Who's going to ask questions about a guy that's about to be executed anyway?"

"We have to do something," Jonas said, running his hands over his close-cropped hair. "Munroe, can't you call in a favor? Get Corrigan a stay of execution or an appeal?"

"With what evidence?"

"We sure have a lot of dead bodies."

"Yes, but what does that prove? Just that someone's trying to kill us. The reasons why are nothing but speculation. The only actual evidence we've seen is a flash drive that we can't access and a piece of paper that Almeida took from you. We have nothing that could save John Corrigan's life, and without Corrigan, we probably won't have any way to stop whatever's happening."

"Almeida didn't talk as though this is just about money or covering up a business deal. He acted like something was coming."

"Like an attack?" Annabelle asked.

"I don't know. He called the leaders of our country a pack of bullies and said that an operation ordered by our government failed to kill Ramon Castillo but succeeded in murdering the kingpin's family. He called it a war."

Katherine stood and paced around the small motel room. She unwrapped a king-size Butterfinger and bit off large chunks of chocolate and peanut butter. Between bites, she said, "This is my fault. I didn't dig deep enough, and now an innocent man is going to die because of my incompetence."

Munroe shook his head. "You followed where the evidence led you like any good investigator would. The problem is that, in this case, the evidence lies. Still, the way I see it, we only have one option on how to proceed."

He crossed his arms and leaned back against the headboard. "We're going to have to stage a good old-fashioned jailbreak."

55

Silence filled the small motel room. Jonas Black couldn't believe what he had just heard. "Did you get hit on the head? You're federal agents. You don't go around busting death row inmates out of jail."

"If you have a better idea, then I'm all ears," Munroe said.

Jonas clenched his fists and fought to keep his voice down. "I don't want any part of this. Since I've met you, I've been shot at, nearly beaten to death, drugged, and almost drowned. I should have stayed in the hole and finished out my stretch. I was better off. Listen, I want to save John, and I'd love to see these guys brought to justice. But I have my own problems, and I don't care about any of this enough to give my life for it or get thrown back in prison."

Munroe nodded. "I completely understand, Mr. Black. This is a whole lot more than what you signed up for. We'll proceed without you."

"You can't be serious. No one in this room is going to go along with this plan." Jonas looked to Katherine and Annabelle for support.

Katherine took a deep breath and said softly, "I'm in."

Annabelle added, "Me too. Somebody has to keep Deacon from getting himself killed."

Joey said, "I'm not much good in a fight, but I'll help you on the back end of things."

Jonas raised his hands in despair. "You're all nuts. Do you have any idea of the kind of security that the USDB has? It's a fortress guarded by highly trained soldiers. Inmates have digital smart cards that are matched with their fingerprints. There are readers in every cell, room, and hallway. They don't even have bed checks or roll calls because the computer knows where everyone is at every moment. It's impossible, and even if you could pull it off somehow, it would take months of planning and work. You said that they're waking Corrigan up tomorrow."

"All that's true," Munroe replied. "But Corrigan isn't inside Leavenworth. The prison infirmary wasn't equipped to handle his injuries, and so they moved him to a regular hospital nearby. He's laid up in a medically induced coma. I strongly doubt that they would have a man in his condition under heavy guard."

"All of us would still go to prison for breaking him out."

"Only if we get caught. We'll disable the hospital's security systems and take precautions to ensure that we won't be identified in other ways. No one will know who helped Corrigan escape, and by the time anyone can figure anything out, the man will be exonerated. If Corrigan can help get us the evidence we need, I have enough friends in the government to make the minor detail of his escape a total non-issue."

"And what happens if we can't clear his name? If he can't give you what you need and the investigation stalls out? What then?"

"We'll burn that bridge when we come to it."

Jonas said, "Even if you can get him out of the hospital, the cops will be all over you. They'll block all escape routes and have every officer in a hundred miles out searching."

"I have a few tricks up my sleeve."

Jonas laughed derisively. "Great. Let me know how all that works out for you." Then he stormed from the room and slammed the door behind him.

56

Katherine opened the motel room door and followed Jonas Black outside. She found the big man leaning over the third-floor railing and watching a couple with two young kids hauling suitcases into one of the rooms as the kids ran circles around them. She leaned against the cool white metal next to him. The scent of grease and fish from a nearby seafood restaurant mixed with exhaust fumes from US 40 wafted up on a breeze ten degrees too cool for that time of year. She didn't say a word. If Jonas wanted to talk, then he would.

They stood in silence for a few minutes before Jonas said, "You know the funny thing about this idea? The federal agents are all on board, and the convict is the only one with any sense. I knew from the first time I met Munroe that I shouldn't have trusted him. You know why he wants me around? Why he got me out of prison?"

"Because he thought you could talk Corrigan into cooperating."

"That was only part of it. On my first night out, I overheard him telling Annabelle that I'm just a big, dumb animal. He said that I was an attack dog who he needed to avenge his friend's death."

"That's not true."

"Which part?"

"You're not dumb, Jonas. Munroe just said that because he was angry about his friend's death. Grief can make you do crazy things."

"Exactly, and that's what I'm afraid of. That Munroe will do something crazy, and all of us will pay the price." He looked deeply into her eyes and leaned close. He smelled like he'd gone for a swim in the Potomac, but she guessed that she smelled the same way. "Don't do this. Don't go with him."

Katherine analyzed her feelings a moment, searching for a way to explain them. Then she said, "I have to. The truth is that Corrigan's case was handed to me gift-wrapped, and I didn't question any of it. I had something to prove. I was trying to close more cases that year than any other agent in the office. And I succeeded. But I can't help but wonder how many things I overlooked. I keep thinking of my brother. A soldier who has given so much for his country, and I didn't even take the time to exhaust every possibility. That poor man lost his family, and then I helped put him on death row. He's going to die because of me, and I can't accept that."

"There has to be another way."

"I don't see one. And it's not like we're just going to let him go. We'll simply make sure that he's alive long enough for this mess to be sorted out. I think Munroe's right. We could get him out without being identified. We should at least listen to his ideas on how to escape the area. Corrigan was your friend, Jonas."

"I understand why you feel that you have to do this, but I can't. I have my own sins to atone for."

Katherine thought of the story that Jonas had shared with her at dinner. It had only been a few hours earlier, but it felt like it had been much longer. He had told her about coming home from Afghanistan and being tired and depressed and needing to blow off some steam. He had convinced his brother Michael to come out with him, and after a long night of binge drinking, Jonas had driven them home drunk. He'd fallen asleep at the wheel and wrapped the car around a tree. He survived. Michael didn't.

Jonas quickly wiped at his eyes, and she wondered if he was crying. He said, "I had a lot of time to think about the future when I was on the inside. My only hope, the thing that kept me going, was the thought of getting out and helping to support my brother's family. I have a nephew and a sister-in-law out there that could still use my help financially, even though they'll never forgive me for what I did. I just wanted to find work of some kind and drop anonymous checks in the mail. Their own personal guardian angel. I know that I can never make it right. I can't bring Michael back from the dead, but I can protect what he left behind. I owe him that and a whole lot more. I can't go back to prison, not for Corrigan, not for anything or anyone."

57

As Annabelle helped load their bags into the Yukon for the trip to Kansas, she wondered if she was going along with Deacon's plans for the right reasons. She wished that Gerald was there. He would have known the right path. Any time Deacon had been tempted by his own cavalier and reckless spirit, Gerald had countered with reason and accountability.

A dark blue BMW Z4 Roadster pulled up beside the Yukon and interrupted her musing. It was still the middle of the night, and the expensive convertible's appearance couldn't have been a coincidence. This had to be the friend that Munroe had contacted. A small man in jeans and a polo shirt stepped from the vehicle and approached her. "Where's Munroe?"

"I'll get him. Wait here."

A moment later, she returned with Deacon in tow. Munroe greeted the man warmly, but the stranger did not reciprocate. "This makes us even, Munroe," the small man said. Then he retrieved an aluminum briefcase from his trunk and handed it to Annabelle. The man's gaze darted around the parking lot during the whole exchange. Sweat ran down his forehead, and his hands shook. To Munroe, he said in a trembling voice, "You can't get caught with this. I logged it into the system as being destroyed during a test and disposed of. If this unit turns up somewhere, they'll track it back to our lab and to me. I'll lose everything."

With a smile, Munroe said, "If it wasn't for me, you'd be in prison now anyway. Just remember that. You have to be tough if you're going to be dumb. Well, you've been dumb, now man up and face the consequences."

"This makes us even," the man said again.

"We'll see. Have a good night."

The small man dropped back into his car and pulled away from the lot. Katherine came down the concrete motel stairs and said, "Who was that?"

"Just an old friend who has a contract to develop less-than-lethal weaponry for the DOD."

"What's in the case?"

Munroe smiled. "Something that could prove very useful. I'll fill you in on the details during the drive to Leavenworth."

Munroe climbed into the back of the SUV, and Annabelle and Katherine finished packing up all the equipment and clothing. She was about to close the back hatch when Jonas Black threw his duffle into the back atop the other bags.

"I'm driving," was all he said as he climbed behind the wheel.

58

During the sixteen-hour drive to Leavenworth, Munroe explained his plans, and then they all tried to get some much-needed rest. Jonas had driven for the first eight hours and then Annabelle had taken over so that he could sleep. He was keyed up, but it was an essential skill for a soldier to be able to turn off the rest of the world and sleep when they had the chance. Along the way, they stopped at a specialty shop that sold costumes, stage make-up, and wigs.

Yawning, Jonas leaned up from the back seat and said, "What are we doing here?"

Munroe seemed to brace himself before responding. "We need to get wigs and facial prosthetics for Katherine and Annabelle. That way any eyewitness reports or facial sketches will be wrong."

"But why the hell would they need that? I'm the one going into that hospital to get Corrigan."

Munroe took a deep breath. "No, Mr. Black, you're going to drive the truck. Your size and tattoos make you too memorable."

Jonas slammed his palm against the back of Munroe's seat. "This just keeps getting better and better."

Katherine said, "Mind yourself, Jonas. You know he's right.

You being protective and all is sweet, in an oafish sort of way, but we're big girls. We can take care of ourselves just fine."

Jonas clenched his jaw and checked his watch. "You had better get what you need. We're not going to have much daylight left to get the truck and scout the area."

~~*~~

After finalizing the last elements of the plan, they spent the night in the vehicles. Munroe had suggested that they limit any interactions in the area – including gas stations, restaurants, and hotels. Those would be the first places that the police would canvass when asking questions about a group of people in a dark Yukon. And hotels often kept logs of the license plates of their visitors, which Munroe couldn't allow.

The next morning, Katherine and Annabelle took turns changing each other's appearance using the items purchased at the costume shop. The disguises wouldn't stand up to much scrutiny, but they didn't plan to let anyone get a good look at them.

Then they said their goodbyes and split up. Katherine kissed Jonas on the cheek and enjoyed seeing the big man's tanned face turn red. The two men stayed with the newly acquired rental truck, and Katherine and Annabelle drove off in the Yukon after removing the SUV's license plates.

As the collection of red-brick buildings surrounded by trees that comprised the Dwight D. Eisenhower VA Medical Center came into view ahead, a wave of doubt and fear overwhelmed Katherine and made her second-guess herself. Maybe Jonas Black was right? Maybe there was another way? If she moved forward with the plan, she would cross the line from law enforcement to fugitive. But, despite her doubts, she still couldn't think of a better solution, given the extenuating circumstances.

Neither she nor Annabelle said a word as they parked the Yukon and retrieved the aluminum case that Munroe's reluctant acquaintance had provided. Katherine popped the locks on the case and stuffed one of the tranquilizer guns that it contained into her coat. Munroe had said that the guns fired a 1.5 ml dart with a 72 gm CO_2 cartridge as propellant. The darts that the guns used as ammunition contained a sedative that was supposed to act within a two-thousandth of a second, faster than the nerve-conduction velocity. Which meant that the guards would go down instantly without being able to pull a weapon or trigger an alarm. She handed the other tranq gun to Annabelle, along with a pair of sophisticated-looking earplugs. As she closed the case, she prayed that the tranquilizers and the other strange device lived up to Munroe's claims.

Joey had hacked the hospital's computer network and found Corrigan's exact location along with the codes to the facility's security office. They passed through the lobby and followed Joey's directions down the maze of hospital corridors. Calming pastels and soothing off-whites covered the walls, the colors at odds with the antiseptic smell. Katherine repeated the instructions in her head. *Elevator 4 to the lower level. Right out of the elevator. Take a left at Records and Billing. Security Office on the right.*

Joey's directions were spot on. A heavy dark gray door marked *Security* sat right where he had said with a keypad on the wall beside it. Annabelle punched in the code, and the door opened with a buzz. Katherine had been with NCIS for seven years, and she had never shot anyone, although rigorous training had made her a proficient marksman. She told herself that she wasn't actually going to shoot these men. The guards would just be tranquilized. They would wake up in a couple hours with a slight headache and a vague idea of what had happened. Other than that, they would be no worse for wear. Somehow it still felt like the most criminal and underhanded part of Munroe's plan.

The door opened into a hallway with a bank of lockers straight ahead, the control room on the left, and a small break room equipped with a fridge, a microwave, and two round laminate tables. The place smelled of sweat and burnt coffee. Katherine set the aluminum case near the door and pulled the tranq gun from her jacket.

Having practiced the movements thoroughly in their heads, Katherine and Annabelle immediately swung to the left as they came into the control room. Two men were staring at a bank of monochrome monitors showing the various corridors of the hospital. One of the men turned and reached for a button on his panel, but the women dropped both of the guards with a shot to the side of the neck.

That wasn't so bad, Katherine thought.

Then she heard Annabelle say "Wait!" before screaming in pain. She turned to see the barbs of a taser embedded in Annabelle's chest. The dark-skinned woman shook as the electrical current pulsed through her body.

Katherine wheeled around as the guard that had attacked Annabelle dropped his X26C taser to the floor and tackled her. The man must have been concealed from view down the hall by the lockers.

Momentum carried Katherine forward against an unconscious guard's chair. Strong arms wrapped around her thin frame, pinning her arms to her sides. Lifting her completely off the floor, the attacking guard spun her around and slammed her into the block wall, driving the air from her lungs. The tranq gun fell from her grasp.

But she wasn't about to let some rent-a-cop get the best of her.

Katherine slammed her heel down on the inside of the man's right knee. He buckled to that side but kept hold of her with his arms. With her feet back on the floor, she dropped down, slipped from between his arms, and whirled around in a crouch.

Her palm thrust out and into the man's groin. The hard blow bent him forward, and Katherine followed it with a chop to the side of his neck.

The man stumbled backward, dazed and hunched forward. Wasting no time, she retrieved the trank gun and fired a dart into the chest of the overzealous security officer.

She then moved to Annabelle's side, pulled the barbs from her chest, and helped her to her feet. "Are you okay?" Katherine said.

"Not really," Annabelle whispered.

"Don't worry. Nothing ever goes as planned, and so I actually feel better that we had this happen. Maybe it means that everything will go smooth from here on out."

Annabelle gave her a doubtful look but didn't comment. She just leaned against the wall, straightened her wig, and tried to compose herself. Katherine retrieved the aluminum case and removed the circular device from its padded-foam enclosure. The black machine had a diameter of nearly two feet and looked like a game piece from a giant checkerboard. Following the procedure that Joey had outlined, she hooked the device into the hospital's intercom system and configured the proper output options.

59

After changing into a pair of nurse's scrubs, Katherine commandeered a gurney and followed the corridors leading to John Corrigan's room. When she saw the designation for the proper wing, she inserted the specially designed earplugs that Munroe had received with the circular device. She then pulled out her phone and pressed the button to send the text message that she had already typed out: *At the nest.* Munroe had suggested that all their communications should stay innocuous in case of any later inquiry. They had purchased burner phones for the same reason.

He had also given them a brief description of what the black disk, which was now hooked into the hospital intercom system, would accomplish. The device was a sonic weapon using a principle similar to the Long Range Acoustic Device used by the US military. LRAD systems had countered pirate attacks, controlled riots, and acted as communication devices, but they could also weigh over three hundred pounds. This device was tiny in comparison but still harnessed infrasonic sound waves – those below the frequencies audible to human beings – in order to destabilize the inner ear of anyone in range. The debilitating sound waves would cause those affected to lose focus and balance.

The hospital's secure corridor that held prisoners in need of surgery lay just ahead, and Katherine had yet to notice a change in the behavior of the people around her. But then, as if struck down all at once by an act of God, everyone in the corridor – except for her – dropped to their knees with their hands over their ears.

She rushed forward and typed into a keypad the code that Joey had supplied. The automatic double doors swung open, and she pushed her way past the writhing guards and hospital personnel. She followed the corridor to John Corrigan's room and found the former soldier hooked up to all manner of machinery. Munroe had called in earlier to get an update on Corrigan's condition. He'd learned that the doctors had woken the prisoner with no complications, and Corrigan was nearly ready to be moved back to the USDB. Corrigan twisted against his restraints and rocked back and forth, unable to bring his hands up to block his ears.

Katherine wheeled the gurney into the room, moved to his bedside, and inserted a pair of the earplugs that canceled the sonic weapon's effects. Then she pulled a folded piece of paper out of her pocket and held it up for him to see. It stated that she was there to get him out. He nodded, the surprise evident on his face.

After undoing his restraints, she helped him onto the gurney and quickly pushed it into the hall, clumsily banging the sides of the doorway as she went. With great effort, Katherine forced herself to calm down. Everything was going according to plan. The guards were disabled, and they were almost in the clear.

She pushed the button to open the automatic doors and continued down the hall. She had just started repeating Joey's directions for her escape in her head when the people in the corridor seemed to relax and many stood back up, shaking their heads and looking around at each other in shock and fear.

The sound of running feet echoed from down the hall, and Katherine turned around to see the guards from the secure wing heading in pursuit.

60

Katherine shoved the gurney forward as fast as she could, her legs pumping hard to gain momentum. People dove out of the way of the escaping pair and hugged the walls as they sped by. Eventually, they hit the proper elevator and waited as it slowly rose to meet them. She pulled the tranq gun from her coat and aimed it back in the direction of the running guards. She sighted in and squeezed the trigger when the first man was in range. A high-velocity dart blasted from the gun's barrel and struck the guard square in the chest. He dropped to the polished white floor. As Katherine fired again, his partner dove into one of the doorways to avoid a similar fate.

The elevator doors slid open, and she swung the gurney from the hallway into the elevator. A moment later, she ran down the ground-floor corridor toward the lobby. She could see the sliding front doors of the medical center, but a pair of guards stood in her path inside the lobby. They had their tasers drawn and aimed at her.

The tranq gun held a five-round magazine of darts, and Katherine had already used four. Only enough left for one guard, but perhaps the second man would flee if she disabled his partner.

She jerked back on the gurney, but her feet slid on the laminate floor, and she nearly lost control. The guards raised the tasers and screamed, "Stop or we'll shoot!"

Raising her weapon and using the gurney as cover, Katherine fired at one of the guards, a big man with a beard, the one she judged to be the tougher of the two. The dart burst from the end of the gun, spiraled through the air – and missed the guard completely, sailing just over his shoulder and embedding itself in the drywall behind him.

For a second, she couldn't believe it. How could she have missed? A dart gun probably wasn't the most accurate of weapons, but at this range . . .

The elevator doors dinged down the hall behind her, and more guards rushed into the corridor.

The two guards from the lobby must have guessed that she had spent her last round, and they moved cautiously forward.

Katherine was boxed in with no way to escape and no way to defend herself. It was over. Not just the escape, but life as she knew it.

Then the guards in the lobby fell to the floor, and Annabelle said, "Come on!"

Katherine wasted no time in following. They burst out of the hospital's front doors and helped Corrigan into the awaiting Yukon that Annabelle had positioned in the loading area. Annabelle hopped behind the wheel, and Katherine jumped up into the passenger seat. She saw the guards rushing out of the front doors in the rearview as they sped away.

"What happened back there?" Katherine said. "You weren't supposed to turn off the sonic weapon until we were clear."

"It made a sizzling sound and then quit working. I think it's fried."

Katherine heard the sirens approaching close behind them. Too close, coming too fast. "I hope the next part of Munroe's plan goes smoother than this."

61

Munroe knew that the moment a report that a death row murderer had escaped was broadcast across the airwaves, every cop within fifty miles would converge on Leavenworth – setting up roadblocks, dispatching choppers, checking all methods of transportation: airports, bus stations, train depots, car rental offices. The police would keep searching around the clock until they had run them to ground or were certain that their quarry had escaped the net. They could try to hide out somewhere until the police presence died down, but they didn't have time for that. Instead, Deacon Munroe's plan involved slipping out right beneath the noses of their pursuers.

The twenty-six-foot U-Haul truck that they had rented under a false identity allowed for that to happen. A roll-up door covered the truck's back end. Pull-out ramps allowed the Yukon to drive right into the back. It would be a tight fit, but they had about a foot to spare on each side. Once the Yukon and its passengers had been safely loaded inside, Jonas Black would drive them out right through the roadblocks and past the police.

Munroe waited in the rear cargo area as Jonas bumped over the country roads to the chosen rendezvous point. Munroe's disposable phone vibrated against his leg, and the truck came to a stop. It was the signal that they had arrived. Late the previous afternoon, Jonas had scouted for rendezvous locations and had chosen a spot where they could discreetly load the SUV without any witnesses. And if someone did see them, they would be long gone before that person realized the significance of what they had observed.

Jumping to his feet, Munroe rushed to the end of the truck and threw up the rear door. Then he knelt down, felt his way to a crouch, and hopped to the ground. They needed to pull out the vehicle ramps, and Jonas couldn't do it alone. Munroe heard Jonas's footsteps come around the side of the truck, and with a few words and a bit of guidance, the duo slid both ramps out of their holding brackets in the truck's bumper and dropped their front ends to the gravel and dirt of the rural roadway.

With the ramps in place, they were ready to receive cargo. Now all they had to do was wait for the women to arrive with the package.

62

When Munroe had calmly described his plan, Katherine felt that he had considered most of the variables and that things would likely go off without a hitch. Of course, she also knew that in reality things never went as planned, and so she had anticipated a few hiccups. But nothing like this.

First the device quit working. Then a cop car had apparently been on patrol within a few blocks of the hospital and had immediately taken up pursuit of the escaping SUV.

Annabelle had practiced driving a specific route from the hospital to the rendezvous point. Now that was shot to hell. They had veered off on so many side streets into residential areas and whipped around so many turns in attempts to lose their pursuer that Katherine had no idea where they were, and she doubted that Annabelle had any better sense of their actual location. If they didn't lose the cop soon, police backup would arrive, and they would have no chance of escape.

They needed to lose the tail, but the driver of the blue and white patrol car was well trained. For every turn or corner that Annabelle slid around, the patrol car matched the maneuver perfectly.

"Does this thing have an automatic open button for the back hatch?" Katherine asked.

"I think so."

"Get ready to push it."

Katherine vaulted over the seat, knocking Corrigan out of the way, and then repeated the move into the Yukon's third row. She reached over the seat, pulled up on a lever, and pushed one half of the third row flat. Pulling a latch and lifting up, she unclamped the removable seat from its brace. It now sat unsecured on top of the rear floor.

She looked out the back window at the cop car riding their bumper. Its siren wailed, and the blue and red flashers rotated wildly inside its light-bar. "Keep going straight and open the lift-gate for the back hatch," she yelled to Annabelle.

The rear hatch rose slowly. Katherine didn't even wait for it to open completely. Placing her heels on the seats of the second row and pushing with all her strength, she shoved the unclamped third-row seat out of the back of the Yukon.

It landed on the hood of the patrol car, crumpling the metal, and then the car's momentum pulled the seat up the hood and through the windshield. The car swerved back and forth across the blacktop roadway. The cop fought to maintain control but ultimately lost the battle and smashed into a Toyota Tundra parked beside the road.

Katherine felt a momentary rush of victory and wanted to pump her fist in the air and scream, but then the reality of what she had just done set in. She had run a fellow law-enforcement officer off the road. The car's driver could have been injured or worse. Her joy instantly turned to guilt and regret.

"Close it down," she said to Annabelle and then climbed back to the front seat.

It took a few moments and a few wrong turns to find the right way, but Annabelle must have possessed an impeccable sense of direction because she managed to guide them back on track and find the rendezvous point. The open rear end of the

U-Haul truck beckoned them in, and they crawled easily up the ramp and into the cargo area.

The side doors had little clearance but opened just enough for Katherine to squeeze her small frame through the gap. She hopped out of the truck and helped Jonas slide the ramps back into the holders. While she did that, Annabelle exited the vehicle and started preparing the row of cardboard boxes that would hide the Yukon from any eager young officer who decided to check the cargo hold for himself.

Once the ramps were secured, Jonas said, "What took you so long?"

63

Antonio de Almeida sat at his mother's bedside and read to her from the works of Gabriel García Márquez. His recitation halted abruptly when an insistent knock on her door demanded attention. He stood and opened the door to reveal the pale form of Oliver Pike. "I told you to wait in the car," Almeida said. "I don't understand why such simple instructions confound you."

He was still seething with anger at Pike over the foul-up that the American had created at Munroe's hospital, a debacle which could have been forgiven if the mission had been accomplished.

"You weren't answering your phone."

"I turned it off. I told you that I wanted to spend time with my mother undisturbed."

"Trust me. You'll want to hear this."

"What's happened?"

"It's Corrigan," Pike said. "He just escaped, and he had help. It has to be Munroe and his team. Who else would want to keep Corrigan alive?"

Almeida drew a deep calming breath. He beat down his anger, trying to keep it contained beneath the surface, but his emotions teetered on the verge of boiling over. He walked back to his mother's side and stroked her hair. In a whisper, he said, "It wasn't supposed to be this way. We never should have been forced to hurt anyone. Let alone innocent people."

Pike scoffed derisively. "It happens. Man up and grow a pair of balls."

Almeida's rage exploded. It took on shape and form and could no longer be held in check. He sprang at his colleague, and before Pike could even register the attack, Almeida had a knife to the American's throat as the man's back slammed against the wall. Almeida pressed the edge of the blade into the soft meat of the white man's neck and wanted badly to slice open the veins and let the blood flow.

He stood there for a moment, breathing heavily and debating with himself whether to end Pike's life there and then. Finally he said softly, "Never disrespect me or speak vulgarities in the presence of my mother again. Tell me you understand."

Pike's eyes were hard. "I understand."

The old woman whimpered and rolled away from them. Her gaunt form trembled beneath the blankets. Almeida leaned down and embraced her. "It's okay, Mama. Soon I'll have the formula to a drug that could heal your mind. Won't that be wonderful?"

She mumbled something incoherent in Spanish and then drifted off again into a world that her son could not see.

"Unlike some people in our line of work, I've always maintained a code of honor," Almeida said. "There were certain lines that I would not cross. But the more this situation blows up out of control, the more my boundaries are being tested. I never wanted it to go this far, but I'm afraid that it's time to take things to the next level with Deacon Munroe and Jonas Black. It's time to hit them at their most vulnerable spot. To exploit their weaknesses and their passions."

Almeida closed his eyes, hating himself as he said, "Find me their families."

64

The ladies rode in the cargo area with Corrigan while Munroe and Jonas occupied the cab. The police questioned them at two separate checkpoints, but Jonas explained casually that he was helping his blind cousin move to a new house in Baltimore. Jonas's skills at deception and quick thinking impressed Munroe. The key in such interactions was the level of detail provided. Give up too much information, and the officers would think you were nervous and had something to hide. Embellish too little, and they would think that you were holding back with malicious intent. None of the officers bothered to inspect the cargo area, and the group passed easily through the net that local law enforcement had cast.

Midway through Ohio, Munroe decided that they had come far enough and it was time to have a word with their prisoner. "Find an out-of-the-way motel. Somewhere that won't notice a cash payment."

Jonas, who had been quiet for most of the drive, said, "You think Corrigan will finally be able to tell us the whole story?"

"I doubt it, but hopefully we'll get a few more pieces to the puzzle."

Munroe felt the truck glide off the interstate and up an exit ramp. But then Jonas asked abruptly, "How did you lose your sight?"

The question jolted Munroe. It wasn't one that he had expected – he had found that most people were too polite to ask or simply didn't care. "I suffered a blow to the head that damaged the occipital cortex region of my brain and caused total blindness."

"But how did you receive the blow?"

Munroe avoided the question and turned the inquiry around on Jonas. "Why do you ask? Has someone been telling stories?"

Jonas massaged the steering wheel, the leather creaking beneath his grip, and Munroe guessed that the big man was searching the roadway for a motel. Eventually, Jonas said, "When we were at the Pentagon, I visited the 911 Memorial. I saw your name on the list of Defense of Freedom medal winners. You're a hero."

"Don't you ever say that again. A lot of heroes were born from fire that day. I wasn't one of them."

65

A beautiful Tuesday morning in September. Temperatures in the sixties. Sun shining brightly. The previous night a booming thunderstorm had ripped through DC, but that morning the storm had passed. Deacon Munroe enjoyed the drive to work that day. He rolled down the windows, turned off the radio, and simply watched the cool breeze make the trees come alive as he sat in traffic along the George Washington Memorial Parkway.

He loved DC. It was his city, and every city had a certain rhythm, an energy. New York felt fast-paced and alive with perpetual motion. The energy there made a person want to stay up all night just to drink it all in. DC maintained a more laid-back atmosphere – culture, elegance, power, aristocracy. It suited Deacon Munroe's personality.

The halls of the Pentagon had also come alive that morning with a different kind of energy. Dread and fear permeated the air. Munroe checked his watch. 9:30 a.m. Forty-five minutes earlier, the first plane had struck the North Tower of the World Trade Center. Fifteen minutes later, another plane had attacked the South Tower in what was already being called the worst terrorist attack that America had ever suffered. Some people sat inside their offices, watching the mayhem unfold. Others jogged through the halls on their way to important meetings, those dealing with the blowback from the attacks. Then there were some, like Deacon Munroe, who decided that the best way they could fight back against the terrorists was simply to keep working.

The Navy Operations Center lay behind him. He had just inquired there about a man named Commander Ed Webb. Certain questions had arisen about Commander Webb's complicity in a recent bribery scandal involving prototype naval equipment. The research company developing the equipment had allegedly paid off certain naval personnel to ensure that their project passed inspection.

Munroe had just resigned himself to abandoning the pursuit of Webb for the day when he saw the commander coming down the busy hallway ahead of him among a group of other officers. He flashed his credentials at the approaching group and said, "Commander Webb. I have a few questions for you."

The commander's friends eyed him strangely and moved off down the hallway. The big black man stood ramrod straight, impeccably groomed, his face and head closely shaved. Webb said, "Are you kidding me? With all that's happening today, you want to question me about some stupid misunderstanding?"

"My heart goes out to all those involved in the attacks today in New York, but the world keeps turning. I have a job to do, commander. Same as you."

"My job is to help protect this country. Yours is to harass people like me. Let's get that straight."

Munroe smiled. "Okay. Since we're getting things straight, my job is to hunt down men and women like you when they decide to stop being protectors and soldiers and decide to become criminals and thieves. If that's you, then I'll burn you down. And you will answer my questions whether or not you agree with my timing. I'm not here to—"

The explosion struck. Bright light blinded Munroe, engulfing everything. His feet lifted from the floor, and then he was slammed back down onto his knees. The shock wave tossed him against the wall and stole the air from his chest. Searing heat filled the corridor. Black smoke. Then white smoke. He tried to stand, but a sharp pain shot through his leg. The limb couldn't take any pressure or weight. He couldn't see anything through the thick cloud of noxious fumes that burned his lungs and made him want to be sick. The sprinkler system switched on and pelted him with cold rain.

A man appeared through the smoke, coming from the direction of the Navy Operations Center. Munroe tried to focus through the haze, but his vision had to be deceiving him. The man reached out a hand and said, "Come on!"

But Munroe hesitated.

The Navy officer's arm and chest had been melted by the fire. The man's blackened face looked down at him, the whites of his eyes seeming to glow against the darkness. Munroe could smell the charred flesh. Adrenalin and shock must have kept the officer from feeling the pain since saving Munroe seemed more of a concern to the brave soldier than his own injuries or safety.

Munroe took the burned hand, and the officer pulled him to his feet.

Then a piece of the wall behind them collapsed.

Munroe felt a hard blow to the back of his head as the impact shoved him forward.

The lights went out and never came back on.

From that point forward, scattered voices and strange sounds were all he could remember, but nothing coherent. Just jumbled sensations of pain and fear and confusion.

~~*~~

When he woke, Deacon Munroe found himself in a bed at George Washington Hospital. He asked about the man who had saved his life, but he didn't have a name for the brave naval officer. If the burned man hadn't pulled him to his feet, Munroe realized that he would have been crushed by the falling debris instead of being thrown to safety.

The doctors told him that he had almost died from the jet fuel in his lungs and was lucky to be alive. But he still couldn't see. His eyes were open, but the world was gone. After a few days of observation, his doctor stood by his bedside and told him that the damage to his brain could not be repaired and he would never see again.

Munroe remembered Beth's fingers wrapping around his and squeezing tightly as he lay there in shock and denial and began his daily journey through the five stages of grief. "It'll be okay, Deac. I'll always be there for you. We'll get through this."

Not long after that day, he lost her as well.

66

After finishing his story, Munroe listened to the changing hums of the roadway and the creaks and rattles of the truck for a moment before adding, "I ended up finding out that the man who helped me was the same man I was there to see. Commander Webb. Apparently, as I was rolling around on the floor in confusion, Webb ran back and tried to save some of his friends – that was when he got burned. Then, even in that state, he tried to save a man who was there investigating him on criminal bribery charges while the rest of the world fell down around us. If he hadn't stopped to help me, he would have made it out alive. I'm not saying I blame myself for his death. It's the terrorists' fault, not mine. I was just in the wrong place at the wrong time. But I didn't deserve that medal, and I'm no hero."

Silence settled over the cab of the truck, and Munroe could only guess at Black's reaction. The truck shifted to a lower gear, bumped up a curb, slowed, and then stopped altogether.

"We're here." Jonas Black shut off the engine and said, "You were there at the Pentagon that day doing your job to support your country. While you were fighting that battle, a group of cowards attacked you, killed a bunch of innocent people, and robbed you of your eyesight. You gave up quite a bit of yourself in service to this nation, and then, even after all that, you chose to keep going back to work every day and fighting, despite what they stole from you. It sounds pretty heroic to me."

67

After the women and Corrigan had climbed out through the cargo area's side door, the group piled through the bright red door of another cheap motel room. The Best Value Inn sat two miles from I-70 near Dayton, Ohio and cost less than a hundred bucks a night for two rooms and four beds. More importantly, the neighborhood seemed the type where people didn't ask many questions and minded their own business.

As Jonas helped Corrigan down from the back of the truck, the eyes of his former team leader lit up at the sight of a friendly face. "Jonas Black. They told me you were here, but I almost didn't believe it. From what I heard, you weren't in much better shape than me."

"Yeah, ain't we a pair."

Corrigan slapped him on the back and said, "It's good to see you."

"You too, but maybe you should wait to say that until you hear why they got me out of prison in the first place."

"I figured as much. They thought that I might talk to you. Well, don't worry about it. This has gone far enough. I don't need any convincing."

Jonas led Corrigan into the motel room where the others had arranged the furniture. It was time to have a talk with the man whom they had worked so hard to rescue. The smell of stale cigarette smoke hung in the air. Corrigan sat down in a cheap gray chair beside a small table and looked at each of his four companions in turn before saying, "Where do you want me to start?"

Munroe didn't hesitate. "Fort Meade."

"I'm sure you know the cover story about a cultural-relations class, but the truth is that they approached men and women from all the different branches about participating in a testing program for a new drug called Focus. Not just Spec Ops, either. Guys from logistics and military intelligence as well. It paid quadruple hazard pay, but it was so classified that you could never talk about it with anyone. I thought it was going to be some new type of 'go pill' like the military's been handing out for years."

Annabelle said, "What do you mean? What are 'go pills'?"

Standing by the window and staring out with cautious glances, Jonas said, "Military's been shoving pills filled with amphetamines down our throats since Vietnam, probably before that. Everything from Dexedrine for the boys squaring off against the Viet Cong to Modafinil and ampakines in more modern times. But you run into a bunch of problems with that crap. What goes up sometimes has a hard time coming down. So then you have to take something like Binoctal or some other barbiturate to help you sleep. Rinse and repeat. Up and down. Up and down. It keeps you alert, but it also puts you on edge. You're ready to snap."

Corrigan nodded. "We thought it was just the next-gen amphetamine. A step up from Modafinil. But it was a lot more than that. Black and I and the others from the unit had taken Modafinil on long missions, and like Black said, I knew what that felt like. It helped you stay alert and awake, but you still weren't at one hundred percent, and it had its side effects. This drug, Focus, was a whole other ball game. Quicker reaction times. More energy. Better concentration. It made you feel like you were operating *above* one hundred percent. My thoughts became clearer and more precise. At first, I thought it was just my own perception that the drug altered. Like a scientist thinking that they can come up with their best ideas on acid, or a kid on PCP thinking they can fly. But the researchers conducted all manner of tests, the same kinds of things we would do in training or assessments, and across the board, we posted numbers well beyond peak performance."

"Where were these tests conducted? Someone would have noticed at Fort Meade," Munroe said.

"They housed us at Meade, but for the tests, they loaded us into a truck and took us to a facility that didn't look military. Somewhere out among the trees. I don't know exactly where."

"How far?"

"I'm not sure. Probably a half-hour. Forty minutes."

"So, if this drug is so great, where did everything go wrong?"

"They had us taking the drug in cycles. Testing how long we could stay on it, upping dosages, tweaking formulas. We weren't supposed to be around anyone, in case we had any problems with the drug."

Corrigan's eyes filled with tears, and he continued in a trembling voice. "But it was my daughter's birthday, and I had missed so many already. The tests had all been going well. No one had displayed any dangerous side effects. And so I bribed one of the COs to let me travel back to Pendleton for the weekend. Apparently, they had changed the formula in the latest batch, the most aggressive version of the drug yet. It had some pretty major problems. I was told later that it shuts down the rational side of your brain and stimulates the part responsible for anger. It left whoever took it with only the most basic fight-or-flight instincts. All I remember from that night was feeling like I had the flu for a few minutes – and then nothing. Just rage and fear. I woke up covered in blood."

Katherine leaned forward and said, "But why let the military use you as a scapegoat? You could have told the whole world about the drug and that what happened wasn't your fault. You might have still done some time, but definitely not murder one."

The former sergeant sat straighter and wiped the tears from his eyes. His eyelids lowered, and his breathing changed. "Because I didn't want to cause a scandal for the military or expose a top-secret project. I'm a soldier and—"

"You're lying," Jonas said abruptly. "What's the real reason?"

Looking as if he'd been slapped, it took Corrigan a moment to recover. When he did, he looked Jonas straight in the eyes and said, "I didn't tell anyone because it *was* my fault. I insisted on going to my daughter's party even against the recommendations of the researchers. I was reckless. Other members of the program had similar reactions, but they were contained on base and kept under observation. No one was seriously injured. My family is dead because of my stupidity and irresponsibility. I deserve to be on death row."

The air conditioner hummed next to the window. A shower in a neighboring room hissed out a steady drone of white noise. A car honked in the distance. Beyond those background noises, a deep silence swallowed the room. Everyone seemed to be digesting all the new information. Black could tell that Katherine and Annabelle wanted to comfort Corrigan in some way but had no clue how to do so.

Then Munroe's voice cut through the silence. "This doesn't add up."

"I'm telling you the truth," Corrigan said defensively.

"That's not what I mean. If you accepted your fate and the military swept all this under the rug, then why is everything coming to a head now? Why murder General Easton and Wyatt Randall and Gerald and whoever else?"

"What about the money from the cartel?" Annabelle asked.

"Maybe evidence of the cartel connection could be enough, but it still doesn't seem right. Someone who controlled a drug like this shouldn't have a problem getting the bureaucrats to look the other way on that."

Corrigan said, "The military was more than happy to cover everything up and move forward with their new super-drug. Think of the tactical advantage to any country that could supply their troops with Focus. Your soldiers could instantly outperform everyone else. The problem is that Wyatt Randall discovered that Brendan Lennix didn't just plan to make billions off the new drug. The Castillo Cartel, who had bailed Lennix out of bankruptcy, forced Lennix to use the formula for the bad batch of the drug to create a chemical weapon that could be released as an aerosol. That's the evidence that Randall took to General Easton and why the general came to see me."

Jonas leaned his head against the wall as the implications of such a weapon became frighteningly clear. "Can you imagine dropping that crap into a bunker? The soldiers inside would slaughter each other, and all you'd have to do would be to mop up."

With a grim look on his face, Munroe added softly, "Or imagine if a terrorist released such a weapon into the air at a crowded football stadium."

Part Five

68

Sitting behind his massive glass and steel desk, Brendan Lennix cradled the empty ten-thousand-dollar bottle of Macallan 1939 in one hand and a picture of his family in the other. Three kids and a beautiful wife. Their smiling faces taunted and judged him. What would they think of him if they knew the truth?

All he had ever wanted was to make the world a better place. He wasn't a monster or a megalomaniac. He didn't long for world domination or destruction or even wealth and power. He simply wished to cure disease and make people smarter.

Focus wasn't just any other drug. It was a revolution, his legacy to the world. The next step in human evolution wouldn't stem from mutation, as in the *X-Men* cartoons that his son liked to watch. The future of mankind truly hinged upon a movement that some called "cosmetic neurology."

Lennix imagined a world where a simple pill could make the populace more intelligent and more productive. The possibilities didn't end there. As researchers probed deeper into the potential of the human brain – using the extra edge of the newly expanded mental and emotional capabilities and brilliance that Focus unlocked – they could find ways to reduce hatred and elevate compassion. Endless possibilities. A new frontier of thought. A better world.

The demand was certainly there – from an aging population fighting memory loss and dementia; from overwrought parents bent on giving their children every possible advantage; from anxious employees in an efficiency-obsessed, smartphone-equipped office culture where work never really ended.

It would have been beautiful, but now Ramon Castillo had twisted and corrupted Lennix's vision. The idealistic entrepreneur had made a deal with the devil to achieve his goals, and the devil had come to collect payment for his side of the bargain.

Lennix picked up the burner cell phone he used for off-the-books communication and stared at the display. An unsent text message containing an address stretched across the screen in small digital letters.

Pike had come to him requesting the address of an FBI safe house. Lennix Pharmaceuticals, through their new contracts, had employees that could retrieve secure information from several government servers. Once they had been given access to one part of the system, Lennix's expert computer specialists could poke around in other areas. He had used them to get all kinds of information, but nothing like this. Nothing that would directly result in the deaths of innocent people. Innocent kids, just like his own.

It seemed that pushing the send button on the message would forfeit his soul, his lofty ideals, and his dreams of a better world. But what choice did he have? They would kill him if he didn't cooperate. He was sure of that. But his concern wasn't only for his own life.

With one last look at the picture of his children, he pressed the button to send the message.

69

From the passenger seat of a gray cargo van parked across the street, Oliver Pike scanned the average-looking colonial-style home located in the Windbrook neighborhood of Clinton, Maryland. He estimated that the girls would be in one of the upstairs bedrooms and that they would have four FBI protectors in the house: three on the lower level and one on the second floor. He relayed that information to the strike team in the back of the van. Almeida added, "Remember. We need the girls alive. No screw-ups."

The five members of the strike team, all clad in black tactical gear and balaclavas, gave curt nods of understanding. These men weren't simply street thugs. They were all former special-operations soldiers that Pike had recruited with Brendan Lennix's money. Almeida returned the nods and said, "Get to work."

The five members of the team piled out of the van and glided across the street like living shadows. They moved with confidence and grace and blended effortlessly with their environment.

Pike climbed into the back seat and, leaving the sliding side door open and facing the property, readied his Stealth Recon Scout sniper rifle. A long sound suppressor extended from the weapon's muzzle. As the strike team set breaching charges on the front and back doors, Pike watched the property through his scope, looking for signs of life.

Through his headset, he heard the voice of the strike team commander. "Ready to breach." The commandos would blow the doors, toss in flash-bang grenades, and then sweep through the property, killing anyone that wasn't one of the extraction targets.

He pushed his throat mic and said, "Breach the doors."

Through the scope, he watched the front door blow inward, the flash-bangs explode, and the black shadows melt into the chaos.

~~*~~

A stocky, muscular Hispanic man named Miguel checked his watch and stroked the coarse hair of his mustache as he stared at the dumpy little ranch-style in Stafford, Virginia. Miguel had been given specific instructions about what time to enter the house. Almeida didn't want to tip off the FBI that they were coming to the safe house, and so the two extractions had to be coordinated. The thickset man was just glad that he had to deal only with a boy and his mother and not a house full of trained FBI agents.

He nodded to his partner and said, "It's time. You go in the back. And remember, we need the boy alive and unharmed."

"What about the mother?"

"Doesn't matter."

~~*~~

Sitting on the bed with her back against the headboard, Makayla Munroe drew on her sketchpad and thought about how much this whole situation sucked. Chloe lay on the carpet beside the room's other bed. An earbud cord dangled beneath Chloe's chin as she frowned at her algebra homework. Makayla had finished her assignments an hour earlier. The homework made things suck even more. What was the point of being stuck in protective custody if you didn't even get out of homework?

The pencil drawing in the sketchbook showed a girl in a hooded sweatshirt. The girl stared at Makayla over her shoulder with haunting monochrome eyes. Wisps of hair blew out from beneath the hood. Her lips bunched together in a tight line. The girl looked sad.

Makayla felt a resonance from the picture, the same kind of energy that her dad had always talked about when he visited an art gallery. It was her best work yet. She wished that her dad could actually *see* her pictures but wondered if he would feel that energy from it like he did with the works of the masters.

A series of impossibly loud explosions sounded from beneath her feet. A cacophony of gunshots followed. It sounded like World War Three down there. Chloe stared toward the door, eyes wide with fear, the earbud cord still dangling.

Chloe seemed frozen in terror, and Makayla was also afraid. But, strangely, the fear didn't paralyze her. Her mind instantly started thinking about what to do and didn't allow her to worry about what would happen if they were captured.

What would her dad do?

Something unexpected.

Makayla dropped the sketchpad on the bed and grabbed her sister. "Come on. We're getting out of here."

~~*~~

Will Black finished a set of push-ups and then stood and flexed in front of the mirror attached to his dresser. Freshman football practice started in a little over a month, and he needed to bulk up if he wanted a spot on the team. Everyone said he was big for his age, and he could be a linebacker, but he preferred offense. He wanted to be a running back and score touchdowns. He just hoped that he had inherited some size from his Uncle Jonas. When Will had been young, he remembered his dad calling Jonas "Mountain." Then Jonas would smile, throw out an insult, and call Will's dad "Foothill."

He wondered if he would ever see his uncle again.

A knock on the front door, barely audible over the heavy-metal music blaring out of his speakers, drew his attention. He turned down the stereo and heard his mom open the door. A few seconds later, she screamed. And then the unmistakable sound of a gunshot echoed through the small house.

~~*~~

A female agent, her hair tied back in a tight ponytail and with a black pistol in her right hand, swept into the room just as Makayla opened the window. "What are you doing?" the agent said. "Get away from the window and stay down." Then the woman shut the door behind her and slipped back into the hallway.

Makayla pushed the window open the rest of the way and looked out. They could climb onto the roof over the back porch and then drop to the ground. "Come on, Chloe. We're leaving."

Her sister looked at her as if she'd grown a second head. "The agent said to stay here."

"I don't care what she said. We stay, and we're dead."

Chloe started to cry and stepped toward the bedroom door, away from the window. "No – we do what we're told!"

Makayla grabbed her sister by the arm and said, "You're going out that window. Even if I have to throw you out."

~~*~~

Will stood frozen in shock for a second. What was happening? A robbery? Quickly regaining his composure, he realized that it didn't matter. His mother was in danger, and he needed to help her. But how?

Then he remembered his father's old shotgun. A Remington 870 pump-action twelve gauge. His mother had never really wanted him to go near the gun, but she had told him where she had hidden the weapon for events such as this.

His mother's bedroom was just across the hall, but the possibility of being shot as soon as he opened his bedroom door made it seem like much farther. Taking three quick breaths, Will inched open his door.

Footsteps in the hall. Coming toward him. He had to move.

Wrenching open his door, he sprinted across the hall and slammed his mother's door shut behind him. Then he locked it and moved to the closet. Someone slammed into the bedroom door and shook its frame, but he ignored that.

Get to the gun, Will kept telling himself.

Inside the closet, he felt around on the top shelf, pulling down items of his mother's clothing. His fingers wrapped around something metal, cold, and round. The barrel of the shotgun. He pulled the weapon down and aimed it toward the door.

The entire door frame shook from another impact on the other side.

Will suddenly realized that he had no idea how to work the gun. His mother had never shown him, and he wasn't even sure that she knew. Was it loaded? Was there a bullet or shell or whatever it was called ready to be fired?

He felt around the gun for a safety and found a button near the trigger. He pushed it to the position that showed red. That surely meant that it was ready to fire.

The door shook again, but this time it burst inward. Pieces of the door frame exploded into the room as the wood cracked under the weight of the stocky Hispanic man coming through the opening.

The man raised a gun.

Will pointed the barrel of the shotgun in the man's direction and yelled, "Don't move!"

The man raised his hands but didn't release the weapon. "It's okay, kid. We don't want to hurt you. Be cool."

"What do you want? Where's my mom?" Will shook the shotgun at the intruder for emphasis.

The man took a step forward, and from fear, Will jerked back on the trigger.

He expected a huge boom, followed by the sight of the intruder flying back out of the room in a spray of blood. Just like he'd seen in the movies.

But nothing happened.

He pulled the trigger again and looked down at the weapon in horror.

As he did so, the Hispanic man leapt forward, ripped the shotgun from his grasp, and slammed the butt of his pistol against the side of Will's head. Pain exploded through his skull, and he saw flashes of colored light.

He fell against the wall and slid to the floor beside the closet. The intruder stood over him. The Hispanic man stroked his mustache and smiled. Then he pumped back the shotgun's grip, making a loud crunching noise. "You didn't jack a shell into the chamber, kid. Better luck next time. Now get up. We're going for a ride."

~~*~~

Sitting beside Pike in the van, Almeida listened to the concussive sounds of gunfire from inside the house, patiently waiting for a situation report from the strike team once the agents inside the dwelling had been dispatched. He looked over at the neighboring homes. He wondered what those people were thinking at that moment. Did they have any suspicion that they lived next door to an FBI safe house? He supposed not, otherwise the place wouldn't actually be very safe.

At his side, Pike said, "I think I just saw the kids drop into the backyard."

Almeida's gaze shot to the rear of the house, and he indeed saw movement. In one motion, he pulled his pistol and jumped from the van.

~~*~~

A tall wooden fence surrounded the backyard, obscuring the neighboring homes, but Makayla had seen from the window that an alley and more backyards lay on the other side of the fence. She threw open a gate to reveal the alleyway. She shoved her sister through first, but then she heard pounding footsteps coming from the front of the house.

"Run, Chloe!"

She let the gate swing shut behind them and sprinted down the alley beside her sister. Chloe was slow, and Makayla easily passed her.

The sound of the gate being pulled open echoed down the alleyway, but Makayla dared not turn back. She ran faster than she ever had in her life. Her lungs felt as if they were going to explode, and her calf muscles burned, but she kept pushing forward.

The end of the alley was in sight just ahead. But what would they do once they reached it?

"Mak!" Chloe screamed.

"Stop or I'll shoot your sister," a voice said from behind her. A man's gravelly voice.

Makayla stopped moving forward but didn't turn around. The end of the alley lay just ahead, beckoning her, taunting her.

"Don't get any ideas," the man said. "I don't want to hurt you. Please don't make me."

She turned back and looked into her sister's terrified face. Tears streaked down Chloe's reddened cheeks. Makayla didn't know what to do. Didn't know what to say. But the words came to her by instinct. "It's okay, Chloe. Everything's going to be okay."

70

Sitting at his desk and surrounded by superhero memorabilia, Joey Helgeson jabbed at his keyboard, typing with a flourish. He thought of the girl from the coffee shop. She was so beautiful and sexy with her blue hair, her nose ring, and the Little Mermaid tattoo that ran up her forearm to her bicep. He read the letter back to himself, but halfway through, he stopped and clicked the delete icon.

He wondered what the hell he had been thinking. He couldn't express his feelings in a letter. No one wrote letters anymore.

He could track her down on Facebook. Everyone was on there. Hack her account, get her e-mail, phone number, credit card, bank account, learn more about her, get an edge . . .

Joey shook off the idea as he realized how quickly his status of secret admirer could be upgraded to full-blown stalker.

His phone vibrated against his leg, and he jumped out of his chair. Ever since that man had invaded his world, he had been on edge. Never feeling safe, not even in his own home. Taking a calming breath, he sat back down and answered the phone.

He immediately recognized the voice, and it caused fear to seize his body.

"Hello, Mr. Helgeson," Almeida said. "I have another message, and so I figured that I would pass it along through my favorite courier."

Joey's voice cracked as he said, "Who's that?"

"That's you, Mr. Helgeson. Try to stay with me. I've kidnapped Munroe's daughters from the FBI safe house, and as a bonus I've also taken Jonas Black's nephew, a boy named Will. Tell your friends that I'll trade the lives of their loved ones for the flash drive and Sergeant Corrigan. Now, listen to the following instructions carefully. In fact, you may want to write this part down."

71

Antonio de Almeida sat in the passenger seat of one of the black Mercedes GL550s traveling to the meeting point. One of his own men drove – Miguel, the same man who had captured Will Black. Pike occupied the back seat with Brendan Lennix. Almeida had insisted that the CEO should take a more active role. The other GL550 contained four men from Pike's team of mercenaries. Almeida had chosen a location in rural Virginia – a dead-end road surrounded by thick foliage – for the exchange. Of course, he never intended to actually trade anything. As soon as they had Corrigan and the drive in their custody, he would order Pike's men to open fire. Munroe and Black had been given every opportunity to walk away, and he regretted that their innocent family members would also be among the first casualties of this war. Collateral damage, however, was an inevitable fact of any conflict.

Almeida rolled down the window. The crisp air carried hints of the fires that had been burning recently in the Shenandoah National Park. They pulled down the long dirt lane to the spot he had outlined to Joey Helgeson. When they reached the proper location, only one man stood in the dirt cul-de-sac – Jonas Black.

The GL550 rolled to a stop, and Almeida stepped out. "Mr. Black, where are your friends?"

"They're waiting at the real site of the exchange."

Almeida laughed. "I can just imagine the way that conversation went down. Either you or Munroe insisted that you establish dominance and change the location to a place where you had complete control of the surrounding environment."

Jonas Black tried to maintain his stony composure, but Almeida could see a quick flash of fear and doubt in the big man's eyes, indicating that the discussion between the members of Munroe's group had gone extremely close to the way he had described. Almeida imagined that Munroe and Black also suspected that he planned to kill them all once he had the drive. But he wasn't worried. The cards he held trumped any scheme or counter-attack that they could have cooked up.

"Where are the kids?" Jonas said.

"They're safe. Once I have what I need, I'll share their exact location with you."

Jonas stepped forward. His body shook, and his fists clenched into tight balls. A barely contained rage burned behind his eyes.

The mercenaries raised their guns and sighted in on him but Almeida held up a hand and said, "Let's not be reckless. If you do as I say, Mr. Black, you will see your nephew again."

"And what about my sister-in-law? She's in the hospital in critical condition from a gunshot wound."

"War has casualties. How much collateral damage is sustained is up to you. Make no mistake, I am in complete control. You and your friends can attempt all the theatrics you wish. Change the location. Threaten me. Try to outsmart me. None of it matters. The end result will be the same."

Almeida raised a hand to the surrounding forest and gestured to the mercenaries hidden among the trees to come forward. Two men, who had blended perfectly with the environment like a pair of chameleons, melted out of the trees and approached the clearing. Each had a long sniper rifle slung over a shoulder.

They unloaded their gear and climbed into the GL550 with the other four mercenaries.

Almeida's gaze met Jonas's. The hatred and rage burned so brightly within the former soldier's eyes that they seemed to glow. Almeida gestured toward the SUVs, and, smiling, he said, "Shall we take a ride?"

72

Jonas Black's blood boiled and his skin crawled as he directed Almeida and his mercenaries to the new rendezvous point. He and Munroe had selected the new location in order to do exactly as Almeida had said and control the circumstances of the meeting as much as possible. For this purpose, they had chosen an abandoned ready-mix plant located down a dead-end road. A place with no innocent bystanders.

He knew that once Almeida had the drive and Corrigan, the Colombian would not allow them or their families to live, not after all the grief they had caused the Castillo Cartel.

"Turn left here," Jonas said.

The GL550 pulled down a long lane. Gravel had once covered the roadway, but the weeds had overtaken it now. An ineffective chain-link fence surrounded the property but sagged in several places. A faded white sign read *Scottdale Ready Mix – Over 300 Years Combined Experience*. Apparently, all that experience hadn't helped to keep the lights on. The massive gray silos and bins that had once held sand and gravel for mixing into the cement stood out against the horizon. Rusty catwalks, metal ladders, and all manner of conveyors clung to the sides of the cement silos and storage tanks. Empty dumping areas for ornamental rock sectioned off by giant white blocks sat to the left, while the office and control room had fallen into disrepair on the right. In the center of the space between the dumping areas and the control room, with the storage bins at their backs, Jonas's three companions – Munroe, Katherine, and Annabelle – stood beside the Yukon, awaiting their arrival.

The GL550 came to a stop fifty feet from the Yukon. As the mercenaries piled from the vehicles, Almeida said, "You may join your friends."

Jonas crossed the gap between the two groups, half expecting Almeida to shoot him in the back. The wind blew loose dirt and sand in his face and eyes, but he kept moving. Once he reached them, Katherine asked, "Are you okay?"

"Ask me in an hour," he replied.

Almeida approached them and said, "I like the scenery. Very dramatic. I understand why you wanted to change the location, and honestly, it makes no difference to me. I'm sorry that it's come to this, but you must admit that you really haven't given me much choice. I truly hated to involve your families."

Munroe said, "Where are they?"

"The drive first."

"How do we even know that they're still alive?"

Almeida held out an open palm to his side, and the wiry white man beside him placed a small device in the upturned hand. Almeida tossed the device across the gap. Jonas snatched it from the air. Almeida said, "Push play."

Jonas held the large touch-screen cell phone up for all of them to see the video and for Munroe to hear it, and then he pushed the icon marked with a green triangle.

The camera pointed down into a large hole in the earth. A track hoe was visible in the background of the scene. A storage container rested within the massive hole. The container had been buried with only the front opening still exposed. Jonas couldn't see anything else in the background. The camera was probably angled in such a way as to obscure the rest of the area. Two men pulled open the doors of the shipping container.

Then the camera panned around to show the three kids. Jonas hadn't seen Will in years, but he recognized him immediately. The boy looked like Michael – dark hair, intense eyes, tan complexion – only with a stockier, more muscular build. Munroe's daughter Chloe looked scared beyond reason, and Jonas was glad that Munroe didn't have to see the look on her face. The older girl, Makayla, maintained a hate-filled look of defiance.

Jonas knew what was coming next before it happened. Almeida's men shoved the kids into the hole, forced them to enter the darkness of the shipping container, and then swung the doors shut. He heard the teenagers banging on the doors and screaming for help. The sound of the track hoe starting up masked the screams as the massive yellow piece of heavy machinery pushed dirt into the hole and smoothed out the mound.

Jonas's heart broke. He thought of the kids out there buried alive, alone and afraid. Almeida had been right: the Colombian held all the cards.

When the video was over, Almeida spoke first. "I'll take the phone back now." Jonas angrily pitched it into the dirt and gravel in front of the Colombian. Almeida picked up the device, dusted it off, and continued. "That video was sent to me just a few moments ago. It displays a technique that we've often used in Mexico to help encourage cooperation. My colleagues have disposed of bodies at the location in the video many times. None of them have been found. Your family members have somewhere between fifteen and twenty hours before they suffocate – if they stay calm, that is. And so I'll ask you again . . . where is the flash drive?"

73

The darkness felt heavy around her. It pressed down like a living thing with substance and weight, choking the air from her lungs. But Makayla Munroe knew that it was all in her head, just common claustrophobia. Still, all the rational thoughts in the world couldn't hold back the rising tide of fear. The darkness was crushing her. She wondered if this was the way that her dad felt all the time.

After banging on the doors hysterically for a few seconds, they had all dropped to the floor of the container and sat in silence as they tried to get to grips with the impossible situation. Then Chloe started to sob in one corner. The cries sounded hollow and tinny as they echoed around the interior of the sealed metal box.

"You need to stop crying," the boy said.

Makayla quickly jumped to her sister's defense. "Leave her alone."

"I'm not trying to be a jerk here. They've buried us. We only have so much oxygen. Crying is just going to use it up faster."

Chloe screamed, "Why does it matter! We're going to die in here!"

"Chloe!" Makayla said. "He's right. You need to calm down.

Think about it. If they wanted us dead, they could have just killed us."

"So what *do* they want?"

"I don't know, but I bet they're the same people that attacked Dad. He has something that they want. They're probably holding us for ransom."

"What do we do?"

The boy said, "We need to lie down on the floor and stay calm and quiet. That way our bodies will use less oxygen."

"How do you know that?" Makayla asked.

"I saw it on TV. One of those *what would you do?* shows. I remember thinking that I would try to hold my breath. You know, the less breaths you take, the less oxygen you would use. But the show said that was wrong, that you actually die faster that way."

Chloe started sobbing again.

"Let's not talk about dying anymore. We're not going to die," Makayla said.

She groped her way blindly across the metal floor, using her sister's cries as a guide. She found Chloe and wrapped her arms around her small frame. She cradled her and stroked Chloe's hair as she said, "It's going to be okay. Dad will get us out of this."

74

They had little choice but to give in to Almeida's demands, but Jonas knew that they still had a few tricks up their sleeves that could save their lives. After receiving the call from Joey, they had formulated a plan and collected some choice hardware from their local arms dealer, Tobi Savoy. Jonas reached into the Yukon and retrieved the remote control for one of the gadgets that Tobi had provided. As he worked the controls, a tiny motor came to life in the weeds, and a small helicopter drone lifted off. Military or law-enforcement personnel could use the small drone, which was little more than a toy with a souped-up engine and camera system, in order to survey a battlefield or other area from above without the need for more expensive – and more visible – aerial surveillance.

Jonas piloted the drone to land directly in front of Almeida. When it touched the ground, he said, "The drive is taped to the bottom."

Almeida's eyes narrowed, but then he smiled and picked up the drone. "Very cute." Almeida's face didn't change as he turned over the drone and saw the drive attached – along with a block of C4 plastic explosive.

Jonas said, "Tell us where they're buried, or I'll detonate the bomb."

"You wouldn't risk killing me and losing your only chance to save your families. You would never find them in time, unless I tell you where to look. And none of my associates here know where they are. It was an entirely different group of men that buried the children. I'm the only one who knows."

Almeida pulled the drive from the bottom of the drone and tossed the little helicopter and the explosive toward Jonas. It landed in the dirt a few feet away.

The Colombian handed the flash drive to one of his men, who plugged it into a laptop. Almeida rattled off a sixteen-character string of letters and numbers that Jonas assumed was the password. The man read the password back, and then hit another key on the keyboard. Then the other man smiled and gave Almeida a quick nod.

Munroe said, "We still have Corrigan, and we won't turn him over until we know where you buried the kids."

Almeida shrugged and replied, "Keep him. It makes no difference to me."

A white man in an expensive suit who Jonas recognized as Brendan Lennix stepped forward and said, "What are you saying? We need Corrigan!"

"Please be quiet, Mr. Lennix."

Lennix stepped closer to Almeida, and his features curled into a snarl. "How dare you talk to me like that, you—"

"Brendan, you are a Catholic, is that correct?" Almeida didn't seem to lose his composure for even a second. "When was your last confession?"

"What does that have to do with anything?"

"I'm sorry, but Vaquero informed me that once we had the flash drive in our possession we would no longer be in need of your services. As a stockholder of Lennix Phamaceuticals, he's lost faith in your leadership." Almeida aimed his Glock pistol at Lennix's chest. "Consider this a hostile takeover. You may have a moment to prepare your soul."

Lennix stood frozen in fear for a second and then ran toward a nearby patch of trees that was surrounded by tall grass. Almeida shot him twice in the back. Lennix looked down at the blood spreading outward from the exit wounds as though he couldn't believe this was really happening, and then he fell into the weeds, staining them with red.

With a nod toward Jonas Black and his friends, the Colombian said to his men, "You may kill them now."

Upon the order of their commander, the six mercenaries raised their Heckler & Koch MP5 sub-machine guns and took aim.

75

John Corrigan's head pounded as though his skull was about to burst, and the parts of his body that *didn't* hurt were fewer than those that did. Despite all that, he was still a soldier. Years of intense training had taught him to fight through the pain.

He thought of the countless hours he had spent trapped in a cell analyzing what had happened to his loved ones and wishing that he could have exacted revenge for them, avenged their deaths in some small way. He just needed someone to line up in his cross hairs like any other enemy, but the only person to blame was himself.

Now, as he looked through the scope of the SIG Sauer SSG 3000 sniper rifle from his perch atop the plant's tallest storage silo, he finally had an enemy that he could see and fight. It felt good to be back on the offensive, to be a soldier again. When he saw the mercenaries raise their weapons, Corrigan didn't hesitate.

He dropped two of the men before the others could even register the danger and dive for cover.

76

Jonas tackled Munroe to the ground, dragging him toward the cover of their black SUV. Sharp tendrils of pain pierced his side where he had been hit, but, thankfully, his body armor had blocked the 9mm bullet from piercing the flesh. He would take a stinging pain over a gaping hole any day. The noise of squealing tires and churning gravel sounded from beyond the front of the Yukon, and he rose swiftly from cover to see Almeida's Mercedes escaping up the rock lane. He cursed and slammed a fist against the Yukon's rear panel. The one man who could save their loved ones was getting away.

Bullets tore into the black SUV, and shards of glass rained down over their heads. Jonas could smell gas, but he also knew that, unlike in the movies, a person could shoot at a car all day and it wouldn't explode unless they were using some kind of tracer or incendiary round.

Equal parts rage and fear pushing him forward, he handed the detonator for the C4 to Katherine and said, "You'll know when to blow it." Then he cupped a hand over the flesh-colored earbud, which he had slipped in when he grabbed the remote control for the drone, and said to Corrigan, "Do you read me?"

"I'm here."

"Cover me and keep them pinned down. I'm going to try something."

When Jonas heard the distinctive report of the sniper rifle, he sprinted around the vehicle, heading for the helicopter drone. The mercenaries fired blindly from cover, and the bullets slammed into surfaces all around him.

In one clean motion, he slid to the ground beside the drone, scooped it up, rose to his knees, and hurled it and the C4 into the air. The gadget flipped end over end as it shot forward and finally bounced off the windshield of the mercenaries' Mercedes GL550.

One of the mercenaries realized the danger and stood to run, but Corrigan dropped him with a .308 round to the back.

The C4 detonated, and the Mercedes blew apart in a massive fireball. A searing wave of heat and flame blew Jonas flat against the ground. He rolled into a ball and covered his face with his arms. Charred and flaming debris pelted him and showered the ground around them all. The smell of burning flesh and gasoline assaulted his senses. A high-pitched ringing filled his brain, and he couldn't think straight.

He felt hands grabbing him and looked up to see Annabelle and Katherine dragging him toward the Yukon. He pushed them away, screamed something that even he couldn't understand, and stumbled toward the driver's door of the SUV.

One word kept repeating through his disoriented thoughts. *Almeida. Almeida.*

Throwing the SUV into drive, Jonas spun away without another word and tore up the lane after his quarry. At the end of the gravel track, he took a right onto a blacktop road, heading in the direction of DC. He couldn't see any other cars ahead or behind. His skin burned, and an ache set in all over his body. The Yukon smelled of gasoline. Bullets must have punctured a fuel line during the firefight, but at least the big vehicle was still running.

Finally, after a few more moments of driving and no sign of Almeida, Jonas turned the Yukon around and headed back, defeated.

77

Deacon Munroe had learned long ago to focus on the things that he could change and ignore the rest. Right now, he didn't have the ability to chase after Almeida, but he could damn sure analyze the clues and find out where the Colombian was heading.

"Katherine?" Munroe said.

In the darkness to his right, she said, "I'm here."

"What happened to Brendan Lennix? Is he still alive?"

"I don't know. He fell into the weeds over there."

"Guide me," he said, holding out his arm.

She led him over to the weeds and said, "Here he is. He's still alive. Barely." Katherine left Munroe and checked Lennix's wounds. "It's not good."

Munroe knelt down and groped his way to the man's side. "Lennix, I know that you didn't want any of this. You're a businessman, not some kind of terrorist. Tell me, do you know what Almeida did with the kids?"

Lennix coughed and tried to speak, but the words came out as weak gasps. But the man didn't give up. He grabbed Munroe's hand, and, squeezing it tightly, he managed to say, "Sorry."

"I know you are. Help make it right. Tell me about the kids. Anything that can help us find them."

The dying CEO rasped out a series of wild incoherent ramblings in a harsh, gurgling whisper as his body trembled and went rigid. Munroe understood a few of the words, but the rest was indecipherable. "Don't know . . . Bankrupt . . . Deal . . . Devil . . . Almeida's after the . . . Weapon . . . Declaring war . . ."

Then Brendan Lennix's body relaxed, and his eyes fell shut for the last time.

78

Munroe heard the scrape and rattle of an approaching vehicle and knew exactly what it meant. Almeida had escaped and with him their chances of finding his daughters. The pain and fear and anxiety at the thought of losing them threatened to overwhelm him. His chest grew tight, but he fought back the roiling tide of a panic attack. He needed to focus, to concentrate on the things that he *could* control.

The SUV came to a stop, and the door creaked open. Jonas Black simply said, "Almeida's gone."

Munroe heard the footfalls of someone jogging up behind them and reasoned that it was Corrigan, who must have abandoned his sniper's perch.

"We need to get back to DC," Munroe said as he struggled to make sense of all they knew and to determine what Almeida had planned.

As soon as they were back on the road and had left the scene of the bloody firefight behind, Munroe said, "Let's go over what we know from the beginning. Wyatt Randall made a revolutionary discovery and took it to his old friend, Brendan Lennix. But Lennix had just avoided bankruptcy by making a deal with the Castillo Cartel, which has been worming its greasy fingers into US businesses and organized crime for years. So then Lennix has everything he needs: the new drug and the money to fund its development. He sells it to the DOD, and they begin testing its effect on soldiers under controlled conditions."

Speaking loudly over the noise of the wind pouring through the vehicle's broken windows, Katherine added, "But then the incident happens with Corrigan, and the military and Lennix cover it up. They don't want anything to taint the release of their new miracle drug."

Munroe pointed in the direction of her voice and said, "Right, which from a certain perspective would have been fine – except that it didn't stop there. Castillo sees the potential for the bad batch of the drug to be developed as a weapon and makes a deal or coerces Lennix into creating it. Either way, Wyatt Randall learns what Lennix is doing and doesn't want his discovery corrupted into something ugly. Maybe he's also conflicted about Corrigan's upcoming execution and that served as a catalyst. So Randall steals the research, maybe even destroys the other records, and runs to the top man in the Marine Corps. I'll bet he was trying to use the evidence and Easton to stop Corrigan's execution. Couldn't live with that blood on his hands. General Easton starts poking around and gets himself killed, his death protecting the secret and the billions of dollars in revenue that would be lost if all this was exposed."

Jonas said, "So now Almeida has the research for this drug Focus – which he could sell to our enemies – and he also has a powerful chemical weapon."

Munroe drummed his fingers on his thighs and tried to figure out what he was missing. He thought of what Brendan Lennix had said before he died. Lennix had mumbled that Almeida was *after* the weapon, not that he *had* the weapon. Lennix seemed to be trying to tell them that Almeida didn't have all the pieces yet.

"Randall didn't know about the weapon until recently. Maybe

he didn't have access to that data. He might not have known how it was being weaponized, just that it was. The directory listing on the flash drive was *John Corrigan, Wyatt Randall, Compound 119, Site B, Money Transfers, and Trial Results.* We obviously know about the first two. Compound 119 is probably the drug, the lab name for Focus. Trial results and money transfers are self-explanatory. So that leaves Site B."

"I think they called the testing facility Site B," Corrigan said.

"That must be where Almeida is headed. Where the weapon is being developed and stored. If we can find that facility, then we can find Almeida. If we stop Almeida, we can make him tell us where the kids are buried."

Jonas Black said, "That's great. We just have to find a secret research facility in the middle of nowhere, stop a group of para-military mercenaries from stealing a chemical weapon, and do it all before three teenagers suffocate to death."

79

When he was dealing with a complex problem, Munroe broke it down and focused on one step at a time. If he thought too much about the big picture, it could be overwhelming and hinder the process. Now he ignored for the time being the end goal of saving the kids and concentrated instead on the next logical step. Finding Site B.

With this in mind, Munroe said, "Corrigan, we need more information about this facility. Anything you saw or heard? Anything distinctive?"

"They transported us inside the back of a truck with no windows, and so I can't tell you anything about the drive there. We're trained to rest when we can, and so, to be honest, I slept for a lot of the time during the ride."

"What about once you arrived?"

"A lot of trees. A small nondescript brick structure above ground and then two levels below which was where the actual labs were located."

"Did you hear or see anything while you were there? Anything in the woods? No matter how small or insignificant. Anything that stood out to you?"

"I noticed a lot of geese. Oh, and they told us to watch out for unexploded ordnance in the woods."

Munroe cross-referenced these details with what they already knew. Within a half-hour to forty minutes of Fort Meade . . . Geese . . . Lots of trees . . . Unexploded ordnance. "When you were in the woods, did you ever see any old telegraph poles?"

Corrigan hesitated a moment but then said, "Maybe. There were some old poles among the trees in a few spots. They looked sort of like telephone poles. I never paid much attention to them."

The last pieces of the puzzle fell into place. A theory on Site B's location started to take shape. "My wife Beth was big into the outdoors. We used to do a lot of hiking and nature walks with the girls. And one of her favorite spots to visit was the Patuxent Research Refuge."

Katherine asked, "What's that?"

"It's a wildlife refuge and research center located just south of Fort Meade. In fact, the North Tract of the refuge used to be part of the base before the military donated that land. They still find unexploded ordnance there from time to time. Stuff left over from when the Army used it as a testing range. You even have to sign a waiver before you hike up there. Then there's the telegraph poles. The major thoroughfare from Baltimore to Washington, DC used to run right through the land now occupied by the refuge. It's been unused for so long that no trace of a road or path remains in most spots, but a lot of the old telegraph poles are still standing."

Katherine seemed to be the first to follow Munroe's logic. She said, "So all we need is a map of the old road, and then maybe we can trace it back to a facility located in the refuge's North Tract."

Jonas immediately added, "Almeida already has a head start. We can drive the Yukon to the closest town and get some gas or even steal a car and—"

Munroe reached out into the darkness and found the big man's shoulder. "We can't do this alone anymore. It's bigger than us now. We can't risk Almeida escaping with this weapon or the drug. We have to call in the cavalry."

Jonas shoved Munroe's hand away. "We don't have time for that! Someone might suspect that we're responsible for Corrigan's escape already. Then there's what happened to you at the hospital. By the time we've waded through all the questions and bureaucracy and convinced the right people about what's really going on, Almeida will be long gone."

"You're right, Mr. Black. But I have an idea about how to make all that go away."

80

Joey Helgeson sat inside his black 1969 GTO Judge convertible at a small gas station off I-395, waiting for the others to arrive. Recent events had convinced Joey that life was too short not to take chances. He thought of that while he smiled, sipped his Starbucks coffee, and contemplated the phone number written across the cup's side with a black permanent marker. His eyes went wide as the bullet-riddled Yukon pulled up beside him.

Collecting his papers, Joey walked to the passenger window. The tinted glass slid down to reveal Munroe's face. Joey had never seen his boss look so pale and worn-down, and the Yukon's interior stank of sweat and gasoline.

"Did you find him?" Munroe asked.

"Yeah," Joey said. "His secretary said that he's a big Jefferson fan and sometimes goes to the memorial in the afternoon to clear his head. I hacked the GPS in his cell to verify it. That's where he is now."

"Good – let's give him something else to think about. Did you find the info I requested?"

Joey passed two Manilla folders through the window to Jonas. "The bank statements and the list of sites are in there."

Munroe nodded. "Mr. Black, we'll keep the bank statements but please hand the other folder back to Annabelle."

Jonas passed the folder to the back seat, and Annabelle asked, "What's this?"

"Marine clay," Munroe said. "Almeida told us that they had buried bodies in this location many times before, but none had been found. That suggests a certain kind of access and use. Not just some random farm or new location. Someone would see them and wonder what they were doing there. Unless it's their own place. It could be a central base of operations or some business or site that they own. Something of that nature. And at the Easton and Randall crime scenes they found traces of marine clay, brick dust, plaster, insulation, and glass particles."

"Construction sites? Places undergoing renovations?"

"I've had Joey doing some research for me since right after the Randall scene. Marine clay typically occurs in the Coastal Plain, most commonly in Fairfax County, Virginia east of Interstates 95 and 395. That narrows down the geographic region. He's also been researching companies and locations in that area to find the most likely sites where they could have buried the kids."

"Sounds pretty thin," Jonas said.

"Thin is all we have right now. Joey's checked with a few of my contacts at the DEA, but they weren't any help. Which could mean nothing, since those guys like to play their cards close to the chest. We're going to attack this thing on both fronts. If we find Almeida, we can find the kids. But if we fail, maybe Annabelle will fare better with the traditional approach. Annabelle, take Corrigan with you and use Joey's car."

Joey's voice cracked as he said, "What?"

Munroe ignored him. "Don't get too deep into anything or put yourself in danger. If you think you're onto something, call in the troops. I'm counting on you to find my babies."

Annabelle reached forward and squeezed his shoulder. Munroe pressed his cheek against her hand. They held the contact a moment, and then she and Corrigan got out of the vehicle and moved toward the GTO.

"Keys in it?" she asked Joey.

"Uhhh . . ."

She didn't wait for his response as she climbed inside the vintage car, started it up, and sped away from the lot. Munroe said, "Take a cab back to your office, Joey. We may need you to run some more data for us."

Then Munroe rolled up the window and the Yukon headed back toward the interstate. Joey stood there a moment in shock before pulling out his cell phone and surfing the Internet for the number of a cab company.

81

With Jonas Black guiding him to the right spot, Munroe sat down on a stone bench inside the rotunda of the Jefferson Memorial. Thomas Jefferson fascinated Munroe, and the memorial had been a favorite spot of his for years, although he had seldom visited it since losing his sight. Still, he could picture it in his mind – the grand dome, the massive rotunda, the circular marble steps, the colonnade of Ionic columns, the nineteen-foot-tall bronze statue of the former president. Munroe had always found that the neoclassical building reminded him of the Roman Pantheon.

Without looking toward the man he had come to confront – Under Secretary of Defense Damian Lightoller – Munroe said, "Jefferson drafted the Declaration of Independence and wrote the Virginia Statute for Religious Freedom. He was the man who penned 'all men are created equal,' and yet he owned over six hundred slaves during the course of his life. Not much has changed in DC. What's that old joke? A mother asks her son where liars go. The boy instantly replies, *Washington, DC.* You fit right in, don't you, Mr. Lightoller?"

"I don't like being insulted or threatened, Munroe."

"Don't worry. Where you're headed, you'll get used to it."

"What does that mean?"

"Prison, Mr. Lightoller."

"We're through here." Lightoller stood, but Munroe grabbed his arm and jerked him back down to the bench. Lightoller pulled away and said, "Don't touch me!"

Munroe maintained his calm and soothing Southern tone. "I knew you had lied to me that day at the Pentagon, but I wasn't ready to confront you about it at the time. Now I am. I had a friend at the Pentagon Police pull your phone records, and I found that, immediately after I left your office, you placed a call to Brendan Lennix. And – what a coincidence – I was almost killed shortly thereafter."

"That doesn't prove anything."

"No, but I also had an associate hack into your bank account, and that *does* tell an interesting story." Munroe held out the Manilla folder that Joey had provided.

Lightoller snatched it from his grasp, flipped through the sheets, and said, "This is illegal!"

"Is it? Well, don't worry – we'll get a warrant before we come after those records for real. That way it's all on the up and up. You've been taking bribes and kickbacks for some time. You were most definitely involved in covering up the murders of John Corrigan's family, and who knows what else will crawl out when we start kicking over all your rocks."

Lightoller shifted nervously on the bench. "You can't do this."

"Oh, I believe I can. Brendan Lennix is dead, and when all this comes out, they'll need to hang it around someone's neck. Guess who that's going to be. I suspect the charges will involve fraud, bribery, and conspiracy to commit murder – among others. Not to mention the violation of the Chemical Weapons Convention, which if you recall is a pesky little international arms-control agreement outlawing the production, stockpiling, and use of chemical weapons."

"I had nothing to do with any of that. I helped cover up the scandal with John Corrigan, and I might have received some funds through improper channels, but I didn't have anything to do with murder or chemical weapons."

Munroe shrugged. "That'll be for the courts to decide."

"What do you want, Munroe?"

"Finally, to the heart of the matter. From what I hear, you're a rising star and have become an expert at playing the game. You've made some influential friends who have invested substantially in your future. I need you to call in every favor you have."

"For what?"

"John Corrigan is going to turn himself in, and you're going to get the execution postponed. Then you're going to pin the breakout on Lennix and his gang of mercenaries. I'll give you their location."

"They're dead?"

"That's right. Finally, you're going to pull strings with the FBI to get me full control of a strike force from the FBI's Hostage Rescue Team and a chopper to transport me to Lennix's secret facility up in the Patuxent Research Refuge. I need all that in less than an hour."

Lightoller laughed condescendingly. "You're out of your mind. What you're asking for is impossible."

Munroe stood and adjusted his dark sunglasses. "You never know how fast you can run until you're being chased, Mr. Lightoller. Make no mistake about it: you are most certainly being chased right now."

Part Six

82

Flown by the HRT's Tactical Aviation Unit, the Sikorsky UH-60 Black Hawk transport helicopter swooped low and fast over the Maryland countryside. Munroe could barely think over the noise of the whirring rotors and the howl of the wind, coupled with the strong smells of sweat and burning fuel. His two companions, Jonas Black and Katherine O'Connell, hadn't spoken a word since climbing into the chopper. He imagined that they each had a lot on their minds.

Over his headset, the assault team leader said, "ETA five minutes!"

A full HRT unit couldn't be assembled in the time they'd had, but Lightoller had been able to round up a six-man fireteam and a pilot. Plus, Jonas Black would be going in with them. The seven highly trained operators should have no problem taking the facility – or so Munroe hoped.

With nothing to do but reflect, Munroe couldn't help but think of his girls. They had both been under five years old the last time he had seen their faces, and he imagined how different they must look now. He had a picture in his head of them as little girls, playing in the backyard with their mother. He tried to imagine them as older versions with some of their mother thrown in, but he couldn't help but still think of them as those little girls.

And now they were out there in a hole somewhere, alone and scared to death and waiting for him to save them, wondering if he would make it in time. He tried not to consider the possibility that he might never hear their voices again, their laughter, their bickering.

He was on the verge of tears when the team leader called out that they had arrived at Site B.

83

Almeida loaded an aluminum carrying case with the weapon canisters and a few of the small prototype dispersal devices while Pike transferred the information from the lab's database onto a portable hard drive. The data would be used to reproduce the weapon, and the samples in the case would be used for the following day's attack.

Overhead, he heard an all-too-familiar sound. The roar of an attack chopper approaching low over the trees.

His mind instantly flashed back to his childhood and the raid on the compound by American commandos. Almeida had heard the sound many times since then, and he had ridden inside several of the flying metal beasts himself, but none of those memories were as vivid as the ones from the night when his friends had burned alive. Sometimes he wondered if his mother was suffering a kinder fate. She no longer had painful memories. Several years from his early life would be better forgotten. Those spent on the streets of Bogota. Scrambling to survive. Starving. Selling his young body in exchange for food. But those years had hardened him and molded him into the young man of whom Ramon Castillo had taken notice and raised up out of the gutter to a position of power, influence, and privilege.

Years later, he had tracked down his mother and his siblings and had given them the safe and comfortable life that his mother had never been able to provide for him. He didn't hate her for that. She had done the best she could with what she had been given. Although Almeida had never known his real father, Castillo treated him like a son. And now Vaquero had chosen him to lead them to their greatest victory, and to avenge the death of Ramon's family at the hands of American tyrants. Unlike the jihadists, Almeida had no interest in killing innocent civilians: he would strike instead at those truly responsible for the country's actions.

"What now?" Miguel said, hefting a large metal container from a back storage room.

Almeida gave him a strange look and examined the large container. Chrome edging. Black aluminum surface. Recessed flip handle. Butterfly locks. It reminded him of an expensive weapons case, the type that would hold a shoulder-mounted missile launcher. "What is that?"

"Vaquero told me to retrieve this. I thought you knew."

"Of course," Almeida said, although he had no idea what could possibly be in the container or why Vaquero would have told Miguel about it but not him.

"Escape plan alpha?" Pike asked as he unplugged the hard drive and attached another circular device to the side of the server. He pressed a red button on top of the device, and it came alive with a mechanical whir.

"Yes – check the corridor and the back stairs. I'll prepare the distraction for our guests."

84

The pilot set the transport helicopter down in a large clearing behind the facility, the intense rotor wash beating down the weeds and tall grass. The night was especially dark, and the lights of the brick building in the distance provided the only illumination.

Jonas Black dropped from the helicopter with the strike team, and they converged upon the compound with smooth, efficient movements. HRT impressed him with their professionalism. They fanned out through the tall grass in perfect formation and covered all the angles. Since Jonas was a former Recon Marine turned makeshift DCIS agent and could identify Almeida and his men, it hadn't been too difficult for Munroe to convince the team leader to allow the big man to accompany them inside the compound. Each member of the team wore a black Nomex flight suit with *FBI* stenciled on their chest and back and toted a Knight's Armament PDW. The weapon fired new intermediate-caliber 6x35mm TSWG ammunition that boasted increased lethality over a 9mm round, improved controllability, reduction in size and weight, and a maximum effective range of three hundred meters. Jonas had to admit that it felt good to be geared up and back in an actual combat situation with the best equipment and the best men. Like he was a real soldier again.

Over the headset, one of the team said, "The perimeter guards are down. Looks like .308s. Head shots."

The team leader said, "You hear that, people. Possible sniper. Eyes open. Red 4, 5, and 6 take EP-1. Red 2 and 3 with me on EP-2. Could be hostages. Check your fire."

The team leader, Red 1, had told Jonas to stay on his six during the mission, so that was what he did. The team split into two with one group heading toward entry point one (the main door), and the other moving to entry point two (a door on the side of the building).

The nondescript brick structure looked standard in every way. The kind of place a casual observer wouldn't give a second glance. The two groups breached the doors simultaneously and methodically checked the first floor. The interior seemed as ordinary as the building's shell. Speckled laminate flooring. White walls. Reception desk. Cluttered cubicles.

"Clear," different members of the team announced as they secured each room.

With the first floor checked, they reached the stairwell that Corrigan had described to them and descended into the bowels of the facility. The next level down contained expensive-looking lab equipment, strange machinery, large vats, and administrative offices. Again, all clear.

Since they had yet to see any signs of occupancy beyond the dead guards, Jonas guessed that Lennix had temporarily shut down the program after Randall stole the research files. He hoped that Lennix had also moved the weapon. But then again, the businessman had probably planned to continue production once the situation was resolved and the threat neutralized.

When they reached the second level down, a security desk and an airlock confronted them. A dead guard slumped behind the raised white desk, his head resting in a pool of his own blood. As Jonas examined the airlock, a strange sense of dread crept over him. He supposed that it just reminded him too much of one of those disaster movies where a runaway virus kick-starts the apocalypse. He dismissed the idea. This facility dealt with chemical, not viral, weaponry. At least, he hoped so.

Moving through the airlock in groups of two, the entry team discovered the main lab. Bright white walls and floors. Futuristic-looking equipment. It was colder inside and carried a distinct chemical smell that Jonas couldn't identify. Several workstations lined the room, topped with computers and microscopes and a multitude of other devices that Jonas would never try to identify. Sealed offices sat along a raised platform along one wall, and other corridors led off to additional rooms. He looked down one of the corridors and saw what appeared to be a storage area filled with black metal cases.

The team fanned out and searched the lab and storage rooms. Jonas's heart pounded, and his body pulsed with surges of adrenalin. Not because of the fear that they would be attacked, but from concern that they wouldn't be – that they were too late.

Each announcement of "Clear" felt like a physical blow. Almeida had escaped with the weapon. A lot of people were going to die, including Jonas Black's nephew and Deacon Munroe's daughters.

"We've missed them," one of the team said.

"Stay frosty," the leader replied. "There are still a lot of places to hide."

What would Munroe do? Jonas asked himself.

Look for clues. Find something they left behind. Find out what they took. Find something out of—

As he scanned the room, something on one of the desks in the room's center caught his eye. He walked over and examined the small box. Its front and back surfaces bore red and white letters and a surgeon general's warning ran along its spine. A pack of cigarettes. Why would someone have a pack of cigarettes in a laboratory? Had it belonged to one of the scientists? Jonas looked around the room again and noticed more cigarette packs scattered among the equipment and tools on the workstations.

"Agent Black," the team leader said. "Don't wander off. We're going to do another sweep and check the server."

"Okay," Jonas said, distracted by his strange discovery. Something about this made him very uneasy, but he couldn't identify exactly what it was. Thinking back, he remembered seeing another pack on the security desk.

"Black!" the team leader shouted. "Don't touch anything! I swear if you screw something up . . ." The man's angry voice trailed off and he stormed away down one of the other corridors.

Jonas couldn't understand what that guy's problem was, but if he didn't ease up Jonas would cave his skull in. As he thought of killing the FBI agent, he tugged at the collar of his Nomex flight suit. It was incredibly hot in the lab. But hadn't he felt cold when he entered the room? That didn't make sense.

Another table held a can of air freshener.

On another sat a dismantled cell phone.

Jonas picked up the cell phone and examined it. Someone had rewired the electronic guts, attaching them to a small silver tube that resembled a CO_2 cartridge. He twisted it in his hands and saw that two extra holes had been drilled in the side.

What were these things?

He couldn't concentrate. He couldn't find the answers. It made him so angry.

He wiped a sleeve across his forehead where sweat had begun to pour down.

Then it came to him. The innocuous devices were actually dispersal units for the weapon, objects that could be hidden in plain sight. He grabbed one of the cigarette packs and pulled it apart. Tiny electronic components scattered across the desk.

Radio-controlled? No, he realized suddenly: motion detectors.

The dispersal units could be placed on a table or in a bathroom or hallway where people would walk by. The motion detector would sense the movement and release the chemical weapon as a clear gas. The person affected wouldn't even realize that they had been dosed.

Jonas's heart wanted to pound its way out of his chest. He felt dizzy. He braced himself against the table and tried to shake the disorientation from his brain.

What was happening?

In a sudden burst of clarity, he realized that things were about to go very wrong.

"Everyone get out of the lab! We've been exposed!"

85

As the *all clear* signs continued from inside the complex, Munroe instructed Katherine to lead him closer to the building. He wanted to be ready when and if they received the final confirmation from the team leader that they could enter. If they had missed Almeida, maybe they could at least find some clue to his next move.

He wondered if Annabelle was faring any better. In her last update, he learned that she had checked off several sites from Joey's list without detecting any suspicious activity. Now darkness had fallen, and most workers from the sites had left with the sun. She was going to continue to check the sites through the night, even if she had to break in to do it, but Munroe knew that was a long shot.

He struggled to think of a method to narrow the search, but anger and fear kept clouding his mind.

His emotions kept getting in the way. He needed to stop thinking about the girls and start thinking about the evidence. He needed to look at it clearly and objectively as he would for any other case. Maybe there was something that he had missed. Some small piece of the puzzle that would make all the rest fit together.

The evidence. Facts.

While Jonas Black and the others had watched Almeida's video of the kids' burial for any visual clue to where the children were being held, Deacon Munroe had done the only thing he could. He had listened. As the video had played, he had focused on the sounds. The background noises that most people ignored. Those tiny nuances were his world, and he had memorized every one that was contained in that video. Unfortunately, he hadn't identified any distinct noise that could pinpoint a specific location in a wide geographic area.

The two most distinctive sounds were an irregular and metallic banging, like that of sheet metal, and a rhythmic *tut-tut-tut*. But he had also heard the buzz and chirp of insects and birds.

In his mind, he pictured a blank chalkboard. On it, he wrote each piece of hard evidence from the crime scenes and the details he remembered from the video of his daughters being buried. He studied each line.

A banging noise. Sheet metal?

A rhythmic tut-tut-tut *sound.*

Prominent insect and bird sounds. Wooded area? Rural? Trees nearby, at the least.

Marine clay, most common between Interstates 95 and 395.

Brick dust.

Plaster.

Insulation.

Glass particles.

Chlorpyrifos, the pesticide. Used on golf courses.

Munroe hadn't focused on the chemical at first because it didn't relate to the others in any obvious way and hadn't been found at both crime scenes. But there was something about it that gnawed at him. Some possible connection between all the pieces of evidence. Some shadow of memory dancing at the edge of his consciousness but refusing to take shape.

He pulled out his phone and dialed Annabelle. She answered

and explained that they hadn't made any further progress. The desperation was evident in her voice, and it echoed his own feelings, but he had one more lead for her to pursue. He said, "I want you to check out every golf course close to our target area."

86

After Pike had shot the perimeter guards, Miguel had driven their vehicle down the road and parked it just inside the woods. Almeida had instructed him to do so for this very contingency. After studying the blueprints contained on the flash drive, he knew that a maintenance hatch led up from the lab to the rear of the above-ground facility. This made it easy for them to slip past the incoming assault team and escape into the trees with their prize.

As they moved quickly through the darkness toward the vehicle, Almeida thought again of the strange container. Vaquero had told him that, since the death of his son, he had wanted Almeida to take over the business when he died. If he could trust him with the empire, why not tell him about a simple container?

Almeida tried to put such thoughts aside. Anything was mere speculation at that point. Instead, he thought of the assault team and wondered if they had discovered the surprise he had prepared for them. He hated that such an action had been necessary to cover their escape.

Thinking of those poor men, he said a quick prayer and asked the Lord to watch over them during the coming storm. He hoped that at least some of them would survive.

87

The team leader yelled for everyone to get out, but it was too late. Jonas dropped to the floor as another member of the squad opened fire into the ceiling. Like a spark igniting a powder keg, the sound of gunfire triggered the instincts of every member of the team. The room exploded with bullets as six highly trained men armed with machine guns blasted imaginary enemies in a wild frenzy.

Jonas fought to keep his sanity, but with every passing second, his thoughts grew cloudier, and the rage inside him boiled up.

The workstations blew apart under the barrage. Computer monitors, microscopes, papers, glass, plastic, metal – the debris erupted from the tables. Someone targeted the overhead lights, plunging half the room into darkness. The air smelled as though it was on fire.

Jonas heard screaming over the ringing in his ears, but then he realized that the sound was coming from deep in his own throat. Now he was up and running. For a moment, he felt disconnected from his body. Instead of occupying his own skin, he floated weightless away from it.

One by one, the team members ran out of ammo and lacked the knowledge of how to reload. Jonas heard more yelling and felt something wet and warm on his hands.

He pulled back as he realized that he had just knocked one of the other men unconscious, and blood covered his fists.

Something hit him from behind. He fell to the floor and looked back to see the team leader using his gun as a club. Pain shot through his back as the man struck him over and over.

Jonas's arms and legs flailed in uncontrolled, undirected fury. But his boot finally connected with a knee, and the team leader toppled over one of the workstations and fell to the floor.

Jonas had to get out. He couldn't think of anything beyond that. But he knew that to stay in this room was to die.

The airlock was up ahead, and he sprinted toward it. Fighting off insanity, he managed to get through the opening and pounded up the stairs. One foot in front of the other. *Run. Run as fast as you can.* Something behind him. Chasing him.

Anger and fear were everywhere. All around him. The world was red with pain and terror.

Suddenly, the cool night air stung Jonas's skin. It gave him a brief second of clarity. He felt grass and dirt between his fingers. His whole body trembled. His skin burned. He was on fire. Then he howled in a primal rage.

A voice called out to him. Through the haze of red, he recognized it. Someone spoke to him again. Katherine? Where was she? He needed to tell her to get away from him, but he couldn't form the words.

With all his remaining strength and sanity, he yelled, "RUN!"

88

Katherine watched in horror as Jonas Black burst from the front door of the research facility and fell to the ground, shaking and screaming. She rushed forward to help him, thinking that he had been shot or injured. "Jonas! What happened?"

He reared back and bellowed out something unintelligible. Then he swiped at the air and pounded the ground as if he was fighting some imaginary enemy that only he could see.

From behind her, Munroe said, "Katherine, step away from him slowly."

She realized then that she was witnessing what had happened to John Corrigan when he had killed his family and to General Easton when he had murdered his wife. The weapon had been released inside the building somehow, and Jonas Black had been exposed.

Out of instinct, Katherine reached for her gun and cursed when she remembered that Almeida had taken it and she had yet to obtain a replacement.

Jonas continued to pound his fists against the dirt and hadn't seemed to recognize her presence. Looking over her shoulder, Katherine saw that Munroe was standing near a hard-topped brown jeep that bore some generic green and white logo. It was probably something used by the security staff. If she and Munroe could get inside the jeep, they could drive away and let the effects of the drug on Jonas wear off. Or, at the very least, they could lock the doors and hide.

Moving as slowly as possible, she stepped away from Jonas. She tried to keep her breathing under control, but she knew all too well what would happen if he saw her. The photos of the crime scene in John Corrigan's house flashed before her eyes. Would that be her fate? Torn apart, beaten to death by a madman.

Her heart rate spiked with every step backward, but every movement also brought her closer to safety.

Almost there, just a couple more feet.

Munroe had already opened the door and climbed into the cab. Katherine resisted the urge to rush the last step.

Jonas Black's head abruptly jerked toward her. She froze. Every muscle in her body trembled. As she looked into his eyes, she knew that Jonas – the man she had grown to care about – was gone and something else had replaced him. Some primitive evil that dwelled in the souls of all men had sprung to the surface and seized control.

He leapt forward. Katherine screamed and jumped up into the driver's seat of the jeep. Her hands fumbled over the steering column, but the keys weren't in the ignition. Changing tactics, she slammed down the lock, sealing out the thing that Jonas Black had become.

But the big man was on his feet and charging. He lowered his shoulder and slammed into the door panel. The whole vehicle shook from the impact. He clawed at the handle and then slammed his shoulder into the door again. Except that this time, the window took the brunt of the attack and shattered inward under his weight.

Katherine screamed again and reached across Munroe to open the passenger-side door. Jonas Black pushed his body up and partway through the window. His fingernails dug into Katherine's back as he clawed at her like a wild beast. She pushed Munroe out the door and then fell on top of him.

Quickly regaining her feet, she dragged Munroe up from the dirt and pulled him toward the surrounding trees.

She looked back to see Jonas pulling his entire large frame through the window of the jeep, scratching and clawing his way after them.

Within a few seconds, they entered the forest, but the sound of Jonas Black tearing the jeep apart urged Katherine forward. They had to keep going. They had to get as far away as possible and then hide. They couldn't fight the massive former Recon Marine, especially in his present crazed subhuman state.

Munroe stumbled over the uneven terrain, but Katherine kept him on his feet as she pulled him deeper beneath the dark canopy. The moon was hiding that night, and dark clouds blotted out the stars, providing almost no light.

The deeper they traveled into the trees, the darker it became. The thick canopy choked out the light and left Katherine barely able to see a foot in front of her face. She pulled Munroe to the side and said, "We need to find a place to hide."

Behind them, the sound of large feet crashing through the brush echoed over the rises and falls of the forest floor.

Jonas Black was coming for them.

89

Katherine pulled Munroe over fallen trees, up rises, down hills, deeper into the wilderness of the refuge. Then he stumbled and toppled forward, taking her down to the moist ground with him. "Enough," he said finally. "We can't outrun him."

"What else can we do? We need to keep moving or find a place to hide."

Munroe quickly analyzed their situation. Jonas Black obviously had strength and ferocity on his side, but the big man had also lost all capacity for rational thought. They could hide, but he was right on their tails. More than likely, he'd pass right by them, but what if he didn't? If he found them, they would be defenseless. As in any battle, they needed to exploit their opponent's weaknesses and utilize their strengths. So what advantage did they have over their enemy?

"How dark is it?" Munroe asked.

"Like coal. I can barely see shadowy outlines of the trees. But we don't have time—"

"Perfect. I want you to leave me. Run ahead a bit and find a place to hide. Make some noise and draw him to you. I'll ambush him."

"Are you out of your head? He'll tear you apart!"

"Not in the darkness. Our large friend is essentially just as blind as I am. Except that I'm used to it, which gives me the advantage."

90

Annabelle stepped down the steps from the dining terrace of the Hill Crest Golf Course and Resort, the only golf course between I-95 and I-395, and moved back toward the GTO. The sound of music and laughter traveled around the veranda from the facility's ballroom. She took a deep breath and inhaled the scent of freshly cut grass mixed with the searing aromas of prime rib. Expensive automobiles filled the parking lot, and the resort's condos and suites were nearly at capacity.

She dropped into the driver's seat of Joey's car, feeling dejected and overwhelmed. "Anything?" Corrigan said from the passenger seat.

"No. I pushed them, but I didn't see anything out of the ordinary. Plus, even if the cartel was involved with this place, they wouldn't bury the kids here. There's too much activity. Too many people. There are probably judges and lawyers and cops in there drinking and partying right now."

"Sometimes the best place to hide is right out in the open. It's the last place you look. Maybe Munroe's contacts at the DEA would know something about this place?"

Annabelle's voice cracked as she said, "Maybe." She white-knuckled the steering wheel, and the tears she had been fighting back for hours broke free and poured down her cheeks. She loved Makayla and Chloe like they were her own flesh and blood, and Deacon would never recover if they didn't find the girls. Their loss would be more than he could handle. It would end him. The people she loved most in the world were counting on her, and she had failed them.

"I'm sorry," Corrigan said. "This is all my fault."

Annabelle wiped away the tears. "You're as much a victim in this as anyone."

"If I had been a better father, none of this would have happened. My family would be alive, and Black's nephew and Munroe's daughters would be home safe right now. You know, I was ready for my execution. I was ready to see my family again."

Annabelle didn't know what to say. How could she comfort a man who had held the bloody bodies of his children, knowing that they had died by his hand?

She pulled out her phone and texted Joey the results of her inquiries at the golf course. She asked him to let Deacon know. He would be expecting a call from her, but she couldn't stand to hear the pain in his voice.

Without another word to Corrigan, she shifted the GTO into gear and pulled away from the parking lot.

~~*~~

Ramon Castillo watched the security feed as the black muscle car rolled away from the resort. It didn't seem that the agent suspected anything, but that could have been a ruse. And the fact that she had come so close was extremely troubling. He wondered what else they knew. Did the government know what was coming?

One of his men shifted anxiously from one leg to the other as he stood in the corner of the room awaiting orders. Castillo calculated the risks and weighed the options as he would for any other business decision.

"Bring my car around to the back. I'm going into the city."

"What about those two?"

"Go after them. Find out what they know, and then kill them."

91

Wielding a fallen log as a weapon, Deacon Munroe crouched low behind a tree and waited. He wished that he had brought his fold-out white cane, but he had left it back in the vehicle. When in its folded state, it could be used as quite a nasty little club.

The sounds of the forest surrounded him, the chirping and croaking and humming of a hundred thousand small creatures. Being in the woods reminded him of playing hide-and-seek with Gerald among the trees and dilapidated outbuildings of the family plantation. Gerald had mastered the art of hiding. He was fearless. Once, Munroe had searched for hours and finally given up, declaring Gerald the winner. He had heard Gerald laugh from somewhere above and had looked up into the rafters of the old barn. Gerald had climbed into the braces and hung there like a monkey, laughing his head off.

Many of the noises ceased as Jonas Black came closer. The big man's pace had slowed from exertion, but he still sounded like a rhino crashing through the brush.

Munroe heard another sound through the trees, maybe fifty feet away. A rhythmic banging. Katherine making noise as he had instructed.

Experience had taught him to gauge distance accurately from

sound, and the crunching of dried leaves betrayed Jonas Black's exact location.

Munroe stepped out from behind the tree, took a deep breath, and swung the log at his pursuer's head. The heavy club sliced through the air and struck something hard.

Too hard. It didn't give like flesh. He must have accidentally struck a tree. The impact sent pulses of pain through Munroe's forearms. The log snapped and dropped from his grasp.

And then Jonas Black was on top of him, howling insanely. The big man pounded Munroe with the ferocity of a gorilla, not with precise punches but with wild flailing movements. Munroe felt himself float upward as his attacker hefted him over his head and tossed him through the air.

He landed on the moist ground and rolled down a slope. He heard Jonas raging after him. Scrambling to his feet, Munroe stumbled through the darkness. His instinct was to run but knew that would lead to his death. Instead, he found another tree and slipped behind it.

Jonas stumbled and rolled down the slope after him like a wild beast. But then, unable to locate his prey, the big man's hysteria peaked, and he everything around him.

If he wasn't stopped soon, he would either kill one – or both – of them or cause terrible injuries to himself. Munroe knew that he had to be subdued, and it was up to him to accomplish the task.

Heart pounding, Munroe waited for the right moment. He gauged the big man's location from his heavy breathing and the sound of his pounding combat boots. Jonas moved past Munroe who jumped out from his hiding spot and leaped onto his opponent's back. He snaked his arms around Jonas Black's throat in a chokehold.

His feet left the ground as the big man thrashed wildly through the trees.

Ethan Cross

Munroe held firm, squeezing tightly around the other man's muscular neck as he was thrown back and forth like a rag doll. Finally, he wrapped his legs around his assailant's enormous frame and locked his ankles together.

Jonas Black ran in circles and slammed his back into the trees, trying to shake off his attacker. Pain shot down Munroe's spine with each impact as branches ripped his skin. But Munroe refused to let go, and after a moment, Jonas finally relented. Defeated, the big man fell to his knees and slipped into unconsciousness.

92

Annabelle barely paid attention to the dark and lonely roadway as it stretched out ahead of her. Her mind was elsewhere. She couldn't shake a memory of Munroe's girls when they were young. Chloe dressed up like a princess and giggling with delight. Makayla scowling in disapproval. Deacon sitting cross-legged on the floor in front of a miniature pink table with a multitude of brightly colored barrettes in his short hair.

A large Dodge Ram truck sped past the GTO, and as it merged back into the right lane, its headlights illuminated a blue sign that read *Hill Crest Landfill – Construction/Demolition Debris Only*.

Annabelle's eyes immediately shot to the right. Another vehicle came up quickly behind her, and its beams cast a pale glow out over the massive open area filled with mounds of dirt, construction equipment, and huge concrete cylinders. Everything clicked into place. The girls were out there somewhere, beneath that ground. She could feel it in her bones.

She fumbled to pull out her cell phone and call Deacon to let him know of her discovery. She glanced down to dial – and Corrigan yelled, "Look out."

Annabelle looked up to see the red glow of tail lights. The Dodge Ram that had passed her had abruptly locked up its brakes and skidded to the side, blocking the roadway.

Dropping the phone, she slammed down on the GTO's brake pedal. The tires squealed, and the air filled with the stink of burning rubber.

Her eyes flicked to the rearview mirror. The lights behind her and the vehicle attached to them kept coming, showing no signs of stopping.

Annabelle twisted the wheel to the left in an attempt to leave the roadway and get into the ditch, but the maneuver came too late. The vehicle behind her, another Dodge truck, caught the GTO's rear and spun the car in a tight circle. They caught the gravel shoulder, hit the ditch, and rolled over.

Glass, dirt, and rock filled the air around the vehicles as metal twisted and compressed.

Annabelle felt her head strike something hard and solid as the air left her lungs. Then the lights went out.

93

Munroe searched the pockets of Jonas Black's Nomex flight suit and found several pairs of flex cuffs. He used them to tightly secure Jonas's wrists and ankles and then called out to Katherine. Using the light of her phone, now that they weren't being chased, she was able to lead them back to the compound. It was a slow and back-breaking walk as they carried Jonas's unconscious form out of the trees. They stood on each side of him, grasping each other's arms and forming a cradle beneath the unconscious man.

When the lights of the compound came into view and they were clear of the trees, they dropped Jonas roughly to the ground and caught their breath. All in all, the entire operation had been a complete and utter disaster. Almeida had escaped with an extremely dangerous chemical weapon. The HRT members were all probably dead or at least out of commission. And Munroe's daughters and Black's nephew were slowly suffocating in a dark hole.

"What now?" Katherine said, breathing hard.

"Is the chopper still there?"

"Yes."

"Then let's carry Mr. Black over to it."

"Why? What are we going to do when we get him there?"

"We're going to hitch a ride."

~~*~~

After throwing Jonas Black into the rear of the helicopter, Munroe and Katherine climbed inside and approached the pilot. He was young, with blond hair and a pink scar down one cheek. Even with the damage to his face, Katherine thought that he looked like a teenager.

Munroe said, "Get us back to DC."

The pilot looked toward the compound, confusion evident on his face. "I can't do that, sir. I've lost communication with the team and—"

"So call in backup," Munroe interrupted.

"I did. A SWAT team from the Baltimore field office was already getting prepped. They're on the way now."

"Then the situation here's under control. When we're in the air, you can call and tell them to go in with tasers or other non-lethal weapons. The six men from your team have been exposed to a chemical weapon and will have to be subdued. And we need to get into the air and back to the city – or that same weapon will be released against the US Capitol Building."

Part Seven

94

After switching vehicles, the three men exchanged their tactical gear for tailored suits and headed into the heart of Washington, DC. Almeida knew that he should have been pleased. They had the weapon, and their goal was in reach. But the black case that Miguel had retrieved from the research facility still bothered him.

Unable to hold back the question any longer, he pulled out his cell phone and dialed the number for Ramon Castillo's disposable phone. Castillo greeted him warmly and asked for an update. Almeida told him of their progress, but finally he said, "Miguel retrieved the black case for you."

Castillo hesitated. "I know. I should have told you about it. It's not that I don't trust you."

"Then what is it?"

"Miguel and I have another mission to complete. I just didn't want to distract you from your own assignment. He's going to tell you to drop him off at a location away from the Capitol. Please do as he asks."

"What is this other mission?"

"I don't want to say over the phone. We'll talk about it when we regroup after our victory is complete. Trust me, my friend."

"Of course, Vaquero. When we speak again, the American system of government will be in chaos."

Almeida hung up the phone, but despite Castillo's assurances, he knew that something was very wrong.

95

Inside the FBI Director's private bathroom located on the seventh floor of the J. Edgar Hoover Building, Jonas Black splashed water over his face and popped two more Tylenol into his mouth, although he probably should have been in a hospital. The headache wouldn't let up, and he hurt all over. But, thankfully, he hadn't broken any bones, and he hadn't hurt anyone else – at least, not permanently. Things could have gone much worse.

He checked his watch and gritted his teeth. In just a few hours, the kids would run out of air. They had let Almeida escape again, and Annabelle's last report had told them that Munroe's latest idea about a golf course had proved futile.

Even with the door to the bathroom shut, he could hear Munroe arguing with the others. After one last splash of water, Jonas slipped his leather jacket over the filthy T-shirt that he had worn under the Nomex flight suit and stepped back into the fray.

"I'm telling you, this is his target," Munroe said.

Dark cherry desks and tables and brown leather couches and chairs sat atop a cream-colored carpet. The wood-paneled walls matched the cherry color of the furniture and gave the room a cultured but dark ambience. The other three men and women sitting around the conference table – including FBI Director

David Cortez, Director of the Secret Service Peter Hulett, and the Secretary of Homeland Security Linda D'Addario – didn't seem convinced by Munroe's arguments.

"You have no actionable intel to suggest that he even intends to attack, let alone what the target will be," said Cortez, a short black man with wire-framed glasses and a bookish appearance.

"Think about it. A man who has made claims of this being a war started by our government is now in possession of a chemical weapon. And you think that it's a coincidence that all this happens the same day that the US Senate is about to enact a new bill declaring several of the Mexican cartels, including the Castillo Cartel, as foreign terrorist organizations."

The new legislation allowed the US government to take the fight against the cartels to a whole new level and gave law enforcement in the United States enhanced tools to combat those groups. Among other things, it permitted the government to freeze money tied to the cartels and enhanced the criminal penalties against those found to be aiding them. It also made it much easier for the US military to take full-scale action.

Director Hulett ran a hand through his gray hair and said, "So, on your hunch, you want us to shut down the US Capitol Building and evacuate the Senate?"

Munroe didn't flinch. "That's right. There's also a major event taking place on the National Mall today. I heard something about it on the radio. I'd like you to cancel that as well, just in case."

"I thought you said he wouldn't attack a civilian target?"

"I don't believe he will."

Director Cortez shook his head and sighed. "It can't be done, Munroe."

Leaning against the bathroom door frame, Jonas Black spoke up. "I know first-hand how dangerous this weapon can be, and if you don't do something to stop it, C-Span is going to be broadcasting a bloodbath."

Linda D'Addario looked more like a second-grade teacher than the head of a government agency with a budget of nearly fifty billion dollars. She pursed her lips and said, "We understand your concerns, and we don't doubt the serious threat that this weapon poses. However, the US is a constant target. We receive threats all the time with more substantiated evidence than this. We can't just shut down the government because the facts suggest that an attack *might* be coming. If we did, our government would cease to function."

"You can't just ignore this threat," Munroe said.

Cortez responded first. "We're not ignoring anything. Security around the Capitol is on high alert. All our agencies are out in full force. Plain-clothes agents have been positioned around the Capitol and the surrounding blocks. We've distributed Almeida's picture. If this man comes within a thousand yards of the Capitol, we'll nail him."

"It won't be enough."

Linda D'Addario said, "Listen, Agent Munroe, we're doing all that we can. We all know about the situation with your daughters and our hearts go out to you. We know how bad you want to catch this guy. But we can't rush major decisions such as this based on emotions and gut feelings. We—"

Munroe gave a terse nod and stood. "Very well, I appreciate your time. But I would like my suggestions and concerns on this matter noted officially. Mr. Black, it's time for us to go."

~~*~~

Katherine had cleaned up as best she could in a public bathroom and then waited in the lobby while Munroe and Jonas tried to convince the bureaucrats to take action. She didn't expect that they'd succeed. The directors of the agencies usually didn't work their way up from the bottom like any other organization. These men and women were political appointees, and shutting down Congress wouldn't be good politics.

Jonas appeared around the corner with Munroe in tow, and she stood to greet them. "Well? Any luck?"

Munroe said, "They've beefed up security around the Capitol, but I don't think it will be enough."

"I told you. Those people are political animals. If they evacuate and they're wrong, it would derail their careers."

Munroe stiffened. "Derail," he said softly. He grabbed the phone from his pocket, held a button, and issued the voice command "Call Joey."

Munroe had contacted the computer genius earlier from the chopper and ordered him to the facility near Fort Meade. He wanted Joey to get into the laboratory's server and find out whatever he could, while the FBI went through any physical files or manifests. Unfortunately, Almeida had used an electromagnetic device to fry the server once he had retrieved the digital files for himself.

Katherine listened intently to Munroe's one-sided conversation. "Joey, I need you to do something for me. Can you hack in and retrieve the schedules for all the Senators and their chiefs of staff for this morning? . . . No, it's not treason. Use somebody from my father's office, if you need to . . . Okay, once you're in, I want you to find out if any of them have meetings with a constituent. Anyone from a business, interest group, campaign donor. Then check out who those people really are. We're looking for someone who's not who they claim to be. Hurry, we don't have much time."

When Munroe hung up, he said, "I need the two of you to get to the Senate office buildings. I'll stay here and coordinate. I'd just slow you down."

"Why? What are you thinking?" Jonas asked.

"My father's office is in the Hart Building. Katherine reminded me of that place when she said 'derail.' There's a special train just for the Senators and their staff that transports them underground from their offices to the Capitol Building. Most of the Senators will be taking that train today. Imagine if someone placed those motion-sensor dispersal units in the train cars or in the hallway leading up from the train."

Katherine followed his logic. "Of course, security will be thinking that they'll try to do something while the Senate's in session, in order to expose all of them to the weapon at once. But you wouldn't have to do it that way. Jonas said that it took several minutes before the madness had fully set in. That may even depend on dosage, and maybe they can adjust that on the dispersal devices."

"Which means that each Senator could be exposed while riding the train and not even know it. A bunch of ticking time bombs."

96

Jonas Black and Katherine sprinted up to the Hart Senate Office Building, the newest of the Senate structures. It had been designed with a contemporary look and a white marble facade that matched the older structures surrounding it. Immediately inside the door sat a metal detector and security checkpoint manned by three guards. Knowing that the replacement PT845 that Tobi Savoy had provided would set off the detector, Jonas displayed his DCIS credentials while Katherine flashed her NCIS creds. To the guards, he said, "We're here on a matter of national security."

The first guard, a man with a linebacker's build, looked him up and down, examining the filthy clothes and bruised and bloody face. Jonas shrugged. "Casual Friday." Then he held up a picture of Almeida. "Has this guy been through here?"

"No, I haven't seen him. But wait here a minute – I think I should call this in."

Katherine stepped up and glared into the man's face. "We have reason to believe that there is an imminent chemical-weapon attack happening right under your nose. You call whoever you want, but you need to let us in there right now."

The linebacker blinked rapidly and then stepped aside.

They sprinted around the corner toward a bank of elevators

to the right of the entrance. The open-air marble interior of the building shone brightly with natural light from massive skylights high above them. A giant black metal sculpture filled the lobby area and rose all the way to the the top floor.

"What room did he say?" Katherine asked.

"703." Munroe had called while they were en route with the discovery that a Texas Senator's chief of staff had scheduled a private tour of the Capitol building with a wealthy campaign donor.

They stepped into the elevator with a group of high-school students wearing oversized suits and bright red ties. The kids eyed Jonas cautiously. He tapped the button for the seventh floor and frowned impatiently as the elevator started its slow ascent. He ignored the high-school kids, who were still staring at his filthy beaten-up form.

The doors hadn't even opened all the way at the seventh floor when Jonas and Katherine bounded out and sprinted around the open-air walkway to Room 703. A Texas flag rested beside the door of a glass-fronted reception area. Pictures of Texas scenery and wildlife adorned the walls. A twenty-something girl with short brown hair and glasses sat behind a walnut reception desk. "Can I help you?" she asked in a perky high-pitched voice.

Jonas didn't bother with pleasantries. He just flashed his ID. "The Senator's chief of staff. Where is he?"

The girl's face turned ashen. "He just left for the Capitol Building."

97

Munroe sat on a stone bench in the corner of the J. Edgar Hoover Building's lobby. Leg bouncing nervously. Arms crossed. Phone clutched in his right hand. Waiting. He tried to consider all the angles. He thought of Almeida and the weapon. The attacks. The kids, slowly suffocating. But there wasn't anything he could do until he received word from his team. He was at the mercy of others, and it was killing him.

Finally, his phone rang. The distinctive ringtone told him that it was Joey. "Were you able to access the server?"

Joey said, "I'm still working on it, but they nuked the drives. We may not get anything. That's not why I called."

"What did you find?"

"They fried the server for the database and research files, but the security system runs off a totally different box. That server's fine, and so I was able to access the camera records and see how Almeida and his men escaped and what they stole."

"And?"

"They made off with the data files, a bunch of those small dispersal units, and a big black case. I had no idea what was in there, but I saw that they took it out of one of the back rooms, and so I checked it out. Luckily, there were more of them back there. The case contained a hand-launchable SUAV. Kind of like a RQ-11 Raven, but with a lot of design changes. It has tanks and a spraying apparatus more like the Yamaha RMAX."

Munroe said, "You lost me."

"Unmanned Aerial Vehicle. It's a small drone plane. But think of this one as one part really expensive high-tech remote-control plane and one part crop duster."

The implications became clear. The researchers had created a device to distribute the weaponized compound over a base or population center or even a crowd of people. "Joey, I've been out of the loop lately with all that's been happening. Remind me what event is taking place on the National Mall today?"

"It's the dedication ceremony for the new education center of the Vietnam War Memorial. But the big draw is that they expanded the center to include photos and stories of and tributes to service members killed in Iraq and Afghanistan and even other wars. So the dedication is kind of a big veteran event that's drawn soldiers and their families from all over the country. They have all kinds of activities and things for the kids and—"

"Did you hear anything on the number of people they expect to attend?"

"I think the news said that it's supposed to be close to double the turnout of those anti-war protests back in 2002 and 2003. I could look those numbers up for you, if you want."

Munroe took a deep breath and said, "No need – I remember those days. The protesters numbered in the hundreds of thousands."

98

Oliver Pike, dressed in an expensive suit and sporting a fake beard, smiled and accepted the visitor badge from the Senator's chief of staff. The rows of fluorescent lighting above their heads hummed and reflected brightly off the smooth concrete floors and bare white walls. He glanced over his shoulder at the train tracks and the chrome and glass loading area. Small wooden signs on poles dotted the space, each labeled with phrases like "No Running" and "Do Not Hold Doors." Beyond the loading doors, the tracks extended down a well-lit tunnel that curved off toward the Capitol.

A pair of security desks manned by three guards sat opposite the loading area. To Pike, a guard said, "Sir, please remove everything from your pockets and place the contents on the desk."

Pike rummaged through the pockets of his suit jacket and pants, and placed the items on top of the desk – wallet, cell phone, three packs of cigarettes, lighter, and Tic Tacs. The guard ran a scanning wand that was designed to detect the presence of explosives or known toxins, as well as the DNA of selected bacteria and viruses, over the items.

The tests came back negative, as Pike had expected, but the thing that amazed him was that the guards didn't actually search him to be sure that he had placed all the items on his person atop the desk. He could have had a bag full of anthrax in his coat and still walked right through.

With the test complete, he placed the innocuous-seeming dispersal devices back into his pockets. His mission would be simple. No one would notice or worry about a pack of cigarettes or a cell phone sitting on a table or on a seat on the train. The devices were a work of genius. They even had timers for the activation of the motion sensors and controls for the dosage levels. He could set them and be well away before they activated and could configure the level of exposure to ensure that the maximum number of Senators and staff would be affected.

As they stood in front of the sliding glass doors of the loading area, Pike heard the whir of the onrushing train. The Senator's chief of staff droned on about the train and the building and thanked him for his company's generous contributions. Pike smiled and nodded at the appropriate times, but his focus was on the mission. Initially, this was to have been a two-man operation, but at the last minute Almeida had decided to send Pike alone, with an extra bonus added to his payment – which suited him just fine.

He could see the small train approaching. An hour from now, he would be safely away – and the US Senate would literally be torn apart.

99

As Jonas Black sprinted down the concrete ramp leading to the Senator's train; he saw two men standing near the loading area. The small blue and white train was gliding down the bright tunnel ahead. In another few seconds, it would be docked and accepting passengers. Pulling his gun, he shouted to the guards, "Stop those men!"

The guards turn toward him but didn't seem to understand.

Jonas ran faster, leaving Katherine behind and heading straight for the train. The glass doors slid open.

One of the two men grabbed the other and shoved him into Jonas's path, but Jonas didn't slow down. The second man collided with him, but he bulled through the impact, swiping the man out of the way with a raised forearm. Despite the disguise, Jonas recognized the first man as the mercenary who had been working for Almeida.

Jonas took aim, but the man dashed onto the train before Jonas could get off a shot.

The doors began to shut, but, without losing momentum, Jonas turned sideways and slipped through the narrowing opening.

The inside of the train car was small and intimate. Two padded bench seats faced each other, one in the front and one in the back. Each comfortably sat two to three passengers. Less than six feet of standing room separated the two seats.

As Jonas slipped inside, he lowered his shoulder to tackle the other man, but the terrorist sidestepped and used Jonas's impetus against him. The man shoved him against the glass on the car's far side. His head struck the window, and pain shot down the length of his body.

The train pulled away from the station and rocketed through the underground tube toward the US Capitol Building.

Ignoring the pain, he whirled around and raised his gun, but his opponent was ready. Jonas fired twice, but the other man caught his arm and redirected the shots through the glass door of the train. The smaller man twisted back his wrist, and Jonas involuntarily dropped his pistol.

The mercenary moved with the speed and agility of an expert in hand-to-hand combat. They exchanged blows in quick blurs of motion, but Jonas couldn't deflect the man's rapid thrusts and open-palmed strikes. He was too fast.

Changing tactics, Jonas used his superior weight against the smaller man. He thrust his whole body forward, slamming the other man back against the train's glass doors which had already started to show spiderweb cracks radiating out from each bullet hole.

The mercenary recovered quickly, kicked the inside of Jonas's left leg – dropping the big man to one knee – and lunged forward. But Jonas wrapped his attacker in a bear hug and squeezed with all his strength.

The man screamed.

Jonas felt ribs separating and cracking.

But then the mercenary landed a headbutt. The blow succeeded in headbutt loosening Jonas's grip enough for the man to pull one arm free. He grabbed the side of Jonas's head and started to jam a thumb into his eye socket.

Reacting on instinct, Jonas lifted the mercenary's smaller frame and threw the man away from him as hard as he could. The man struck the car's door again, but this time the glass gave way.

Tiny shards flying out all around him, the man careened backward out of the opening and, with a wet thud, slammed into one of the tunnel's pillars.

100

Deacon Munroe couldn't believe this was happening. His daughters were running out of time, and the nation was possibly on the verge of the worst terrorist attack in the history of the world, one that could destroy the US government and Washington, DC as they knew it. He felt helpless to stop the attack and powerless to save those he loved.

As his mind raced for answers, he asked Joey, "This drone could be launched from anywhere, right? But could we track it? Shoot it down somehow?"

"Actually, that's the good news."

"We could use some of that."

"These SUAVs aren't fully functional. From what I can see, it looks like they were just using the basic design to test the dispersal mechanism. They're not even equipped with the typical camera-and-computer-based controls. It just has a rudimentary joystick system."

"Okay, what does that tell us?"

"It means that they'll have to control the drone with actual visual contact. Like you would a remote-control plane."

Munroe considered this and said, "You're saying that they'll need to be close. They can't be on the actual mall. Security will be too tight. So they'll have to be somewhere high up. A vantage point

341

tall enough to visually control the UAV as it sweeps over the crowd."

"Exactly, but most of the buildings around there are government facilities or museums. They're not very tall and access would be tricky."

"It would have to be somewhere public," Munroe agreed. "Somewhere full of people where they could blend in and sneak around or even pose as police or maintenance staff and reach a rooftop."

The line went quiet as they both searched desperately for possibilities.

Think, dammit. Think.

Then Joey said, "What about the Old Post Office Pavilion? It's a shopping center now, and its old clock tower is used as a public viewing platform."

Munroe analyzed the facility as if he were planning such an attack. Lots of people to blend in with, but not overcrowded. Low security. Easy access to the roof, upper floors, and a high vantage point. Connected to a Metro station for a quick escape. It was the perfect location.

He said, "I think you may be right, Joey. Get in touch with Black and Katherine. Tell them to meet me on the roof of the Old Post Office immediately."

"What are you going to do?"

"I'm less than a block away from that place right now. I'm going to check it out."

"By yourself?"

"I think I know where I might be able to find some help. Just get in touch with Black."

Munroe hung up the phone and then stepped into the center of the FBI lobby. He heard the sound of footsteps and the low chatter of people on their way to their offices. "Excuse me!" he shouted. "Is anyone here a field agent?"

101

When the Senator's train stopped, five armed guards greeted Jonas Black. He held up his hands and said, "Take it easy, boys. We're all on the same team." He showed his ID, but they didn't seem convinced. A concrete walkway that allowed staff members to walk the distance to the Capitol if they wished followed the train tracks back to the Senate offices. Katherine sprinted down the tunnel, forced to take the long way. When she arrived, she helped calm the fears of the guards and convince them of the true threat.

The situation defused, Jonas retrieved his gun from the floor of the train car. He hadn't even caught his breath when Katherine said, "I just got a call from your friend Joey. He said they're going to hit the event on the National Mall. Munroe needs us at the Old Post Office."

Jonas ejected the magazine of his PT845 pistol, checked the remaining ammo, and inserted a fresh mag. He said, "What's the quickest way to get there?"

102

With the help of two FBI special agents whom he had recruited as they were walking through the lobby, Munroe made his way to the Old Post Office Pavilion, which sat just across Pennsylvania Avenue from the J. Edgar Hoover Building. Under his direction, the agents guided Munroe to the elevator leading up to the building's top floor and the public viewing area inside the old clock tower. He remembered that a man in a glass booth who took the money for tickets also controlled the elevator. To the ticket taker, he said, "Have you seen anyone come through here carrying a large case?"

"Yeah, a couple of maintenance guys. They headed up to nine. Said they needed to fix one of the air-conditioning units on the roof."

"Activate the elevator and get us up there now."

"What's this about?"

"Now!"

Before the elevator arrived, one of the agents said, "Please wait here, Agent Munroe. We'll check it out."

The elevator dinged open, and Munroe stepped toward the sound. When the resonance of the sounds changed, he knew that he was inside the elevator. He felt the stares of the agents upon him. "I'm not sitting on the sidelines this time."

Neither man protested. They simply pressed the button to go to the top of the building. When they arrived, they helped Munroe down the corridor to the roof access.

He felt the change in pressure and sound as they stepped into open air. The cool breeze swept over him, and the sunlight warmed his face. The hot sun caused the roof to smell of oil and asphalt. The space hummed with the industrial sounds of air conditioners and other exhaust vents and spinning fans.

The agents led him forward, but then his helper pushed him down next to the metal surface of one of the air conditioners. "Stay here and be quiet. I think there's someone up ahead. We're going to take a look."

Munroe's heart pounded, and he suddenly felt weak and exposed. The unfamiliar surroundings, pungent smells, and loud droning sounds overwhelmed him.

He listened carefully as the agents left him and moved across the roof. He strained to hear, but the humming of the air conditioners was so loud that it blocked out all the other sounds. Or maybe the agents just weren't making any noise. Then, in the distance, he heard one of them shout, "Don't move! Put your hands behind your heads!"

Munroe released a deep, calming breath. He didn't hear any gunshots, just the agents shouting more orders. They seemed to have the situation under control. Castillo's plot had been thwarted.

Then a voice said, "Hello, Munroe. Wait here. I need to take care of something, and then I'll be back to deal with you."

Munroe's hope faded as he recognized the gravelly South American accent of Antonio de Almeida.

103

Suspecting the terrible attack that was Ramon Castillo's true goal, Almeida had slipped a tracker into Miguel's pocket and followed him to his rendezvous with Castillo himself. The two men had changed into the blue jumpsuits of maintenance workers and had carried the black case into the Old Post Office Pavilion. Almeida didn't follow them to the rooftop immediately as he considered how to proceed. He stood near the railing that overlooked the mall's food court and watched the laughing families and smiling children. Castillo had saved him from the streets and the terrible suffering that accompanied that life. Vaquero had raised him up to a position of respect and had become his mentor and adopted father. Almeida couldn't betray that trust, that love. But how could God ever forgive him if he let such a terrible atrocity take place?

When he saw Deacon Munroe enter with two black-suited men, his decision was made for him. Somehow Munroe had deduced the truth and the location of the attack. The agents would probably surprise Miguel and Castillo and put an end to the attack, but Almeida could never allow his adopted father to be captured. His intense love and loyalty for Vaquero drove him to act.

He followed the three Americans to the rooftop and watched

as the two agents left Munroe and took Castillo and Miguel into custody.

The glass of a massive skylight filled most of the roof, but oily rock and large metal extrusions covered the rest of the roof's surface. Almeida navigated around the obstructions, and after greeting Munroe – whom he had come to respect as an adversary – he glided up silently behind the FBI agents and shot them both in the head.

Castillo's eyes went wide with shock at the sight of him. "Antonio, what are you doing here?"

Gesturing toward the dead men, Almeida said, "I thought you might need some help. It looks like I was correct."

"But you should be at the Capitol."

"I sent Pike. He's a capable and resourceful man. You lied to me, Vaquero. Your goal was never to stop the passage of the bill or to make the American politicians pay for interfering in our business and waging war against us."

Castillo turned to Miguel. "Continue the preparations." Then, looking toward the National Mall, the cartel boss stroked his beard and said, "You're right. This was always my plan, Antonio. I admire you. Your innocence. But the time for restraint and mercy is over. I had hoped to discuss all this with you once the wheels of progress were already set in motion, but here we are. This is just the beginning. We already have forces stationed in every corner of this country. The men who sell our drugs and control our business interests on this side of the border. We'll provide those assets with this new weapon, which they'll release at strategic targets in every city across the nation."

"But that's not what we had discussed. You agreed that there was no reason for innocent people to suffer. That the politicians were responsible and would be the ones to pay. Killing women and children will not bring back your family."

Castillo backhanded Almeida across the face. "Don't speak to me like I'm some common fool. Trust of their government in America is at an all-time low. We will supply the drug, Focus, to America's enemies, and at the same time, we will cause the nation's people to doubt that their government can protect them. The sharks of this world will smell blood in the water, and they will come. What we set in motion here today will lead to the downfall of the United States. They may not crumble completely, but they will never be the same. They will be weak and more easily controlled. Don't you see, Antonio? If we kill their leaders, the people will mourn them. But six months from now, other tyrants will have replaced the current regime, and the cycle will repeat. But they'll remember when I burn this city to the ground. We won't let them forget because another attack will follow. And another. And another."

Castillo grasped Almeida's shoulder and leaned in close. "You've been like a son to me, and I have no other sons left. They've stolen them from me. I need you. You're my general. I need you by my side."

Tears formed in Almeida's eyes, but he held them back. Swallowing down the last doubts of what he must do, he said, "I'll always be by your side, Vaquero. Tell me what to do. If this is the start of the war, I want to fire the first shot. I want to initiate the attack."

Castillo beamed with pride as he squeezed Almeida's shoulder again and gave it a reassuring shake. "I'm so glad to hear you say that." He reached into the black case and handed Almeida a small but sophisticated control device. "Take this up to the clock tower. We'll launch the drone from here, and then it will be up to you to guide it over the National Mall and drop the payload." He indicated a switch covered with a red safety cap. "Just flip this switch, and the world will never be the same."

Almeida nodded and then headed back across the roof. He reached the spot where he had left Munroe, but the blind man was gone. Almeida followed the path inside and saw Munroe feeling his way along the railing back toward the elevators. The entire center of the building was open to the air, and Almeida could see the mall and the food court far below. The echoes of the people blended together into an indecipherable buzz of humanity.

Hand over hand, Munroe pulled himself forward, still refusing to give up. Such strength and perseverance. Such determination in the face of adversity. Unfortunately, Almeida knew that these qualities made Munroe too much of a threat to be left alive.

Almeida hated himself for it, but he raised his Glock pistol and fired two shots into Munroe's back. The blind man's body arched with the impacts, and he fell forward onto the carpeted walkway.

People inside the shopping center and ahead in the museum section of the Old Post Office screamed at the sound of gunfire and scattered like sheep.

Saying a quick prayer for the brave man to find peace in the next world, his gun in one hand and the control device in the other, Antonio de Almeida stepped over Munroe's lifeless form and headed toward the clock tower.

104

The Old Post Office Pavilion reminded Jonas Black more of an old cathedral than it did an office building and mall with its Victorian architecture, dormer-covered roof, and massive clock tower. After dodging in and out of DC traffic and sometimes finding his way onto the sidewalks, he finally skidded the forcefully commandeered black Lexus to a stop in front of the historic landmark, earning a tirade of honks from the other drivers. Mall patrons were flooding out beneath the colossal arches marking the building's entrance.

Jonas and Katherine pushed their way through the panicked crowd to gain access to the structure. The nine-story atrium contained shops, offices, and a food court. All of it topped with decorative metal support struts and an enormous skylight. Jonas felt that the naturally lit atrium resembled an old train station.

The shrieks of tourists echoed across the building's black and white checkered floors, and the smell of grease and uneaten food wafted up from the food court on the structure's lower level.

Once inside, they found the elevators and made their way up to the ninth floor, the uppermost level of the building's main section. Joey had filled them in on the nature of the attack, and so Jonas said to Katherine, "You check out the roof. I'll head up to the clock tower."

105

Annabelle awoke with a stabbing pain behind her eyes. Every muscle seemed to ache, and dried blood clogged her nostrils. Her eyes opened, but a veil of black cloth obstructed her vision. She tried to move her arms but found them secured behind her back.

She heard a harsh voice rasp, "I think the *chica* is awake."

The light hurt her eyes as her captors pulled off the hood. They were in some type of machine shed. Tools and workbenches lined the room. Oil stained the floors, and the space smelled of diesel fuel and sawdust.

Corrigan was seated in a chair to Annabelle's left. Duct tape secured his hands to the arms of the chair. His breath came in labored gasps. Blood ran from his left hand and pooled on the floor. Bile rose in Annabelle's throat as she realized that he was missing two fingers.

Two men stood near Corrigan. One was white, with salt-and-pepper hair and the look of a mechanic. The other was handsome, with dark skin and feral eyes like those of a hyena.

The hyena said, "It's about time you joined the party. You've been out for a while. Your friend here is stubborn. He just keeps repeating his name and rank. But I think you and I will get along much better."

He walked over and caressed a curly strand of Annabelle's hair. She cringed involuntarily and turned her head away from him. He stroked her cheek and licked his lips with a sickening hunger. He said, "Yes, you and I are going to be very friendly."

The hyena cupped one of her breasts. Annabelle pulled back but could do nothing to halt his advances. The other man said, "Hey, we're supposed to find out what she knows, not rape her."

The hyena smiled. "I didn't hear anyone say that we couldn't have a little fun with her. Don't worry, she'll be ready to tell us everything soon. Won't you, *chica*?"

"Almeida wouldn't approve of this," the white man said.

"Too bad that he's not here. If you don't have the *cojones*, you can step outside."

The other man looked at Annabelle for a few seconds. She met his gaze and pleaded with her eyes. But then he lowered his head and moved to the door.

The hyena pulled out a switchblade and pressed it against her throat. He bent down close to her ear. Annabelle could feel his hot breath on her neck. He smelled of cigarettes and expensive cologne.

He whispered, "I hope you like it rough, *chica*."

106

Antonio de Almeida looked out through the safety wires at the top of the old clock tower. He had the entire viewing area to himself, since the tourists had scattered and had been evacuated at the sound of gunfire. It was quiet and calm. A comfortable breeze. A beautiful day.

Looking toward the National Mall, he watched Miguel's small form as the man reared back and launched the drone plane. The control device was rudimentary, with two joysticks that controlled the drone's throttle and its pitch and yaw. Almeida took command of the SUAV easily and guided it toward the target.

He could imagine Castillo's elation and excitement at being so close to his goal. Vaquero's vengeance for his family would be complete within a matter of seconds.

Almeida, on the other hand, felt dead inside.

The prototype plane could not compete with its military counterparts in terms of speed and capabilities, but it was still swift and maneuverable. Almeida expertly guided it over the red-roofed buildings of the EPA and the Andrew W. Mellon Auditorium. Then past the National Museum of American History.

He used the world's tallest stone structure, the Washington

Monument, as a guide. A sea of people surrounded the massive obelisk and stretched past the various war memorials, the Constitution Gardens, and the Reflecting Pool, all the way to the Lincoln Memorial in the far distance.

This was the kill zone, the area where the drone's terrible payload would be unleashed upon the unsuspecting crowd.

Within a matter of minutes, they would turn upon one another, tearing each other apart in an orgy of unbridled fury and pain. A scene straight from the depths of Hell. The affected masses would then spill out into the rest of the city, raising the death toll. Perhaps they would even storm the gates of the White House nearby.

Almeida watched the drone, little more than a dot in the sky, as it drew closer and closer to the target.

All he needed to do was guide the small aircraft to the right, bring it down over the crowd, and flip the switch to release the chemical weapon contained inside. The action would be so simple, and yet so devastating. With the flip of a tiny switch, a basic little plane that could have been constructed in someone's garage would alter the course of history and cause untold pain and suffering.

But Antonio de Almeida didn't guide the plane to the right.

He didn't flip the switch.

Instead, he let the drone fly right past the Washington Monument, over the sea of innocent people, and above the trees bordering the National Mall.

He looked down at Ramon Castillo, the only father he had ever known, as he used his right thumb to push the small joystick forward, causing the drone to pitch down into the blue waters of the Tidal Basin.

107

Corrigan watched with anger and revulsion as the dark-skinned man groped Annabelle, but he didn't bother to protest or bluster. This wasn't the kind of man who could be reasoned with. Instead, Corrigan wanted their captor to forget about him and focus on Annabelle completely.

The man turned his back to Corrigan as he slowly popped the buttons off Annabelle's shirt. Being careful not to draw the man's attention, Corrigan lowered his mouth to his right hand and started to tear off the duct tape binding his wrist, using only his teeth.

Annabelle glanced over and saw what he was trying to do. Tears glistened on her cheeks, but he tried with his gaze to tell her to hold on.

Corrigan's body hurt so badly that he could barely concentrate, and he struggled to focus all his strength. His stare was fixed on the gun tucked into the dark-skinned man's waistband. If he could just free his wrist . . .

The tape came loose, and he tore it free violently.

The other man turned around at the sound, surprise and then anger in his eyes.

Corrigan didn't waste time trying to free his left wrist. On adrenalin alone, he shot to his feet and rushed toward their captor, dragging the chair with him.

The other man didn't reach for his gun. Instead, he lunged at Corrigan with his switchblade.

Corrigan didn't care. He ignored the knife completely, focusing only on accomplishing his mission and retrieving the gun.

White tendrils of agony spiked through his midsection as the blade penetrated his skin and tore through his body. He ignored the pain. Nothing could stop his unrelenting push forward.

Their bodies collided, and the dark-skinned man stumbled back.

Corrigan ripped the 9mm Beretta from the rapist's waistband. The man's eyes went wide. Corrigan didn't hesitate. He raised the gun to the man's temple and pulled the trigger.

The rapist crumpled to the ground like a discarded marionette. The door to the shed flew open as the white man rushed inside at the sound of gunfire.

Corrigan shot him twice in the chest, and he fell back into the dirt.

Then, with his final mission complete, Sergeant John Corrigan dropped to his knees. He reached for the blade protruding from his abdomen, but he lacked the strength to pull it free. He fell over onto his side – the chair still attached to his left wrist the only thing keeping him from falling flat on the concrete – and closed his eyes.

He heard a little girl laugh and felt someone holding his hand. Then he released his grip on this world and slipped into the next.

108

As Katherine moved down the carpeted walkway and searched for the roof access, her heart sank when she saw Munroe lying in the center of the path. She rushed forward and slid to a stop beside him. The blind man lay crumpled on his side against the wall.

His dark sunglasses hid any signs of life in his eyes. She couldn't tell if he was breathing.

She reached down to check for a pulse and jumped as he spoke. "I'm not dead yet. Don't worry about me. Get to the clock tower. Stop Almeida."

"Black's on his way there now. He sent me to check the roof. What happened to you?"

"I think that bastard shot me in the back. Luckily, I finally gave in and followed Black's advice to wear the damn Kevlar vest. That big gorilla saved my life, and he wasn't even here. But leave me. Go check the roof. Castillo and another man are out there. Maybe you can stop them before they even launch that drone."

Knowing that Munroe was right and that stopping the attack was the most important thing, Katherine left him behind. But she had only gone a few feet before two wild-eyed Hispanic men emerged from a door ahead, saw her – and raised their weapons.

~~*~~

Antonio de Almeida had betrayed his family and knew that Vaquero would make him pay dearly for it, but he didn't regret his decision. He had done a great many horrible things in his life, but he couldn't be responsible for the deaths of so many innocent people. He was a soldier, not a monster. One day, probably soon, he would stand before God and be judged, and he knew that the Creator would never forgive him for such terrible wickedness. In the end, the approval of his Heavenly Father mattered more to him than that of his earthly one.

At his back, the elevator door dinged and slid open.

He reacted from pure instinct. He raised his Glock pistol, opened fire, and then sprinted for the nearby door that led to the stairwell.

~~*~~

Jonas Black jerked back as bullets clanged against the metal interior of the elevator. He swung out briefly, gun at the ready, and scanned the room. In his vision's periphery, he saw a dark form slip through a door to his left.

Still cautious, he kept an eye out for any more attackers in the viewing area. Finding none, he rushed to the door and pounded down the set of gray concrete stairs that twisted through the clock tower.

Ahead, he heard the escaping footsteps. Around a turn, he caught sight of Almeida and jumped down with reckless abandon, covering four and five steps at a time.

Rust-colored stains dripped down the white walls. A fingerprint-smeared window in the stairwell wall showed the back of the clock's face and the inner workings of the tower's famous bells. Metal catwalks snaked around the interior of the space.

Almeida was just ahead.

Jonas couldn't fire, couldn't risk killing Almeida, knowing that this man could be their only way to find and save the kids.

He dove headlong down the stairs and crashed into the other man.

They pitched forward and rolled into an old white access door. It gave way, and they tumbled out onto the catwalks inside the clock tower. Each man came up swinging.

In the real world, a fight between two trained operatives was swift and violent. No standing back. No assessing the situation. No planning a clever move. Nothing artistic about it. It was instinct born of training and strength and leverage and endurance and a little bit of controlled fury.

They struck each other with expertly placed blows. Almeida kicked Jonas in the knee, nearly cracking the bone. As he stumbled forward, Jonas banged Almeida's head against the catwalk's metal railing.

Jonas wrapped his massive forearm around Almeida's neck and squeezed. He pressed Almeida against the railing. One good push, and the Colombian would topple over the barrier and fall to the sharp metal protrusions of the bell mechanisms thirty feet below.

"Tell me where to find my nephew!" Jonas screamed.

Then a ceramic knife appeared in Almeida's hand as if by magic. He stabbed it into Jonas's thigh and slammed an elbow against the side of his head.

Pain rippled out from Jonas's temple, and white spots dotted his vision. A terrible shooting agony burned down his leg and dropped him to his knees.

Almeida thrust a knee into his face. His vision grew dark, but he refused to go down.

He lashed out and grabbed Almeida's ankle, yanking the other man's feet out from beneath him.

Then Jonas Black clambered over Almeida's body and pounded his opponent with pure, uninhibited rage. He used his size and weight to pin Almeida to the floor, and – with elbows, palms, and fists – he slammed Almeida back against the metal catwalk, over and over.

Finally, when Jonas felt the fight leave his opponent, he grasped the ceramic knife protruding from his thigh. With a yell of agony, he pulled it free, slicing and tearing the skin and muscle. Then he placed the small ceramic blade against Almeida's throat.

"Now. Where are they?"

Through blood-smeared teeth, Almeida said, "I stopped the attack. I couldn't let Vaquero kill all those people."

Jonas hit him again with an elbow. Almeida's face was a bloody mess, and Jonas guessed that he didn't look much better. "Good for you. You want a medal for *not* mass-murdering a bunch of civilians? I'm going to ask you one more time. Where are the kids?"

"Let me go," Almeida whispered.

Jonas hit him again.

"Let me go, and I'll contact you and tell you where to find the container. There's still time to save them. But not enough to interrogate me. Your only choice is to release me."

109

Katherine dragged Munroe into a nearby office as bullets tore apart the walls around them. Without aiming, she raised her gun and returned fire to keep their enemies from surging forward.

She quickly examined their surroundings. A conference room. Calming, neutral tones. A large oak table covered with sophisticated video-conferencing equipment. Modern art hanging from the walls. No exits. Nowhere to go and nowhere to hide.

Pulling Munroe to his feet and yanking him along with her, Katherine rushed to the far end of the conference table, kicked the leather rolling chair out of the way, and crouched below the table's edge. She prayed that the oak surface would stop a bullet.

With her head against the floor, she checked for the sound of onrushing feet, but no one approached.

Apart from their heavy breathing, the room was utterly silent. She waited. Listened.

But no attack came.

"Don't move," she whispered to Munroe.

"I'm not going anywhere."

Standing up with her Glock 19 gripped in her right hand, Katherine blew a stray strand of red hair from her face and moved slowly to the door.

Checking toward the roof access first, she saw no one. Then

she sidestepped to the other side of the door frame and checked in the opposite direction. No one.

Still cautious, Katherine crept out onto the walkway in a low crouch. But the two Hispanic men had vanished.

~~*~~

Jonas Black pressed the ceramic blade tighter against Almeida's throat. The sharp edge dug into the skin and drew a line of blood. He clenched his teeth and fought for a solution. Almeida was right. The Colombian was tough and well trained, and they would never be able to break him before the kids suffocated.

It was an impossible choice.

Release a dangerous terrorist or allow your family to die.

"Even if I let you go, I have no guarantee that you'll tell us where to find them."

Almeida coughed on his own blood as he said, "There are no guarantees in life, Mr. Black. Just calculated risks. But I'm telling you the truth. I want the killing to stop. I can't take it anymore. Do you think that it brings me pleasure, thinking of those children suffocating? Well, it does not. I want a second chance to do something good with my life. To do penance for my sins. If you show me mercy, Mr. Black, you will see your nephew again."

"The police probably have this place surrounded. You'll never escape, whether I let you go or not."

"That is my problem. I have an escape route planned, but if I'm captured, I will still disclose the location."

The knife shook in Jonas's fist. It would be so easy to slit this man's throat. One quick slash and watch his blood flow out of his body and spill through the grating of the catwalk.

But he had no choice. Or did he?

Jonas struck Almeida three times in rapid succession and rolled him over.

362

Then he took his cell phone from his pocket and, covering the movement with another blow, slid the device into the pocket of Almeida's pin-striped suit. Now, when Almeida ran, Joey could track Jonas's cell phone in order to locate the terrorist.

It wasn't a perfect plan, far from it. But at least it was something, and it made Jonas feel better about what he had to do next.

Using the railing, he pulled himself to his feet and limped away from Almeida. "Go. Get out of here. The sooner you're gone, the quicker you can call Joey and tell us where to find the kids."

With great effort, the broken Colombian got to his feet and hobbled across the catwalk toward the stairs.

Jonas seethed as he watched his enemy walk away. He added, "If you cross me on this, there won't be a place in this world where I won't find you."

Almeida didn't look back but said, "I know. You'll see your nephew soon." With those words, he reached the small access door and stepped toward the stairwell.

A gunshot rang out through the clock tower. The loud noise echoed off the metal of the catwalks and the bell and clock mechanisms in a ringing cacophony.

Jonas watched in horror as Almeida fell back against the railing, a bloody hole in his forehead. Then the Colombian toppled over the edge and plummeted through the air. His body struck the bell mechanisms thirty feet below with a resounding clang.

Ramon Castillo and another Hispanic man stepped out from the stairwell. A smoking Walther pistol dangled from Castillo's left fist. The second man covered Jonas with a large black handgun while the cartel leader looked over the edge at Almeida's broken body far below.

"I loved him," Castillo said. "That's why I gave him a quick death." He turned to Jonas. "You will not be so lucky."

Castillo pulled out a Ka-Bar combat knife from his blue

jumpsuit and stepped toward Jonas. The other man kept his pistol trained on him. Jonas tried to pull himself up to his full height, but he couldn't maintain the pressure on his wounded leg. Still, if Castillo thought that killing him would be easy, the kingpin had another thing coming.

He braced himself for the attack, but then two more shots echoed through the inside of the old clock tower. This time, it was Ramon Castillo and his accomplice who fell dead to the floor of the catwalk.

Katherine O'Connell kept her pistol trained on the two men as she stepped through the access door, kicked the guns out of their hands, and checked for pulses.

Jonas said, "Took you long enough."

"There's a Ben and Jerry's down in the food court," Katherine replied. "I stopped to get a sundae. Hope you don't mind."

"You deserve it. When this is over, I'll buy you all the ice cream you can eat."

"Promises, promises. Don't let my size fool you – I can eat a lot."

As he looked over the railing, Jonas said absently, "I believe it."

The brief moment of relief and joy he had felt at having Katherine save him had passed. Now he stared down at the body of Antonio de Almeida and wondered, with their only lead gone, who was going to save the three frightened kids who were slowly dying at that very moment.

110

Munroe remembered taking his daughters and wife to the Old Post Office for lunch once when Makayla and Chloe had still been small. He had heard that the shops and food court would soon be ousted in favor of converting the entire space into a luxury hotel. He hoped that he would be able to take the girls there one last time before the developers defaced the landmark.

Paramedics had set up shop in front of the pavilion and closed off part of Pennsylvania Avenue. Although the medical personnel had patched up both Munroe and Jonas Black, they still wanted to rush them off to the hospital. But neither of them had time to lick their wounds. Not with the kids still in danger.

Even though he had no idea how to find them.

Then Munroe heard a voice shouting his name. Jonas called the man over, and an out-of-breath FBI agent said, "I've been trying to find you. It's about your kids."

~~*~~

The landfill office smelled like stale coffee and ramen noodles. A few old desks, their surfaces chipped from age, and two leather couches sat inside the small trailer. Mounds of paperwork topped each of the desks. A dry-erase calendar board and a large map of the landfill that had been scribbled on in red pen covered one wall.

Two employees, the Operations Supervisor and the secretary, occupied one of the couches, restrained in handcuffs. Two men in blue windbreakers stenciled with the letters *FBI* flanked the frightened workers.

During the chopper ride, Jonas Black had listened as a young FBI agent explained to him and Munroe that they had received a call from Annabelle, and based on her intel, FBI and local SWAT units had mobilized and converged on two businesses – Hill Crest Landfill and Hill Crest Golf Course and Resort. Annabelle was currently being treated for wounds suffered during a car crash, but Jonas intended to thank her properly later. Unfortunately, his friend John Corrigan had sacrificed himself to save Annabelle and the kids, and he would never have the opportunity to thank John for that. But he didn't have time to mourn his friend now. They had more pressing concerns.

Jonas studied the map and said, "This place is huge. Can you give us any idea of where to start?"

The Operations Supervisor, a small blond man who looked like an accountant except for his thin handlebar mustache, said, "I told you. I wasn't involved with anything illegal. I just run the dump. If somebody helped them do this, it wasn't me."

Katherine suggested, "Maybe we could bring in all the workers and find out which one's been working nights?"

Munroe said, "The kids will be dead by that time. We don't care about any of that right now. Sir, we just need any clue that you can give us."

"We've been working mostly in the Southeast Tract. That's probably where they would have done it."

"That's exactly where they *wouldn't* have buried them. They wouldn't want your men digging them up by accident. Is there a section that your employers wanted you to avoid?"

The blond man thought for a moment and said, "They've told us not to work in the top-right quadrant of the Northeast Tract because that bumps up against the golf course, and they don't want the noise from our equipment disturbing the golfers."

"Excellent. Would we see fresh digging?"

"It rained here last night, and that place is really just a big mud-hole. You could tell if something had been dug up if you looked close, but not really from a distance."

"How big is that area?"

"Maybe forty or fifty acres."

Jonas growled in disgust. "Needle in a damn haystack."

"We need to think outside the box," said Munroe. "If traditional methods fail, find an alternative solution. And there are always alternative solutions. Let's take a drive out to the Northeast Tract."

111

The FBI van bumped and rattled its way across the uneven terrain, heading to the Northeast Tract. Jonas Black helped Munroe out of the van, and then the blind man stood and listened as the others piled out and searched the area. "Everyone, shut up and don't move."

The background noises that Munroe had detected in Almeida's video – the clanging metallic sound and the rhythmic *tut-tut-tut* – hadn't helped him to pinpoint a location from a wide geographic area. But now that they had narrowed the search to a very specific region, he hoped that those area-specific sounds could help narrow the search further.

He strained to hear something familiar, something to indicate that they were in the right place. But there was nothing. Maybe he had been wrong. Maybe . . .

A clanging of sheet metal echoed from somewhere in the distance, but it was much farther away than in the video. Munroe pointed in the direction of the noise and said, "Mr. Black, take me to that sound."

Jonas guided him across the rocky, muddy ground, the clanging growing closer and closer as they went. Finally, Munroe said, "Stop. What's making the noise?"

"Looks like a rusty little maintenance shed. A piece of

the corrugated metal siding is torn free and flapping in the wind."

They were close, but Munroe still didn't hear the *tut-tut-tut* sound. "Describe the rest of the area to me."

"It's just kind of a huge open mud-pit," Jonas said. "A lot of grass and weeds covering the surface, showing that they haven't buried anything in this section for a while. Maybe we could get a bunch of volunteers together and walk the tract to see if we can find a spot where the vegetation is disturbed?"

"We don't have the time! We need to narrow down the search. Keep describing."

"There's the old shed, but that's about it. The tract butts up against a line of trees to the east."

"Where's the Operations Supervisor?"

"Right here," the man said from fifteen feet away.

"What's on the other side of those trees? Is that the golf course?"

"That's right."

Munroe listened for the *tut-tut-tut* sound, but it wasn't there. "Take me closer to the trees."

Once there, he stood still again and fought to hear anything familiar. It seemed right. The shape, pitch, and volume of the clanging noise matched. He heard the chirping of insects and birds in the trees. But still no *tut-tut-tut*.

What was he missing? What had changed since the previous evening? What had been different in the video? Then he realized that the time of day was different. It was now early afternoon, and the video had been shot at dusk.

"Ask our FBI friends if they have the groundskeeper for the golf course in custody. If so, get him on the phone."

The sound of Jonas's heavy footsteps moved away quickly, and Munroe heard him speaking with the agents and explaining the situation. Within a few moments, he returned and placed a cell phone in Munroe's palm.

"Is this the groundskeeper?" Munroe said into the receiver.

"That's right. How can I help?"

"Are you doing any extra watering around dusk?"

"Yeah, there's a section of new grass by the trees that I've been giving some extra TLC to. Have the sprinklers there scheduled for dusk and in the middle of the night. Why are—"

"Turn those sprinklers on. Right now."

A few moments later, Munroe heard it. The faint, rhythmic *tut-tut-tut* of a sprinkler system – but it was too far away. He pointed in the direction of the sound and said, "Black, that way!"

He stopped several times and listened, found the nature of the sounds inconsistent in some manner, and moved on. Finally, after they had raced across a few acres, he stopped and said, "This is it! Everyone spread out and look for anything out of the ordinary. Anything to indicate that—"

One of the FBI agents yelled, "Here! This is freshly dug ground!"

~~*~~

Jonas Black watched as the track hoe clawed furiously at the earth, exposing the metal shipping container. Munroe had found the kids. Jonas still couldn't wrap his mind around *how* Munroe had accomplished it, but in that moment, he couldn't have cared less. The most important question still remained: *Had they made it in time?*

When the entrance was clear of dirt and clay and the old construction debris that had been buried with it, Jonas jumped down into the hole first – pain spearing out from his knife wound shot through his leg on impact, but he pushed past it – and yanked at the the doors of the container. The edges of the metal door panels dragged against the dirt and didn't want to open, but with the adrenalin pounding through his veins, he forced them to move.

Light from above filled the container, and three teenagers shielded their eyes and breathed deeply from the new source of air. Jonas rushed forward and embraced all three of them in a bear hug.

He heard someone else dropping clumsily into the hole. Munroe stumbled forward with open arms. His daughters ran to him. Tears streamed down all their faces. Munroe broke out laughing, and the joy infected them all. They alternated between crying and laughing as they rocked back and forth, squeezing each other tightly.

112

With balloons and flowers in his arms, Jonas Black led his nephew through the bustling corridors of Stafford Hospital. Will's mother occupied a private room on the third floor. The doctors said she was recovering nicely and would be able to return home soon.

As Jonas placed the get-well gifts on a table in the corner, Will ran up and squeezed his mother, pressing down on and pulling against the various tubes and cords connected to her body.

"Easy," Stacey said, laughing and returning her son's embrace.

Then she looked over at Jonas. She didn't say a word, but her eyes told him all that he needed to know. She might never forgive him and she'd certainly never forget, but while he couldn't bring back his brother, he had brought Will home. He knew something between Stacey and him had changed.

He couldn't replace his brother or make the pain of Michael's absence go away, but he vowed that he would always be there to watch over the family that his brother had left behind.

113

Sitting at a picnic table in his backyard, Deacon Munroe listened to the sounds of laughter and conversation. It was a gorgeous day. Warm, but not hot, with a gentle breeze blowing down off the mountains. The smell of grilled hamburgers floated through the air. He soaked it in, enjoying the sounds of his loved ones, new and old.

Joey talking about the newest video games with Jonas Black's nephew and some girl who the young genius had apparently met at a coffee shop. Jonas Black himself tossing a football back and forth with Makayla. Annabelle opening the grill and flipping burgers. Katherine O'Connell discussing boys with Chloe.

It was a beautiful scene, and Munroe wished more than anything that he could actually *see* it, instead of just visualizing it in his mind.

He pressed a button on his watch, and a digital voice announced the time. He realized that the sun was probably setting, and so he turned in that direction and tried to remember the colors. He painted the picture in his mind. A scene of rolling green mountains, reds and yellows overlaying a bright blue sky, purple hues outlining the clouds.

It would have been easy to resent the fact that there was so much beauty in the world that he would never see again. But if the events of the past several days had taught him anything, it was to be grateful for all that he did have and to take nothing for granted.

His phone vibrated against his leg, but he ignored it, not wanting to spoil the beautiful tapestry of life and happiness being created all around him.

But then Annabelle's phone rang the moment his stopped. He heard her answer and start walking toward him. "Deac, it's the Secretary of Defense. He says it's important."

She handed him the phone, and Munroe listened to the laughter and joy for a moment longer before bringing the device to his ear.

"Mr. Secretary, what can I do for you?"

THE SHEPHERD

Ethan Cross

Meet **Francis Ackerman**, America's **most terrifying** serial killer.

What **excites** him most is the **game of chance**.

He likes to **play** with ordinary people. **Innocent people.**

Someone just like you.

If you take part in Ackerman's **game**, he'll **stalk you**, then take you prisoner.

Will he let you live? **Or will you die?**

There are so many **different ways to die**, and Ackerman knows them all. **It's part of his game.**

Do you wanna play?

Francis Ackerman does.

And he's found you...

OUT NOW

a r r o w   b o o k s

THE PROPHET

Ethan Cross

OLD ENEMIES

Francis Ackerman is America's most terrifying serial killer. Brutal and cunning, he is ready to take his evil games to a new level.

NEW THREATS

Special Agent Marcus Williams cannot shake Ackerman from his mind. Yet now he must focus on catching the Anarchist, a new killer who abducts women before burning them alive.

HIDDEN TERRORS

The Anarchist will strike again soon. And Ackerman is still free. But even worse than this is a mysterious figure, unknown to the authorities – and his plans are more terrible than anyone imagines.

OUT NOW

arrow books